BOUND TO DIE

B in M

509·922·1646

800· 752· 3199

BOUND TO DIE

Brian Lutterman

SALVO PRESS
Bend, Oregon

BOUND TO DIE

Copyright © 2002 by Brian Lutterman

Salvo Press
P.O. Box 9095
Bend, OR 97708
www.salvopress.com

Library of Congress Control Number: 2001098657

ISBN: 1-930486-33-2

Printed in U.S.A.
First Edition

CHAPTER 1

Somehow Tori knew it was not over yet. She might easily have concluded that the unknowable gods had completed their work, turning her
into a thirty-six-year-old widow, and then, as of the end of the week, an
unemployed thirty-six-year-old widow. Yet she sensed, merely by looking around her, the truth of her grandfather's favorite saying.

The old man was always cheerful and matter-of-fact in maintaining that
"...things always look darkest just before they turn completely black."

They all looked like strangers to her now, these people who milled
around, beers in hand, squinting into the late-afternoon sunshine on the
day of the carnage. Tori McMillan knew many of them, had even been
friends with some of them. But now they seemed like clones, or impos-
tors emerged from pods into a world she now barely recognized.

The only exception was Max Tuten who, regrettably, looked and sounded just the same. "Like I've been saying, Tori. If there's anything you
need, well...."

She looked up at her boss, a tall man two years her junior, with short,
dark hair and tortoiseshell glasses. He looked out of place at the Western-
style gathering, wearing khaki slacks and golf shirt, more like a fraterni-
ty brother than an assistant general counsel.

She said, "How about a job, Max?"

He looked disappointed and hurt. "We've talked about that, Tori. I
mean, things haven't worked out the way any of us wanted, but...." He
waved his hands in vague futility, looking around as if for support from
the small gathering. "I mean, we're giving you a generous package and
all."

That was one way of putting it, she supposed. An equally valid view was that they were paying her a large sum not to sue them under the Family Leave Act. Tori sipped from a plastic glass of club soda. "Tell me again, Max. Why, exactly, am I here? Why am I supposed to schmooze all these people from other companies? Most of them aren't even attorneys."

"Your next job wouldn't have to be as a lawyer."

"I like working as a lawyer."

"Well, it wouldn't hurt to talk to these people. You could make some contacts."

Tori drained her glass. "Go away, Max. Just go."

Max looked at his watch. "I guess I'd better get going. I've got to go over some figures for that presentation tomorrow."

Tori had already lost what little interest she'd had in the conversation. She was again adrift, in those minutes before her now-unfamiliar world went insane.

"Hi, Tori." She looked up to see a tall, middle-aged man, looking awkward in jeans and denim shirt. It took Tori a moment to recognize Larry Stevens, a software engineer from Sattex, her own company.

"Hi, Larry."

The kindly, bespectacled man squeezed Tori's hand. "I'm terribly sorry about Ben."

"Thank you." An awkward silence followed. Nobody—not even the outgoing Larry—ever knew what to say next.

Larry looked at himself. "I feel like an idiot, dressed like this. Whose idea was this Western-theme event, anyway?"

"I don't know."

He shook his head. "A faux Western barbecue at a state park in a Washington, D.C. suburb—I guess it's a natural for a seminar on marketing database software to aerospace companies." He changed the subject. "Is Max here?"

Tori shifted uncomfortably on the hay bale that served as her seat. "He just left."

"Too bad. I like to watch him schmooze, in his eager, puppy-dog sort of way." Larry smiled. He knew, as everyone did, that Tori's scheming, upwardly mobile boss had lusted after her for years.

"So how are you coping?" Larry asked. "I'm surprised to see you here—not too many legal eagles around."

"Max brought me here to job-hunt."

Larry looked shocked. "What the hell—"

"They're letting me go, Larry. I took a couple of months off to...be with Ben. When I got back, my job had been filled and now he doesn't know what to do with me. There are people here from Oracle, Microsoft—places I might look."

"That sucks," Larry said, looking genuinely angry. "Sattex is a big company. There ought to be a place for you there."

Tori shrugged. She knew she should have felt outrage. It would have been nice to feel something. Anything, other than the overpowering grief.

"Are you...in touch with Cindy?" Larry looked uncomfortable and dutiful in mentioning his ex-wife. But he was the reason the two women had met, when he had worked with Tori years ago. Until recently, Cindy had also worked at Sattex.

"I haven't heard from her," she answered, suddenly astonished to realize how little contact she'd had with her best friend during the past few months. It had been disappointing but not totally unexpected when so many of her friends had gradually drifted away during the long nightmare of Ben's illness. But Cindy...

She hadn't even attended the funeral.

"Well," Larry said suddenly. "Take care of yourself. And good luck." He patted her hand.

Tori wandered through the crowd in the state park pavilion, nodding to people she knew, accepting condolences. She was numb to it all. She knew she should talk to someone. To Cindy.

She walked to the edge of the pavilion, which was bordered by a large food service trailer and a portable bar. Then she glanced past the trailer and froze. Walking up the path leading from the parking lot, incredibly, was Cindy Stevens.

But, somehow, not Cindy Stevens.

Cindy, a tall woman with short blond hair, walked with grim determination toward the pavilion. What on earth was she doing here?

"Cindy!" Tori shouted. Her friend ignored her.

Tori looked at her friend's face and realized that she had been right. Something—everything—was wrong. This place. These people. Cindy, most of all.

And the gods had not finished.

Witnesses would later recall hearing someone scream before Cindy

Stevens pulled the gun from her purse. The scream came from Tori, who scrambled through the crowd toward Cindy, but was blocked by rows of picnic tables and by the trailer.

Two people had been hit before the crowd reacted to the half-dozen shots with screams and flight. Tori, blocked now by the crush of the fleeing crowd, watched in horror as Cindy looked around, then shot a third person. Blood sprayed from a woman's neck as she reeled backward.

Perhaps a dozen people were trapped as Cindy, gun in hand, moved relentlessly toward the corner created by the trailer and the bar. Several people fled into the trailer. Most were forced to simply hit the floor where they were.

A woman tried to climb over the bar. Cindy Stevens calmly shot her three times. Then, after looking around briefly, she walked back through the pavilion toward the parking lot. No one followed.

•

FBI Special Agent Nolan Bertelson sat in front of the television in his family room, tie loosened, soda in hand. His day at the Silver Spring Resident Office had been a string of miserable events: a bank robbery in Takoma Park; a diplomat jailed for DUI in Rockville; carping superiors; a mountain of paperwork; appearing to testify in a kidnapping case, then having the trial postponed.

"Dad, can I stay over at Jenny's?" a teenage voice called from the kitchen.

Without looking he asked, "What does Mom say?" No response. His daughter hadn't asked her mother. Bertelson turned his attention back to the television, sitting up as he saw the image of bodies being carried from what looked like a picnic area. He reached for the remote and turned up the volume; there had been a multiple murder at a state park, at a barbecue for a software industry group. He was about to turn the volume up further when the cell phone inside his jacket pocket trilled.

He fumbled with the jacket, which lay next to him on the sofa, finally extracting the phone from an inside pocket.

"Bertelson."

"This is Temple," said the whispery voice that made Bertelson's pulse quicken. He got up and took the phone with him into the bathroom.

"Have you heard about the software group killings?" Temple asked.

"Yes. I've got the TV on right now."

"We've got a problem. All four victims are Bound."

"What?" The FBI agent nearly dropped the phone.

"The killer is a woman named Cynthia Stevens. Her ex-husband was one of the victims."

"That means," Bertelson said, thinking quickly, "security must have been breached."

"Exactly. You need to get on the case immediately, Nolan."

"It's not my jurisdiction."

"You'll be brought in."

"All right. Then what?"

"Find Cynthia Stevens," said the voice he knew only as Temple. "At all costs."

CHAPTER 2

Tori remembered little of the ride home in the police car. She had started to sob and shake uncontrollably after leaving the murder scene, finally pulling herself together as the squad neared her two-story colonial in Chevy Chase. Her brain refused to accommodate itself to the scene she had just witnessed. Seeing Max Tuten's BMW in her driveway jarred her back to reality, however unpleasant.

"Oh, shit," she muttered.

The officer in the front seat beside her, a young woman, glanced over. "Are you all right?"

"It's only my boss."

"Do you have somewhere you can go tonight?"

"I—" She realized with a sickening twinge that she couldn't go to Cindy's. "I'll be okay."

Max jumped out of his car and followed her to the front door. "Tori! I heard there were shootings. My God, it could have been me." He seemed unconcerned that it could much more easily have been Tori.

"Who was it?" he demanded. "They aren't releasing names yet."

"Go away, Max."

He grabbed her by the shoulders and spun her around—too roughly, he realized. "Tori," he said, releasing her, "you've got to tell me who got killed. I know those people."

"Larry Stevens."

The words had a visible effect on Max. "Larry...my God...Who else?"

"I don't know." She turned the key in the lock.

"You don't know? You were there. You have to know."

"Nobody from Sattex. A man and two women."

"Three others," he said, more to himself than Tori.

Tori was not about to open the door and risk letting him in. "I'd like to be alone now, Max."

"What?" Tuten looked up. "Oh, sure. Well, thanks. Don't worry about coming back to work right away—there's no hurry. If there's anything I can do...."

Tori reached into her purse and slipped a key off a ring. "My car is still up there. Have somebody bring it back."

Max, looking defeated and shell-shocked, took the key. "It could have been me," he said again.

After Max left, Tori sat in her darkened living room with a cool cloth on her forehead. She sedated herself with some pills left over from Ben's illness, but they were of little help in shutting out the nightmare scene that repeated endlessly in her mind.

Despite—or because of—the total unreality of what had happened, Tori had behaved coolly at the scene, using her first aid training to try to help the four casualties. The first victim had been Larry Stevens, who'd had half his face blown off. He had been killed instantly. The other three victims had likewise been beyond help. Tori remembered little of what followed, including the sealing of the area, and then questioning by the police. It had been after dark when the thirty or so seminar participants had finally been allowed to leave.

Tori started violently when the doorbell rang. Recovering her senses, she remembered being warned to expect another visit from the police. She got up and walked through the dark to the door, staggering slightly, and looked through the peephole. The man who stood outside was tall and blond, wearing a suit, white shirt, and tie.

 She opened the door on the chain, and the man held his credentials up to the opening. "Ms. McMillan? I'm Sergeant Jaworski from the Montgomery County Police Department."

Tori closed the door, unhooked the chain, and stood back to admit the policeman. "I know you were questioned at the scene," he said. "But I understand you know the suspect well, so...."

She nodded.

"Is there somewhere we could talk?"

She started into the living room, then turned around. "Would you mind talking in the kitchen, Sergeant?"

"Fine."

"I'm going to make some coffee. Could you use some?"

"Sure."

Tori led him through the short hallway toward the rear of the house. She didn't turn on the kitchen's harsh overhead lamp, settling for several under-counter lights. Kyle Jaworski sat patiently at the table, and Tori studied him as the coffee dripped into the carafe. He was very blond, well past the age when most blondes have begun to darken. Even his eyebrows were nearly white. He settled into his chair, glancing around Tori's kitchen as if he had nowhere in particular to be at the moment. He looked cool, intelligent—even elegant.

Tori brought a steaming mug to the table.

"Are you okay?" he asked as she sat down.

Tori considered the question. Still weak-kneed and shaky, she kept reliving the scene, like a flashback, but it didn't seem real. Her brain rejected what her eyes had seen; Cindy Stevens could not have walked up to that group with a nine-millimeter pistol and killed four people, then walked away. It just could not have happened.

"I'm fine," she said.

The detective pulled out his notebook. "I'd like to get a couple of questions out of the way first. Since Officer Simmons interviewed you, have you thought of anywhere Mrs. Stevens might have gone?"

"No."

"Have you thought of anyone else she might have visited?"

"No." She felt self-conscious, wondering if she was slurring her words, if the pills were having an effect after all.

Jaworski made two check marks in his notebook, then said, "I'd like to take a step back and get some basic information from you."

Tori sipped her coffee, using both hands to hold the cup. "All right."

"I understand your full name is Victoria Saunders McMillan. You are thirty-six years old and were born in Fort Hood, Texas, the oldest of three children."

"Yes."

"How long have you worked at Sattex?"

"Four years next month. I also worked as a salesperson for the company for four years before that, while I went to law school at night. I came back after two years with a big law firm."

"What does Sattex do? Something with software, right?"

Tori studied the detective and guessed that he knew very well what

Sattex did. But his face was unreadable; he seemed relaxed and guileless. He also, she realized, looked vaguely familiar. "We develop and sell software for databases, encryption, and communications," she said.

"And that's all done out of the corporate headquarters in Bethesda?"

"Among other locations."

"What is your job?"

"I'm an attorney. I support a department that sells to national accounts. It's mostly negotiating and drafting contracts, and handling disputes that arise from them."

"When and how did you meet Cynthia Stevens?"

"It was about six years ago. I worked with her husband, Larry. He introduced us, and we hit it off right away. I left the company for a couple of years shortly after that, but we remained best friends."

Jaworski took his time with the next question, taking a quiet sip from his coffee cup. "But you hadn't seen her recently."

"No. The last time was about five weeks ago. I'd seen very little of her since she quit working at Sattex."

"She worked there, too?"

"Yes, until last April or May."

"Why did she quit?"

"The usual. A jerky boss. A glass ceiling. She got fed up. We didn't talk about it that much. Actually we'd seen less and less of each other during the past year."

"Why is that?"

Tori hesitated. "My husband was sick. That made it hard to maintain a friendship. I was preoccupied. She felt awkward and intrusive."

"I see. Where is your husband tonight?"

He had gray eyes, Tori noticed. While they gave nothing away, she once again had the feeling that he knew full well the answer to the question he'd asked. "He's in Pennsylvania," she said.

"Pennsylvania," Jaworski repeated.

"Right. In a little town just west of Bucks County. You go north off the main road, left through the gate, and down about fifteen rows. Second grave on the right."

Jaworski gave her a condescending look. "Then I guess this must be doubly hard for you. I'm sorry."

Tori blinked back tears, suddenly realizing that she must look like complete hell.

Jaworski gave her a minute, then started again. "Did Mrs. Stevens find another job after she quit at Sattex?"

"I don't think so. I know she was looking."

"Mr. and Mrs. Stevens were divorced, is that right?"

"For about three years."

"Why did they get divorced?"

Tori took a large gulp from her coffee cup. "They grew apart over the years. They didn't have any huge disagreements, but they had loads of minor ones. They just seemed to get on each other's nerves, and not even to like each other that much any more."

"Was the divorce contentious?"

"Not at all. All the details were worked out very agreeably. They didn't see much of each other after that, but they weren't hostile."

"Were either of them dating anyone?"

"I don't know if Larry was. I don't believe Cindy was—she dated off and on after the divorce, but never anything serious."

"Can you remember the names of anyone she dated?"

Tori thought for a moment. "No."

The detective made a note. "You can't think of any reason Mrs. Stevens would have wanted to kill her ex-husband?"

"No." She stood up. "More coffee?"

"Yes, thanks."

Tori brought the carafe over and topped off their cups. Jaworski studied his notes. When Tori was seated he said, "I'm sorry to have to go over this again, but we need to talk about what you saw today."

She hesitated, then nodded.

"When you saw Mrs. Stevens coming up the path toward the pavilion, did you notice anything unusual about her?"

Tori closed her eyes. "She was grim and wild-eyed. I'd never seen her look that way before." She opened her eyes and looked at Jaworski. "She looked insane."

"How far was she from the pavilion when she pulled the gun from her purse?"

"Probably ten or fifteen feet."

"Who was shot first?"

"Larry."

"What did you see?"

Tori took a breath. "She raised the gun to his face and shot him point-blank."

"Then what happened?"

"She turned and shot the man Larry was talking to."

The detective studied his notes. "That would be Ron O'Hara from IBM."

"If you say so. I didn't recognize him."

"Do you know if Mrs. Stevens knew Mr. O'Hara?"

"I have no idea. I'm not sure if she knew either of the other two victims, either."

"How many shots did she fire at Mr. O'Hara?"

"I think two."

"What happened next?"

Tori closed her eyes again. "It was hard to see, because people were starting to scream and run. But she made her way further into the pavilion. Closer to the trailer and the bar. I heard more shots—maybe three more. But I couldn't see exactly what happened. And then, I did see this, she shot a woman who was trying to climb over the bar. Three more shots, I think. She seemed to hesitate for a moment. Then she just walked away."

Jaworski paused, formulating his next question carefully. "With respect to victims two, three, and four, was she seeking these people out? Or was she just shooting randomly?"

"She definitely aimed at individuals. She wasn't just firing wildly into the crowd."

"But was she looking for those specific individuals? Or could it have been anyone?"

Tori thought about it. "I don't know. She did look around. But I don't know if she was looking for those particular people."

"Is there any reason she should have been?"

"Not that I know of. I don't even know who they were."

"Did you know Mrs. Stevens owned a gun?"

"No, and I was shocked to learn that she did. She didn't like the idea of guns."

"How is it she was able to become proficient at firing one?"

"It didn't take much skill, Sergeant. All of the shootings were at point-blank range. It was a confined area—there was nowhere for those people to run or hide." She studied him again; his detachment, she thought, seemed contrived, as if he cared about the crime and the victims but . . .

couldn't show it.

Jaworski stood up. "Thanks for your time. Be sure to give me a call if you think of anything that might be useful, or if she makes any attempt to contact you. I'll find my own way out."

"Did you know they had a son?" Tori asked.

Jaworski gave a noncommittal grunt, then resumed his departure.

"Don't you want to hear about him?"

He turned back toward her. "Do you think I need to?"

Tori, surprised, wasn't sure how to answer. "I thought you wanted all the facts."

"All the relevant facts, yes."

Tori continued to stare at him.

Jaworski, with exaggerated patience, returned to his chair and took out his notebook. He gave her a small smile. "Tell me about their son."

"They had a boy named Scotty who disappeared about seven years ago."

"I seem to remember something about that."

"I never met Scotty," Tori recalled. "But by all accounts he was a wonderful boy. He just disappeared one day while riding his bike. There were massive searches and televised appeals, but no trace was ever found."

"Yes, I remember now. How did Mr. and Mrs. Stevens react?"

"I didn't meet them until a year after it had happened. But they were still devastated, of course. They leaned on each other initially—went together to the support groups, and so on. But looking back on it, Scotty's disappearance is probably what started their drift apart from each other. Over the years, Larry seemed to recover well. He was very secure, very friendly. I know he did volunteer work for some organization. But Cindy never really bounced back. She took two years off to look for Scotty— putting up posters, staffing hot lines, tracking down sightings. Her career never really recovered from the hiatus. She battled depression off and on after the disappearance. And I think she resented Larry for coping well."

"Was it a festering anger? Something that might have built up, and then boiled over?"

"Not a chance," she said firmly. "Cindy may have resented him, but it never reached that level. Not even close."

"Why didn't they have any more children afterward?"

"Larry wasn't sure he wanted to, and Cindy wasn't sure she could cope."

"Do you have any reason to believe the disappearance may have something to do with the murders?"

"Not really."

He folded up his notebook and replaced it in his inside jacket pocket.

Tori's patience gave way. "I'm terribly sorry to have wasted your time, Sergeant."

"No problem," he said. She couldn't tell if he was being sarcastic.

"You don't care why she did it, do you."

"My opinion doesn't matter."

"You don't care."

He started out the door, paused, and turned around. Again, he gave her a small smile. "Well, I'll tell you, Ms. McMillan. My Polish brain doesn't process all this psychological stuff too well. My job is pretty simple, when you come right down to it. My duty is to catch killers, not to probe their souls out of personal curiosity. And just for good measure, my boss, Lieutenant Kandel, told me just an hour ago to make this a no-frills case. He said, 'Forget the psychology, Jaworski. Just find her.' To me, it looks pretty much like a straightforward domestic killing, with some other people getting in the way."

"I don't believe that and neither do you."

For the first time, Jaworski's good humor gave way. "All right," he snapped. "You tell me, Ms. McMillan. Help me out here. Tell me why the hell she did it."

Tori sat for a long time before answering. "I have no idea in the world."

CHAPTER 3

Jim Traeger hurried down the hallway through the West Wing. The staff meeting had been unusually short and productive. Still, on a couple of occasions he had found his attention beginning to wander. After nearly six years in the White House, his head was no longer completely in the game.

Traeger, a tall, thin man with short hair and wire-rimmed glasses, strode through the outer office, nodding to the military aide and Secret Service agent, both of whom sat with infinite patience outside the door. He gave the door a short, absent knock, then walked into the Oval Office.

President Roark Harris, wearing half-glasses, glanced up from his daily news summary. "Christ, Jim, they're beating me up over this latest shooting. What the hell does any of it have to do with me? Was I supposed to have Federal agents stationed at a state park in Olney, Maryland because some nut might come along and start shooting people?"

Traeger, legal pad in hand, took a seat in front of the President's desk. The greeting was typical Harris. Traeger had worked for him for nearly twenty years, going back to his days in the Arizona Legislature, then moving with him as he became a Congressman, then Governor of Arizona, then President. He was Harris's closest advisor. Yet he was still very much the functionary, the servant, who called the boss "sir" and did not rate a good morning.

The President put his papers down. "We've got shootings in schools, in post offices, in workplaces. Wackos everyplace. How does your brain trust think we should respond to this one?"

The issue hadn't actually come up at the staff meeting just completed, but Traeger knew what the consensus would have been.

"Just the usual, sir."

Harris nodded. "The usual" would consist of a statement expressing shock, sadness, and outrage, coupled with a call for more cops, tougher punishment, and family values.

Traeger hesitated. "I just can't help thinking that we need something better than the usual. Something...different."

Harris gave him a curious look, which gradually formed itself into an indulgent smile. "You've gone soft on me since you came back, Jim. You even volunteer for some social agency, right?"

Traeger returned the smile. He'd been back in his old job as chief of staff for nearly a year after an eighteen-month stint as Secretary of Commerce. And he had changed, more than Harris would ever know.

The President, a big, beefy man, sixty-five years old, with thinning brown hair, leaned back in his chair, hands clasped behind his head. "Hell, I get tired of saying the same shit all the time, just as much as everybody gets sick of hearing it. But what's the alternative? Spending more money on welfare? Federalizing local crimes? That's just not me."

Indeed it was not, Traeger thought, not for a rugged individualist, an Arizona rancher, whose parents had named him after a character in an Ayn Rand novel. And not for a second-term President so popular he would be able to virtually handpick his own successor.

Harris sat up again. "All right, get with Nick and write up something a little softer if you want." The President put his reading glasses back on. "Have you read this paper Amy wrote on succession?"

Traeger nodded, his pulse quickening.

"Well, what do you think?"

Traeger knew he had to be careful. The memo, from the President's Special Counsel, was trying to push the President into an early endorsement of his Vice President, Norman Whitelaw, for the nomination next year. With the country at peace, the economy booming, and Harris, the Reaganesque Marlboro Man, presiding over it all, the nomination would be tantamount to election. Everyone had assumed all along that Vice President Whitelaw would be the anointed successor; the memo Harris was reading urged an early, emphatic endorsement of the Vice President to scare off any potential challengers. And the memo's author, Amy Burke, was fast becoming Traeger's chief rival for the President's ear. Worse, she was a former aide to the Vice President.

Without waiting for an answer, the President leaned forward. "What's _with you, Jim?_

with you, Jim? You've been closed-mouthed about this succession thing ever since you came back."

Traeger took a breath. He had been waiting for the right moment to make his move. Now, with Amy Burke forcing his hand, he could wait no longer. "I believe we need to slow down, to re-think this entire process, Mr. President."

Harris was flabbergasted. "What the hell? Out of the clear blue sky you're sitting here and telling me I should dump Norm Whitelaw?"

Traeger stiffened. "I'm just saying no one has given this process any conscious thought. It's just been assumed."

"What's to think about?"

"We need to consider who will best carry out your policies, implement your agenda."

The President leaned back, rubbing his face. Dumping Whitelaw was unthinkable; the Vice President had been loyal beyond reproach. He had dutifully endorsed the President's mostly-economic agenda, and suffered in silence the Administration's neglect of his pet social causes such as opposition to legalized abortion. He had, by all accounts, done a good job in heading up the war on illegal drugs. It was true that Whitelaw—an austere, rigid, church-going Mississippian—wasn't exactly the President's type of man. But then, Reagan and Bush had also seemed like strange bedfellows and, like Harris and Whitelaw, they had won two elections together after initially opposing each other for their party's nomination.

"Jesus Christ, Jim. I just don't believe this. What's going on here? Is there some kind of movement out there I don't know about?"

"Not that I know of, sir."

Harris's perplexed look changed to wary. "Is this something personal between you and Amy?"

"Not at all."

"Then you just don't like Whitelaw."

"That's not true," Traeger protested. In fact, he did like the Vice President personally, finding him principled, sincere, and genuine. "It's just that we need to think beyond merely winning the election. We need to think about your policies, the reason you were elected."

The President was silent for a full minute. "So what the hell am I supposed to do? You think I—shit, this is about Milt, isn't it."

"I haven't spoken to the senator, or anyone else about it," Traeger replied. He had no doubt that if Harris felt free to pick anyone he wanted, it would be Florida Senator Milton Hokanson, a dynamic, folksy man who was much more in tune with the President's economic agenda—lower taxes, less regulation—and less concerned about abortion and prayer in schools.

"Hell, I like Milt—everybody does," Harris said. "But to dump Norm...."

"I'm only asking you to think about it," Traeger said. "You've been successful because you stand for something."

Harris was unmoved. "Well, thanks a fuckin' ton for dropping this shit-load on me, Jim. I don't know where the hell you're coming from, but I hope you know what you're doing, going out on a limb like this." The President, shaking his head, put the memo to one side. "We'll have to take it up later. And I hope you have a very, very convincing explanation for this."

•

Cindy Stevens listened to the roar of traffic on the K Street freeway above the parking lot where she now sat, motionless, in her car. She had been frustrated in her attempts to get the ringleaders. They had been ready for her. But of course they would be. For three months they had been toy-ing with her, monitoring her, trying to determine what she knew. She couldn't make things right any more; she had long since given up on that. But she could make the bastards pay, at least some of them.

In a few minutes she would go back to finish the job. Their building was well guarded; to go in would be suicide. But that was a problem only if you valued your own life.

She didn't.

For the twentieth or so time in the past half-day, a wave of nausea rip-pled through her abdomen as she recalled what she had done. She gripped the steering wheel and waited for it to pass. How many had she actually killed? She couldn't remember for sure. Larry, of course. Two or three others. All of them she could find. But then she'd seen Tori...

Oh, God, Tori. What on Earth had she been doing there? There had been no time, no way, to explain; only for the briefest and most inade-quate of acknowledgments afterward. But she couldn't drag Tori into it. Those she loved had suffered enough—Tori doubly so. Cindy had given up her job, her friends, everything, for this futile three-month quest. In the end she had done what she'd had to do. But it had not been enough. Not ...

Nearly enough

nearly enough.

She screamed as a face appeared in her window. She fumbled, reaching for the door lock, but it was too late. A strong arm pulled her out of the car, an arm belonging to a large man with crooked front teeth.

Cindy locked eyes with the man for an instant, then she understood with an unimaginable sadness that she had failed Scotty, that she would never complete her mission.

"You...."

The man smiled.

•

It was past seven that night when Traeger settled back in his limousine, a briefcase full of work beside him, for the ride home to Potomac, Maryland. He had hoped the President would be intrigued by his idea. Instead he had been furious. The process had not started well, and Traeger was not in control of it.

Miraculously, both girls were home tonight. He went upstairs and stuck his head into the room belonging to Brianna, fourteen.

"Hi, Bree."

Brianna mumbled something in response. She was wearing headphones attached to an MP3 player.

"How was your day?"

"All right."

Traeger shrugged. Brianna had lately discovered that her parents were the two uncoolest people in the known universe. Traeger went across the hall, knocked softly and opened the door. Caitlin, twelve, lay propped up on the bed, watching a sitcom on TV. She sat up and broke into a smile, showing an expensive mouthful of braces, when her father walked in.

"How's it going, Katy?" He kissed her on the forehead.

"Hey, it's Captain Oddball," she replied. Caitlin had given him the name when an opposition senator, after four days of brutal budget negotiations, had dubbed Traeger "Captain Hardball."

"How was the soccer game?" Traeger asked.

"We lost again, but I got an assist."

"Good job. Will you have dinner with us?"

"Sorry, Bree and I already ate."

Traeger nodded and softly closed the door. Downstairs, his wife, Pam, had dinner ready. He kissed her absently, and they sat down to a meal of grilled chicken and baked potatoes.

"Long day?" Pam asked.

"Yep. They're beating us up on those shootings. The TV and radio coverage won't quit."

"Christ, Jim. You just don't need this any more. We don't need it. Why are you so determined to stick this out until the bitter end?"

Traeger slowly chewed his food and glanced across the table at her. Pam, while still attractive, had recently begun to show her age. Or maybe he had only recently begun to notice it. Tiny lines had formed around her large, pretty eyes, and the skin along her jaw line had begun to sag ever so slightly. If time had caused his former college sweetheart to age, Washington had accelerated the process. She had come to hate the city, with its mudslinging, gossip, and hypocrisy. She had sat dutifully in the front row during the hearings for his confirmation as Commerce Secretary, listening for three days as one witness after another dragged her husband's name through the mud. From then on, she had never ceased lobbying for a return to Phoenix, her hometown, where they had met during college.

Traeger couldn't blame her. But he knew the distance between them had less to do with Washington and his job than with the change that had come over him a year ago. He knew Pam would never understand—could never understand—his new purpose; the mission that had reinvigorated him; the new life that had taken hold during the past year.

Regrettably, they had said, many of the Bound outgrow their spouses.

He resumed eating. "I'm committed, Pam. It's only another year."

"Closer to a year and a half," she corrected. "You know, I talked to Katherine the other day. There's a house for sale in Scottsdale that would be perfect—"

"Pam, please. Until I know what I'm going to do, it's pointless to—"

"And just when will you know?" she asked, her voice acquiring an angry edge.

Traeger wished he could answer the question. The truth was that he didn't want to think about it; his job, though not as all engrossing as it once had been, was still challenging and interesting, and he had never been happier. He worried about a post-White House letdown, even though his career options were numerous and attractive. He had standing offers from two prestigious political consulting firms. Corporations were lining up to hire him. He could teach, or help Harris with his memoirs.

He had accepted that at age forty-one, he would never again hold a job as important, interesting, or powerful as the one he now held.

But all this contemplation about future options was meaningless now; everything would be meaningless unless he succeeded in his mission. And, in any event, he knew the decisions about his future were no longer his to make.

Traeger had finished dinner and was headed upstairs when he heard the distinctive ring from his den. He hurried inside, shut the door behind him, and then sat down behind his desk. Spread out before him was a battery of special communications equipment set up by the Secret Service. But this call, though scrambled, was not from the White House.

"Yes?"

"This is Temple," said the whispered, electronically distorted voice—a man's, he thought, but he was never sure. "I'm sorry, Jim, but it's a go. You have thirty days."

Traeger silently replaced the phone and sat motionless behind his desk for a long moment. Then, feeling suddenly ill, he bolted across the hall to the bathroom and retched into the toilet.

He stood there for several minutes, catching his breath, his gaze avoiding the mirror. His eyes caught sight of a hairbrush—Caitlin's brush. He thought about the day nine months ago when he had taken a hair from the same brush, placed it in an envelope, and sent it to Temple.

Oh, God, no. Not Caitlin. For a moment he hated himself.

But he recovered quickly, as he always did at such times. The larger picture came back into focus, and his equilibrium returned. What would happen with Caitlin was a tragedy. But he would do it gladly, would do it ten times over, for the most important cause in the world.

CHAPTER 4

Tori rambled around the kitchen, fixing a dinner she probably wouldn't eat, ignoring two messages on her answering machine from reporters. She had woken up from a drugged sleep at noon, then forced herself to drink a large glass of orange juice and go for a long walk through her Chevy Chase neighborhood. This lovely old brick house, set on a wooded street, had been their dream home. Now it seemed like a vast, empty prison, incarcerating all her nightmares along with her. Near the end of Ben's losing battle with cancer she had made the decision to go on living. It wasn't as though she had carefully thought about the alternatives, but she knew she had a choice, and that if she gave up, Ben would never have forgiven her. But could either she or Ben have anticipated this?

She remembered the last time she'd seen Cindy, about three weeks before Ben had died. They'd sat in the living room, watching television. Cindy, sitting across the room, had gestured to her; Ben, seated next to Tori in his bathrobe, had fallen asleep. Gently, she'd woken him up, and they'd helped him into the bedroom. She'd tucked him in, and he had looked up at her, his haggard, exhausted face breaking into a smile, his trademark irresistible, lopsided grin. "It'll be all right," he whispered, touching her face.

Back in the living room, Cindy had poured drinks for them. Neither of them spoke for several minutes. The television was now silent.

"He's going to die," Tori said. She waited for Cindy to contradict her, to tell her there was still hope.

Cindy studied the glass in her hand.

"What should I do?" Tori asked.

Cindy let out a short, bitter laugh. "You're asking me?"

Tori watched her, wondering how openly she dared to speak, how much of Cindy's survival over the years had depended on the fiction that Scotty might still be alive. "You've coped," Tori said.

Cindy sipped from her glass. "Tori, this is the most ridiculous conversation we've ever had."

"What do you mean?"

"You're talking to me about coping? What a joke. For seven years I've been a depressed, neurotic, hate-filled, desperate mess."

"Cindy..."

"You, on the other hand, are the most competent, practical, sensible person I've ever met."

Tori fought to keep her anger in check, but her tight voice rose ominously. "So life goes on? Is that what you're saying? I won't miss a beat? Just check off another item on my to-do list: 'Grieve for Ben?' Is that what you're saying?"

Cindy didn't lash back. "All I'm saying is that you may not know what to do now, but you will. You're better equipped to deal with this than anyone I know. Somehow, life will go on." She drained her glass. "For you."

At the time, Tori hadn't asked what she'd meant by those last two words. And she'd never had another chance to ask. In truth, Cindy had been drifting away from her for months. And Tori had observed the drift at a distance, only vaguely aware that Cindy had quit her job, and that she'd been traveling a lot. As Ben's condition had worsened, as the hospice people had started coming in, as Ben's relatives had begun to arrive, she had called Cindy a couple of times, getting her machine both times and receiving no return call. Cindy's absence had never really sunk in, and had never hurt, until Tori had looked around for her at Ben's funeral. She hadn't even come.

Now she returned to her pointless chores and her pathetic to-do list. Max Tuten had left two messages, expressing support and repeating that she should return to work only when ready. Events had placed Max in a position that might have seemed awkward to some men: trying to hit on Tori now that she was single and vulnerable, while at the same time easing her off his department's payroll. But the ever-cheerful Max was undaunted.

She was sitting at the table, staring at the plate of food in front of her, when the phone rang. She let the machine pick up.

"Hello, Ms. McMillan? This is Kyle Jaworski. I'm sorry to bother you, but this is kind of—"

She picked up the receiver. "Yes, Sergeant?"

"Oh, hi." The detective sounded relieved. "I need to tell you something, and I didn't want you to see it on the news. I also have a couple more questions for you."

Tori sat down.

Jaworski continued. "Cindy Stevens' car was found about an hour ago in Georgetown, under the K Street Freeway."

Tori held her breath.

"There was a note," he said.

"Oh, God."

"They're just getting the search started. I haven't seen the note or even heard its exact contents. But the bottom line is she was going over to the Key Bridge and jump off."

Tori didn't say anything.

"Interestingly, there was a report of a possible sighting earlier in the evening. It was on Massachusetts Avenue, just across 395 from the Hill. Anyway, Metro checked it out, but couldn't confirm anything. Apparently the source wasn't too reliable—some homeless guy named Artie. Do you know of any reason she might have been there?"

"No."

"Has she made any attempt to contact you since we last spoke?"

Tori was shocked. "Of course not."

"I'm sorry to have to tell you this. I guess I'd better get going."

"Wait. This will be checked out thoroughly, won't it? I mean, to make absolutely sure this is...what it seems."

He sounded incredulous, even amused, by the question. "Oh, yes. Your favorite true-blue Polish detective will see to it personally. But you should know that any psychologist worth his salt would have predicted a suicide by the killer in this case."

Tori replaced the receiver and put her head down on the table.

•

The next morning Tori drove into the city. The rush-hour traffic had thinned at ten as she drove south on Connecticut Avenue, the bright sunshine mocking her despair. She had turned on the television that morning and she'd had to sit down when they showed the scene. The park, the pavilion, the bodies on stretchers, the grim-looking policemen. As if she . . . *needed help remembering.*

needed help remembering. Cindy's body had still not been recovered. Unlike Kyle Jaworski, the news media had been quick to pick up on Cindy and Larry's previous notoriety as parents of a kidnap victim. Commentators were openly speculating that despondency over Scotty's disappearance had caused Cindy to snap.

That her mission now was stupid and futile she had no doubt. But she had to do something. Going back to work was not an option. There was nothing to do at home. It was the worst time of her life, and she ached to have Cindy to talk things over with. But she didn't, and rather than sitting around thinking about the incredible nightmare of the previous forty-eight hours, she could at least try to find out why it had happened.

She proceeded down Massachusetts, going under and around traffic circles and squares, overshooting her target. On the other side of the I-395 underpass, Tori found street parking for her Audi near the Georgetown law school. A welcome breeze fought the oppressive August heat as she walked across the bridge.

They had made an odd-looking pair—Tori, the lithe, dark-haired, not-quite waif and Cindy, the big, blond Amazon. They had called each other their "partners in crime" and had talked on the phone for hours. They had shared a fondness for outdoor sports, three-hanky movies, and sharp observations about people they worked with. Cindy had adored Ben, and he had cheerfully accepted her into their world, just as he had cheerfully accepted nearly everything that came his way.

Over the years Cindy had seemed increasingly lost, and Tori had felt helpless to do anything about it. Part of her had wanted to kick Cindy in the rear, to tell her to get over Scotty and get on with life. But as Ben's illness had worsened, she had come to realize exactly why Cindy would never get over it. She had felt Cindy pulling away over the past year, but could not blame her for it. After losing first Scotty, then her marriage, she couldn't handle another loss.

Tori stood on Massachusetts and looked up and down the wide, busy street. What the hell was she doing here? Looking for some street person too confused to tell the police anything useful. She walked north on a side street and began looking into the alleys. After two blocks she crossed the street and turned around, walking back toward Massachusetts.

She began walking down an alley. Two scruffy-looking men loitered near a dumpster. She held back; did she really have the nerve to simply walk up and approach these people?

The men looked up at her. She backed up a couple of steps, then jumped as a car horn honked. She heard the squeal of brakes, wheeled around, and grazed the rear bumper of a car that was backing out of a small parking deck.

The driver jumped out of the car, a battered Taurus, and came around to the rear. "Are you okay?"

"I'm fine," Tori said, her face reddening with embarrassment. "I'm really sorry—"

"Nonsense. I should have looked where I was going," the man said in a Texas-sounding drawl. "Are you sure you're okay?"

"Oh, yes, yes...." Damnit. The tears were starting to flow. It seemed that all she had done for the past week—the past year—was cry in front of people.

The man produced a handkerchief, and she took it gratefully. "I'm so sorry," she sniffed.

"No problem," he assured her.

Tori dried her tears and returned the handkerchief, and they stood there for a long moment, studying each other. He was a tall man, middle-aged, with dark, curly hair and glasses, wearing a corduroy suit that had seen better days.

"I've ruined your morning," he said. "Let me make it up to you. I'll buy you coffee. I'm Rick Percival." He extended his hand.

Tori fought off the urge to run and took the hand. "Tori McMillan."

They walked to a coffee shop on Massachusetts Avenue that featured a glass atrium fronting the sidewalk. Rick Percival had taken charge, finding them seats and ordering coffee.

"I'm not trying to get myself off the hook here," he said, "but something tells me you weren't having too great a day even before I tried to run you down."

Tori managed a shaky smile. "I guess not."

"Do you live around here?"

"No. Chevy Chase."

"What brings you to this neck of the woods?"

Tori studied Percival. His face was open and friendly, his manner folksy and low-key. "Just some errands," she said. She wasn't about to mention her search for Artie.

"Judging by your reaction, they must have been some pretty unpleasant errands."

She hesitated, and Percival gave her an apologetic smile. "I'm prying. I apologize. Let's talk about something else."

"Thanks."

"You sound like a fellow Texan."

Tori was surprised. "I was born there—Fort Hood—but I thought all the moving around when I was a kid had removed it from my voice."

"Naw-once a Texan, always. Military family?"

"Yes. Army."

"I grew up in a little town in the Panhandle."

"What do you do now?"

"I work for an outfit called Urban Hope. You've heard of us?"

"A social agency, right? You work with disadvantaged youth."

"Right. We run what we call 'urban missions.' We work with runaways, truants, kids from broken homes. Our national headquarters is here in this building."

Tori looked around, and Percival smiled. "Not the Hilton, is it. That's the plight of a nonprofit—pretty low-rent all around."

"What do you do for the organization?"

"I'm the Executive Director."

"Of the entire organization? Oh, and here I am, chattering away—"

He laughed. "Don't worry about it. I'm a busy man, but who isn't? People are my business, and if I can't take a few minutes for people now and then, I might as well hang it up."

Tori suddenly felt emotionally crowded and overwhelmed. "I-need to go," she said.

He stood up. "Sure. It was a pleasure meeting you. Just tell me one thing."

She nodded.

"Are you married?"

"I'm—well...."

"You're widowed, aren't you. Recently."

She didn't try to hide her surprise. "Only two weeks ago. How on earth did you know?"

He gave her a grim smile. "A guess, but not a very difficult one. I deal with broken lives every day. I know the look. You're a very attractive woman, but there are certain types of devastation that show up on a person's face, that nothing can hide. I'm terribly sorry for your loss, Tori."

"Thank you," she said, fighting back tears again. "You're very kind."

Percival handed her his business card. "My home number is on here," he said. "Call me sometime. Soon. Let me buy you lunch. You talk, I'll listen."

She started to answer, but he gripped her arm. "Think about it. Take care, Tori."

It was when she turned north on Connecticut that Tori noticed the blue sedan in her rearview mirror. For her, the car, which had stayed with her for at least half a mile, provided confirmation that she was losing her mind. *My God, what now?*

She took a left by the zoo and wound through the Kalomara neighborhood. The blue car followed. She felt cold and sweaty as she turned back onto Connecticut. She couldn't see the driver, who was hidden by the sunny glare bouncing off the windshield.

Horns blared and brakes screeched. Tori hit the brakes, but it was too late. She had already run the red light. Undaunted, the blue sedan followed.

Tori started to panic as she neared the Maryland line. She thought of pulling into a police station. But where was the goddamned police station? She couldn't remember. Or maybe she just didn't know.

Light after light, mile after mile, the blue sedan stayed with her.

She smacked her forehead in frustration. Why didn't she call the police? She pulled the cell phone from the Audi's glove box.

The battery was dead. It had been ages since she'd recharged it.

There was only one thing to do now. She pulled off Connecticut into Chevy Chase and headed for home. The blue car followed her down the quiet side streets, parking on the street as she pulled into the garage. She started to close the garage door, then hesitated. The garage wasn't attached to the house; she'd have to either make a run for the house or barricade herself in the garage.

Tori glanced toward the street; the driver wasn't leaving the car. She grabbed her purse and the dead cell phone, then headed for the front door. She glanced back at the blue car; a man was getting out. Frantically, she dug for her house key. Shit. Where was it?

The man was walking up the driveway.

Where was the goddamned key?

She wheeled on the man. "Listen, Mister. I've already called the police on this cell phone—they should be here any minute. And I've got a gun in this purse," she lied.

Her pursuer, a burly man with thinning hair, wearing a dark suit, held up his hand. "Take it easy, ma'am." He reached inside his jacket pocket. "I'm taking my creds out of my pocket."

"Creds? Then you're—"

"Special Agent Nolan Bertelson, FBI."

Tori couldn't believe it. But the credentials appeared genuine. "You—what the hell were you doing?"

"My job, Ms. McMillan. I need to ask you a few questions about those killings you witnessed."

"Jesus Christ!" she exploded. "You are out of line, Mister. That was harassment. It scared me to death and almost caused an accident."

Bertelson was unmoved. "I'm sorry. My instructions were to observe and question you. I still need to ask those questions."

"Forget it. I've told the police everything I know."

"I'm sorry," he said again, his voice even and patient. "But we've been asked to assist the local police in the investigation."

"Look, you tell me why you were following me, and I'll answer your questions."

"We don't explain or bargain, ma'am," he said. "We ask questions. We're the FBI."

Tori, seething, found the key and unlocked the door. Bertelson followed her inside. She sat down in the living room. "Ask your questions. But somebody will hear about this."

The FBI man sat down without being asked and pulled out a notebook. "I've seen your statement to the police, and I have some follow-up questions."

Tori said nothing.

"You have been acquainted with Cynthia Stevens for many years."

"Yes."

"Would you describe her as your best friend?"

"I suppose so, yes."

"Yet you claim to have had no contact with her for approximately three weeks before the shootings."

"That is not a claim," Tori said. "It's a fact."

"Would you care to explain that fact?"

Tori hesitated. Did she really want to get into Ben's death and Cindy's emotional problems? "I have no explanation beyond what's contained in my statement," she said.

Bertelson gave her a sharp look. "All right. And did you have any contact with Mrs. Stevens after the shootings?"

"Of course not."

"And she made no attempt of any kind to contact you indirectly?"

"She's dead, for God's sake. What on earth do you want from me?"

"Just answer the question."

"The answer is no."

"You do understand the federal and state penalties for being an accessory after the fact and making false statements to investigators?"

"Probably similar to those for stalking," she said evenly.

The agent showed no reaction. "You gave a statement to Sergeant Jaworski of the Montgomery County police."

"Yes."

"Did Sergeant Jaworski contact you when Mrs. Stevens' car was found?"

"Yes."

"Did he tell you, then or at any other time, of a purported sighting of Mrs. Stevens on Massachusetts Avenue NW?"

"No." She tried to make her voice sound slightly perplexed and interested rather than flat and certain.

"Today you drove to a building on Massachusetts Avenue NW. You walked for several blocks and appeared to be searching for something or someone. Would you explain what you were doing and why?"

"No."

"Ms. McMillan, it's in your interest to cooperate fully. I'd hate to take you in and have you cited for refusal to answer questions and obstructing justice."

"And if I were you, I'd hate to have to explain both the relevance of your questions and the propriety of your actions. Go ahead and issue your subpoena—I'll take my chances in front of the judge."

They stared at each other for a long moment, and Tori gave silent thanks to Ben, wherever he was. It hadn't always been easy being married to a white collar criminal defense attorney for five years, but every once in a while, it came in handy. And Bertelson had to know she was a lawyer as well.

Bertelson closed his notebook. His features softened, and he assumed a gentle, paternal air. "Ms. McMillan, we know what you've been through, believe me. We are not harassing you unnecessarily. But you must under- stand, these are questions stand, these are questions that must be asked in the course of any professional investigation. Not all of them are pleasant, and every once in a while, I have to lean on people a little bit. You obviously have some familiarity with criminal law—you must know what I'm saying is true."

Tori thought about it. As big a jerk as Bertelson was, he was right.

The FBI man seemed to relax further. "I'm sure you don't recall, ma'am, but we've met before, under equally trying circumstances, unfortunately."

"Scotty's kidnapping," she said.

He nodded. "I was in charge of the investigation, and we interviewed all friends and acquaintances of the Stevens family. I know the family, and I feel for all of them—Mrs. Stevens included. It's hard to imagine a more complete family tragedy. No one wants to complete the investigation and get past all this more than I do."

Bertelson stood up, hesitated, then sat back down. "Don't misconstrue what I'm about to tell you. I like Kyle Jaworski. I've worked with him before. You won't find a smarter young detective anywhere. But this is a murder investigation—a multiple murder. Our personal likes and preferences and personalities have no place here. Several years ago, Sergeant Jaworski's department suspended him for assaulting a Federal officer. He also took a leave of absence for chemical dependency treatment."

Tori tried to imagine the easygoing Jaworski coming to blows with someone. She couldn't.

He stood up again. "I just cannot over-emphasize the importance of cooperating fully with all proper authorities. In this case, that happens to be me. You are the chief suspect's best friend—you are a key witness. We need you. If you think of anything, please call me."

CHAPTER 5

Everyone in the room stood along with President Roark Harris, who
flashed his famous grin. "Thanks, everybody." The National Security
Council meeting was adjourned. Harris returned to his office, accompanied by the Secretaries of State and Defense. Jim Traeger, after a brief
chat with the Chairman of the Joints Chiefs of Staff, started down the
hallway toward his own office. After a few steps he felt a hand on his
shoulder.

"Jim, can you spare a moment?"

Traeger turned around. The hand belonged to Vice President Norman
Whitelaw.

"Of course," Traeger said, making a point of first consulting his wrist-
watch. The tall, elegant Whitelaw, unlike the President, treated him less
like hired help and more like a human being. But Traeger knew the Vice
President, who nominally outranked him, resented the power Traeger
wielded, much as the President resented his own dependence on his politically savvy chief of staff.

The two men entered the Vice President's office, and the door closed
behind them. Whitelaw gestured toward a sofa, while taking a club chair
across the coffee table from him.

Whitelaw, Traeger thought, at least looked like a President, with a long,
patrician face and dark, wavy hair with just enough graying at the tem-
ples. His manner was Southern and courtly, his voice a gentle drawl. The
Vice President sat back, legs crossed. "Nice response on those shootings
up in Maryland, Jim."

Traeger grunted noncommittally.

"More emphasis on sympathy for the victims—he sounded downright

Clintonesque yesterday, feeling their pain. And downplaying the punishment that awaits the wicked perpetrator."

Traeger waited.

"Of course, there's no change in our policy. But that's your particular genius. Changing the spin while leaving the substance untouched."

Traeger looked up. Whitelaw's tone had not been admiring.

The Vice President leaned forward. "We've worked together a long time, Jim. We've gotten along well. You were one of my early boosters. Now you've turned against me, and I'd like to know why."

Traeger started to protest, but Whitelaw cut him off. "Don't deny it. I know all the Hokanson bullshit is coming from you."

The chief of staff, who still hadn't said a word, leaned back and crossed his legs.

"I've been the President's man," Whitelaw said. "I've played the good soldier, done everything he's asked. I've given all the low-road speeches attacking all his enemies, attended every foreign funeral, spoken at every party fund-raiser and dinner in every rinky-dink county in America. I've been completely loyal—he has no reason to do this to me."

"He's not doing anything to you."

"I know he's not, at least not yet. You are."

Traeger shrugged.

"I want you to know two things," Whitelaw continued. "First of all, I've been loyal, and I'll continue to be loyal. I'll do whatever you want in order to make this work. You want me to keep a lid on the abortion people, I'll do it. You want me to preach the gospel of the flat tax in front of business groups every week, I'll be there. Just tell me what you want."

"I'll pass it along to the President," Traeger said, eager to wrap up the meeting.

"Then pass this along, too, Jim: I'm in this race, all the way. No matter what you do, no matter what the President says or does. You dump me and you've got trouble. Trouble with the Christians. Trouble from here all the way through the primaries to the convention."

Traeger's knees weakened. It was the worst possible news. Whitelaw wouldn't go quietly. He stood up. "I don't want trouble."

Whitelaw remained seated. "No, you just want your way."

The Vice President watched Traeger leave, then picked up the phone and punched in a number. After a moment he said, "No luck. I have no idea who's behind this. Find out who he's working for."

•

At three that afternoon Traeger entered the Oval Office to brief the President on negotiations over a labor reform bill pending in the Senate. He was surprised to see two other people already seated in the office.

Roger Clayton, a heavyset, balding, bearded man who favored bow ties and cigars, was the President's longtime campaign manager and remained his chief pollster and liaison to the party. Traeger and Clayton had long maintained an uneasy relationship with each other, each respecting the other and taking care not to intrude on the other's turf.

Seated next to Clayton was Amy Burke, the President's chief aide for political affairs and a protégé of the Vice President. She was thirtyish and attractive in a Southern, debutante/sorority queen way. Her pulled-back, blonde-streaked hair; her just-right makeup; her classic, expensive, tai-lored tweed suit—all were severely perfect.

Roark Harris remained oblivious to the awkwardness. "I thought I'd ask Roger and Amy to sit in on this meeting, to talk about this succession stuff," he said.

The meeting was not even supposed to be about succession, much less to include Clayton and Burke. In fact, Harris, an orderly man, normally would not have dreamed of holding an impromptu meeting. All such functions were set up and cleared through Traeger and his staff. It wasn't hard to figure out what was happening: the President had been consulting others behind his back. And this gathering was less a meeting than an ambush.

Traeger sat down. "I wasn't really prepared to discuss this now."

"You seem to have done a lot of thinking about it," the President observed. "Roger has a poll we should think about."

Of course he would. Roger always had a poll, which by sheer coinci-dence invariably supported Roger's position.

"It says," the President continued, "seventy percent of the people think I'd be disloyal to dump the Vice President."

Traeger thought quickly about how to counter Clayton's poll. He decid-ed to skip the obvious: that half of the poll's respondents didn't give a rat's ass, and those who did had given the matter little thought. "Previous polls," Traeger pointed out, "also show a strong majority saying you should endorse the best person for the job."

Clayton spoke for the first time, in his ponderous, wise-man voice.

"Jim, why are we having this conversation? What precipitated this?"

"The proper question should be, 'Why shouldn't we be having a conversation like this?' Why should the President let inertia dictate his decision?"

Clayton leaned back, stroking his beard. "The President has twice selected Norman Whitelaw to be the number two elected official in this government and a proverbial heartbeat away from the Presidency itself. That, my friend, is not inertia. Those were very, very conscious decisions."

Traeger hesitated. With Harris in the room, he couldn't very well point out the obvious—that Whitelaw was the candidate best able to help the ticket get elected, not necessarily the best qualified to be President. "Of course you're right," Traeger said. "The President made very deliberate and thoughtful decisions for the good of the country. Then why should this decision be any different?" From the corner of his eye, Traeger saw Roark Harris lift an eyebrow. It had been a good comeback.

Traeger pressed his advantage. "You seem to have done a lot of research, Roger. Why don't you outline the case for Norm Whitelaw as the candidate best able to implement the President's agenda during the next eight years?"

"That's not the only consideration and you know it. An agenda is meaningless if you don't get elected."

"I see. So, do you want to make the case for Whitelaw's electability?"

"That case, my friend, is open and shut. He's by far the number one candidate against any major challenger."

"And," the President added, "Hokanson barely registers. He's in fourth place."

"The day you endorse him he climbs to number one."

"That's total speculation and total bullshit," Clayton shot back, finally losing his cool.

Traeger glanced at Amy, who had wisely remained silent, letting Clayton run interference. Even while responding to Clayton, Traeger had been addressing his arguments to Amy; she was a far more formidable opponent. "We need to take a step back," Traeger said. "Winning elections is great; it's what we've all devoted most of our lives to. But we need to ask why. Why do we want to win this particular election? What do we hope to accomplish? Your argument is circular, Roger. You're saying we need to win this election because we need to win this election."

"Fine. You go out and lose it," Clayton said, sounding disgusted.

Amy Burke spoke for the first time. "I don't think you've really answered the original question, Jim. Why now? You could have spoken up on this months ago. Years ago." Amy's tone was, as always, lightly mocking and condescending. Her Southern accent had been diminished only a little by her years at Harvard. She was known to roll her eyes occasionally at Whitelaw's dogmatism, but there was no doubt where her loyalties rested.

"I didn't realize this was going to be a railroad rather than a conscious choice," Traeger asserted. He avoided Harris's eyes; the response was lame and everyone knew it. He had no good excuse. Amy Burke, having zeroed in on his weakest point, resumed her original silence.

The meeting went in circles, covering the same arguments for another half-hour before the President dismissed the participants.

"Jim."

Traeger, already halfway through the doorway, looked back at Harris.

"Stay a minute, will you?"

Traeger returned, taking his original chair.

The President stood up and looked out the window for a long minute. Without turning around he said, "Jim, I should kick your ass out of the White House and all the way across the Potomac for this goddamned stunt."

Traeger said nothing.

"I just can't believe you'd pull this kind of shit at the last minute."

Traeger maintained his silence, and Harris wheeled around to confront him. "Just tell me what's going on here. For six and a half years I've always been able to believe there's at least one person in this town who's got my interests at heart, whose agenda is identical to mine. Now I don't know what the hell to think. What've you got against Whitelaw?"

Traeger, exasperated, felt like throttling his boss. "Mr. President, you know I've never let personal likes or dislikes get in the way of my political judgment. I've got nothing against Whitelaw; I just think Hokanson is a better fit, politically and philosophically."

"Jim, since when do you give a flying fuck about philosophy?"

The question left Traeger momentarily speechless. He shrugged.

Harris sat down. "You said this morning Whitelaw is in the race, endorsement or no. Is he serious?"

"In his own mind, maybe." Traeger tried to sound confident.

The President knitted his fingers together and rested his chin on them. "It sure looks to me like Norm could make trouble for us. He can raise money, and he'd be a pain in some of the early primary states, especially in the South."

"He could create some problems, I'm not denying that. But in the long run, the problems would go away. He's kept a low profile during the past seven years, but if the public heard his real views, he'd be exposed as a social extremist. At best, he's got regional strength; as a mainstream, national candidate, he's not viable."

Harris' face was troubled. "But he's worked hard and loyally for me."

"So has Senator Hokanson. So have a lot of people, and they don't have the sense of entitlement the Vice President seems to have."

The President shot him a nasty look. Sometimes Traeger annoyed the hell out of him. His chief of staff was just a little too smart, a little too quick with the answer to any objection. Harris swiveled in his chair and looked through the blue-tinged bulletproof window out over the South Lawn. "How about Hokanson? Could he make trouble for us?"

"Fortunately, Mr. President, we don't even have to ask that question," Traeger said.

Harris swiveled back around. "Why not?"

"For the same reason we should give him serious consideration. He doesn't want to make trouble for us."

•

Riding home that night, Traeger thought about the President's question. Since when did he care about anything other than politics? The question wasn't tough to answer: Since ten months, three weeks, and four days ago, when he had become Bound.

He knew he could never explain to anyone the change that had come over him, even if he'd been allowed to do so. The change would have startled most of all those who saw him as Captain Hardball. In the entire world of politics, he had been the toughest, the most cynical, and the most tactical. Bottom-line-cut-to-the-chase-no-bullshit.

He understood everything so differently now; saw things so much more clearly. He could see now that Roark Harris' philosophy of rugged individualism was incomplete at best. He knew that a sense of community was essential. He knew caring and commitment were important, that love was the answer. Traeger smiled to himself at how ludicrously touchy-feely these sentiments would have sounded to him only a year ago. In some ways he may have gone soft. But not when it came to completing his mission. He would not, could not, fail.

He wondered, not for the first time, how he had been selected to undergo the experience. He knew that at bottom he had been chosen because he was in a position to help the cause. Yet somehow they had known, better than he himself had known, of the inner emptiness he had felt, of the unacknowledged yearning for meaning and happiness. And so, through this mysterious, serendipitous process, he had been selected to go to something called a Corman seminar.

•

Tori did her stretching on the C & O Canal towpath, just upriver from the Key Bridge. It was less than a mile from where Cindy's car had been found, and only blocks from where she had presumably jumped to her death into the Potomac. The day was hot, even for August in Washington, and only the faintest of breezes disturbed the trees that overhung the gravel path and the still waters of the canal. She leaned against a tree, bracing herself with one hand, while using the other to bring her heel up toward her back.

Several miles up the canal, on a hot July day five and a half years earlier, she and Cindy had stopped their bikes at a spigot to refill their water bottles. They had struck up a conversation with a young man, a handsome, easygoing attorney named Ben McMillan...

Tori had given up trying to stop punishing herself. She couldn't avoid them all—the canal, the Mall, Georgetown, Alexandria, Rock Creek Park. They were all her places, and Ben's. And Cindy's. For the first time she thought seriously about relocating. There was now no job to keep her here. And with Cindy as well as Ben gone, there might be too many of these encounters with ghosts.

Kyle Jaworski came into view as she was stretching her other leg. The detective looked fit but pale, and in contrast to his elegant work clothing, his workout attire—baggy shorts and faded T-shirt—looked out of character. He appraised Tori, who wore shorts and a T-shirt, with an appreciative glance that was less than a leer but far more than cursory.

"Thanks for coming, Sergeant."

He smiled. "I'm sure I can use the exercise."

"Anybody can do an interview in a police station or home." She extended her arms ed her arms and twisted from one side to the other. "I'm giving you the C & O Canal. Have you stretched yet?"

He grudgingly touched his toes a few times, then said, "Let's go." They began at a slow trot, westward along the towpath.

"When are you going back to work?" he asked.

"I'm not."

She noticed his surprised expression. "My job was filled while I took a couple of months off to be with my husband. They don't have a place for me."

"No place at all? Sattex is a decent-sized company."

Tori, suddenly feeling tired and chilled, didn't answer. She had never understood why companies operated that way, but it happened all the time. In truth, she had been ready to leave the company more than a year ago, when Max Tuten had been promoted to assistant general counsel. Her career had come to a standstill, blocked by the men who ran the department, guys who looked good in suits, played a lot of golf, and smoked cigars together afterward. The company had awarded her a nice severance package, and when Ben was alive, they had done well. She would be secure financially.

She just wished Cindy were here.

"So what can I do for you?" Jaworski asked, suddenly all business.

"Somebody has to listen to reason," she said. "You weren't very receptive the other night. Nevertheless, you're all I've got."

"Thanks for the ringing vote of confidence. But I don't understand what you want from me."

"I'm still interested in why Cindy killed those people."

"I thought we'd been over that."

She persisted. "Have you found any connection at all between the victims?"

He hesitated, considering whether to answer. "Ms. McMillan, I normally don't discuss ongoing investigations with witnesses. But I know what you've been through, and I understand your concern. There's no link, nothing to suggest the victims were consciously chosen. They were all management types who work in the same industry, but so was everybody else at that barbecue. Other than that, I couldn't find any link. They're all upstanding citizens, volunteer in the community, kind to animals, etc., etc."

Tori said, "To me, that just makes the whole thing even more inexplicable. But, I appreciate your answering me."

"I'm not that bad a guy," he said. "If I was, I'd be hauling you into the station instead of having you grant me an audience at your favorite jogging spot."

He slowed to a trot, then a walk, as they approached a water spigot. Sweat poured from him, and Tori could see that while he looked pale, Jaworski wasn't out of shape. The muscles now visible under the wet, clinging T-shirt were well defined, and a run of about a mile and a half in the heat hadn't left him unduly winded.

They took turns drinking at the fountain attached to the spigot, and Jaworski leaned down and ran water over his head. He stood upright, shook off the water, and said, "I imagine you've received a visit from the Federal Bureau of Incompetence."

"And it was a real treat."

"You undoubtedly got an earful about Yours Truly."

"The subject came up," she agreed.

"You heard I'm a drunk and that I was suspended once."

"You forgot the assault on the Federal officer."

Kyle Jaworski smiled. "No, that's something I'm not likely to forget."

"Bertelson was the officer, wasn't he."

"And I should've hit him harder, gotten my money's worth out of the suspension. But after that swell anger management training they made me go to, I'd probably just give him a hug if I came across him today."

"Bertelson warned me not to talk to you," she said.

"And yet...."

"And yet here I am. Agent Bertelson and I didn't hit it off very well. In fact, he was following me in a way that bordered on stalking. He scared me."

"Nolan's actually a pussycat. Sensitive and misunderstood."

"He asked about you—what kind of questions you've asked me and when. Why do you suppose he did that?"

Jaworski gave her a small smile, then looked away. "It's all just bureaucratic bullshit. I don't want him on this case, there's no reason for him to be on this case, and yet here he is, on this case. The County Executive wanted to cover his ass, so he ordered the chief to bring them in."

"Why did you hit Bertelson?"

"It was a long time ago. We had...differences."

"That's not a very helpful answer."

"I'd just prefer not to discuss that."

"Then let's try a different question: Why didn't you tell me you worked on Scotty's kidnapping?"

He gave her an uneasy smile. "So you remembered."

"Yes, I did. You actually interviewed me in connection with the case. Why didn't you tell me?"

"It was irrelevant."

"You went on talking about Scotty's kidnapping as if you'd barely heard of it."

"You were the one who brought up the kidnapping."

They jogged the rest of the way to Georgetown in silence. At the foot of the stairs to 35th Street they stood for a moment, cooling down.

After a brief pause she said, "You know, I didn't like Bertelson, but his questions were proper if not tactful. And he hasn't told me anything provably false. You, on the other hand, weren't open with me."

His gray eyes flashed briefly. "As I said, Ms. McMillan, my job is a pretty simple one, and I'm pretty good at it. I don't spend a lot of time sitting around worrying about openness and about delicate ethical sensibilities. My job is to find Cindy Stevens, period."

"And you can tell me, with a perfectly straight face, that the killings had nothing to do with Scotty."

"I don't care."

"You don't...." Tori spluttered.

Jaworski looked out toward the river. "If you think I'm a heartless bastard, you're entitled to your opinion. But I practically lived with Cindy and Larry for close to a year. Whenever I need a reminder of what my job is about, I think about them. And I still think about Scotty. Every day." He walked away without a word.

●

Jaworski berated himself as he climbed the steps to M Street. She was pushing him, hard, into an area he needed to stay clear of at all costs. For years he had managed to shove Scotty Stevens and Nolan Bertelson to the back of his mind. He should have known he would have to face them again, that they had never really gone away.

He had started with the same idealism as any cop. And he was subject to the same grinding, dehumanizing pressures as any cop. But the Stevens case was different, and the evil behind it—faceless, unfathomable—was larger and longer-lived than the crime it had perpetrated seven years ago.

He paused, catching his breath as he waited to cross M Street to where his Mercedes 190 was parked. He unlocked the car, reached in for a towel, and threw it on the leather seat before getting in. He turned west on M Street and proceeded up Canal Road, the sounds of Mozart filling the vehicle. What was he to make of Tori McMillan, of her connection to two unspeakable crimes; of her profoundly unsettling questions about the latest murders? And, most unsettling of all, what was he to make of the woman herself, and of the reaction she produced in him?

He pictured her again, with her raven hair, green eyes, and thin, tapered face. Small and unmistakably feminine, but compact, self-sufficient, tough. She had revealed her fears, suspicions, and frustrations to him, and he could see it had been a struggle for her. But he knew there were more feelings beneath the surface. From the moment he had walked into her home, he'd wanted to know them all, to know her, completely. Maybe it was just as well that he had blown it, behaved like an ass. Reacting to her now, acknowledging his feelings, was a luxury he couldn't afford.

Jaworski counted himself lucky to have escaped the Stevens case with his career—even his life—intact. Afterward, he had been glad to go back to the everyday greed, lust, ego—even madness—that drove other criminals and their crimes. But the inevitable time of reckoning had arrived. If he was careful and lucky, and stayed clear of Tori McMillan, he might survive it again.

•

So preoccupied with his thoughts was Jaworski that he didn't notice, three cars behind him, a blue sedan, driven by Special Agent Nolan Bertelson.

CHAPTER 6

Jim Traeger ate a late lunch by himself in the White House mess, trying to fight off hopelessness. He was losing the President, and losing him
on an issue that could not be lost. He had to turn his boss around. In the
months since he had become Bound, he had experienced peace and happiness beyond his wildest imaginings. He would let nothing threaten it.
Nothing.

"Hey, how's Captain Hardball?"

He looked up; Amy Burke was standing next to him, holding a tray.
"Mind if I join you?"

"Sure."

Amy sat down. Traeger looked at her lunch, a tiny salad and a glass of
mineral water, and wondered why she even bothered. She sipped from her
glass. "I have to hand it to you, Jim. I guess we'd all gotten a little com-
placent around here. You've really shaken things up."

"I wasn't trying to." He glanced around the nearly deserted room to
make sure no one was within earshot. "I just wanted to give people something to think about."

"You succeeded brilliantly. But the new Whitelaw vs. Hokanson horse
race isn't even what interests me the most."

Traeger chewed on a french fry. "All right, I'll bite. What does interest
you the most?"

She leaned forward, and Traeger could smell her light but distinctive
perfume. "What interests me," she said, "is the new Jim Traeger."

He shook his head, spearing two more french fries with his fork. "No,
no. It's the same old me, and this isn't about me, anyway."

"Sure it is, Jim. It's entirely about you." She ate a small bite of salad, chewing it thoroughly. "There's no grass-roots movement out there, Jim. No groundswell of support for Hokanson. No discontent with Whitelaw. And, what's more interesting, you haven't tried to create any of those things. That's the way the old Jim Traeger would have gone about getting it done. Start early, have a complete game plan, round up support, then present your choice as a fait accompli. Instead, you've forced a point-blank confrontation at a late stage."

Traeger managed a smile as he finished his burger. Amy was right, of course. For all his reputation as a hardball player, Traeger never risked an open battle unless he had to. He would never fight an opponent who could be co-opted, outmaneuvered, or bought off. Under normal circumstances, he would have started a comprehensive campaign for Hokanson long ago, a bandwagon that would have appeared to come from a dozen directions. He was proceeding differently now only because Temple's orders forced him to move much later than he normally would have.

Amy drank some more water. "Some people say you've gone soft since you came back from Commerce. But I don't think so. I think you must know what you're doing. You nearly always do." She smiled, and Traeger knew he had to guard against being taken in by her. Amy had courted him, ever since she had begun working for Whitelaw during the first Harris Administration.

"I'm a lame duck, Amy. What do I have to lose by speaking my mind? You—you're going to be chief of staff in the Whitelaw administration. Hell, even if lightning strikes somehow and there's a Hokanson adminis-tration, you'll be right in the thick of things."

She smiled again. "That's why it's so interesting to watch you at work, Jim. Of course this is all about you. You're putting yourself on the line— all your credibility, all your years with Harris—you're staking all of it on one throw of the dice. You are the only thing Hokanson has going for him."

Traeger shrugged. She had left unspoken the obvious corollary: he was also the only thing standing between Norman Whitelaw and the Presidency.

She said, "If you haven't been in on this with Hokanson all along, which is what all my sources tell me, that means he hasn't actually agreed to run."

"True."

"How do you know he will? He'd be taking on both Harris and . . . whitelaw."

Whitelaw."

"I don't think that will be a problem." In fact, Traeger had asked Temple that very question. He'll run, had been the immediate and simple reply.

She leaned toward him again, lightly touching his hand. "This is me you're talking to. You can tell me—what on earth are you up to?"

He looked away without answering.

She finished her salad and patted her mouth with a napkin. "It's quite a performance, Jim. Putting all that on the line without a clue as to your real agenda. Not so much as a hint as to where you're really coming from." She stood up. "Win or lose, you've got balls, Jim Traeger."

•

After a quick dinner at home that night, Traeger drove in his own Lexus to Arlington. He took the Beltway across the Potomac, then caught I-66, heading east. He exited near Glebe Road, and turned toward Wilson Boulevard. Less than a mile from Glebe, he parked in the rear lot of a nondescript two-story brick-and-glass building. Walking briskly up to a back door, he entered the Washington Area Nonprofit Resource Center, showing an I.D. card to a security guard. Traeger treasured these monthly meetings, which most powerful people would have disdained. There was no political profit in serving as chair of the board of the Washington, D.C. region of Urban Hope, but the personal gain had been immense beyond measure.

In a small but pleasantly appointed conference room on the second floor, Traeger welcomed the other board members, who were mostly well-dressed professionals like himself. There were nine attendees, with two no-shows.

Traeger called the meeting to order. The brisk, businesslike proceedings included a review of next year's budget, a call for volunteers for the fall's United Way campaign, the need for a new roof at the Urban Hope center in Anacostia, and plans for a new mission in suburban Prince George's County. It was shortly after nine when Traeger adjourned the meeting. For perhaps twenty minutes most of the board members left one by one. Finally, only Traeger remained.

He was soon joined, however, by four other people, who filtered in after the board members had left. The new group, two women and three men, glanced around the room, nodding to one another. Traeger went to the door, stepped outside, and looked around. Then he returned to the room, locking the door behind him. The five exchanged hugs with each other. Then they pulled five chairs away from the conference table, moving them into a tight circle. Traeger took a candle from his pocket, lit it, then shut off the overhead florescent lights. The group took the chairs, squeezing together until their knees touched.

A woman asked, "Have you heard about Caitlin, Jim?"

Traeger's face, eerie in the flickering candlelight, assumed a pained expression. "Yes. It's a go."

One of the men spoke. "We're sorry, Jim. Truly sorry. If there's anything we can do...."

Traeger nodded. "I know that, Ed. I appreciate it."

For a minute no one spoke. Then Traeger said, "I guess we might as well get started."

The five clasped hands around the circle.

"May the Bound be forever unbroken," Traeger said.

•

Tori looked at the telephone in front of her. There was a perfectly logical reason for what she was about to do. Yet she was not going to do it for any logical reason. She couldn't even articulate the emotional reason for trying to find out what had happened to Cindy, any more than she could have stated why she had undertaken a futile search for a homeless man named Artie.

She had told Kyle Jaworski she knew none of the four shooting victims other than Larry. That was true as far as it went. But she did know the daughter of Michele Tanaka, an employee of a company called Lawsys, who had been trying to crawl over a bar when Cindy had shot her three times. Val Gross, Michele's daughter, had worked as a law clerk for Tori's department the previous summer.

"Hello?"

"Val? This is Tori McMillan."

"Tori! It's good to hear your voice."

"I just thought I'd call to offer my condolences. I'm so sorry, Val."

Tori could hear sobbing at the other end of the line. "That's...so kind of you."

Tori waited for Val to compose herself, then said, "How are you coping?" It was a question she had been asked dozens of times during the past month.

past month.

"I don't know...Not as well as I should be, I know. It was just so sudden. And senseless. I hadn't seen her for a couple of weeks, and...oh, damn. Here I go again...."

Once again, Tori paused to let Val regain her composure. She realized that Val had apparently not heard about Ben's death, and she wasn't about to bring it up. She said, "I'm sorry I never got the chance to meet your mother, Val."

"You would have liked her, Tori. She was a lot like you, actually. Very strong, very positive. She was a very active volunteer, too."

Tori recalled Kyle Jaworski's observation about the victims: They're all upstanding citizens, volunteer in the community... "For what organization?" she asked.

"A little outfit called Friendship House. It's like a job training and education center for high school dropouts—they're located over in Northeast. Mom would go in and counsel these kids, and occasionally teach a computer course. She was on the board, too."

"How did she get involved?"

"It was about six or seven years ago, I guess. After she went to the Corman Seminar."

"What's a Corman Seminar?"

"Oh, it's one of those personal growth retreats—all touchy-feely. The company sent her down to some resort in Mexico for about a ten-day program. She was like a new person when she came back—happy and positive and full of energy. Anyway, one of the things they really encouraged at Corman was volunteering. So Mom got involved in Friendship House...I'm sorry. Here I am, rambling on."

Tori had a dozen other questions, but decided not to press further. She decided not to tell Val that she had seen her mother die, or that the killer had been her best friend. "I should let you go," Tori said. "I just wanted to offer my condolences."

"I appreciate it," said Val. "I've had dozens of people call. I just wish one of them could tell me why Mom had to die."

Tori replaced the receiver, composed herself, then made another call.

"This is Troy," said a whiny voice at the other end.

"Good morning, Troy. How's my favorite human resources rep?"

"Tori? But I thought you were—well...."

"Gone?" Tori suggested.

"Uh, yes."

"Don't worry, I'm on my way out. I just wonder if you could answer a question for me before I go."

Troy Jenkins hesitated. He was being asked to give information to a terminated Sattex employee.

"It's not even about me," Tori assured him. "I'd just like to know a little about Corman seminars."

wary "Why do you need to know?" Jenkins asked warily.

"So I can spill it to a competitor and get you in trouble."

"Jesus—"

"Troy, lighten up. Just tell me whether the company sends people to Corman seminars. That has to be public information."

firm "I can't tell you that," he said firmly.

She kept her voice under control. "Troy, let's pretend for a moment you're a normal human being, and not a scared corporate drone who exists for the sole purpose of enforcing policies and regulations. Just help out a fellow human being, okay?"

"Tori—"

"Just give me the goddamn information."

There was a brief pause. Then, "Yes, we do." Jenkins sounded stunned.

"How many?"

"One or two a year, I'd guess."

"How are they selected?"

"By Corman."

"Not by Sattex?"

"Oh, no. To go to Corman, they have to invite you."

"How do they know about you?"

"They're well connected. They have graduates in every major corporation in America. Government agencies, too. They find the people they want."

"And Sattex always agrees to send them? To give them the time off and pay for it?"

"Tori, nobody ever turns down an invitation to send somebody to Corman. It's a prestige thing."

"Did Larry Stevens go to a Corman seminar?"

Jenkins sounded as if he'd been asked for the number of his Swiss bank account. "Jesus, Tori. What kind of question is that?"

"A pretty simple one, I think."

"For Christ's sake, why do you need to know that?"

"Troy, I just need to know. You could save me a day's work by telling me. Just tell me, and I'm out of your life for good."

She could hear a sigh. "I shouldn't."

Tori tried to think like a bureaucrat. "Make a memo of this conversation for the file. Say I pulled rank on you, bullied you."

After a long silence, Jenkins said, "Yes, he went. A long time ago. Goodbye, Tori."

Tori went upstairs and paused in the hallway in front of a closed door across from the master bedroom. She hadn't been inside Ben's study since he had died. She took a breath, opened the door and went inside. The room was cluttered, and had a slightly musty smell. There were still marks on the carpet from the IV stands provided by the hospice service; during his final year Ben had spent many hours and nights lying on the leather couch, insisting it was more comfortable than the bed. But he had died in their bed, with her, during the night.

She turned on the lights, opened the blinds, and sat down behind his desk. Before the illness Tori would often perch herself on the sofa and simply watch him as he spent long evenings here, writing briefs, practicing summations, dictating interrogatories.

She booted up the computer and accessed the Internet, looking for information on Corman seminars. It didn't take long to discover the basics. Corman Leadership Training, Inc. (CLT), headquartered in Miami, had been founded by Nathan Corman, a prominent humanist psychologist who had ranked in influence with the likes of Rogers and Maslow. The company was considered the nation's premier corporate training firm, with an emphasis on the personal growth of the participants. Many of their seminars were held in Cancún, Mexico.

Finding out who owned CLT was far more difficult. Tori searched several databases, finally learning that the company had been sold by Corman's estate when the psychologist had died ten years ago. The purchaser was FuTek, Inc., a pharmaceutical/chemical/biomedical conglomerate. FuTek sounded familiar to Tori, although she couldn't remember why, so she began another search.

Within minutes, she had learned why the name was familiar. FuTek had been founded by multi-billionaire Dennis Curry, an entrepreneur who had launched his career in the pharmaceutical business at Merck. After growing FuTek into a gigantic conglomerate Curry had, eight years ago, abruptly vanished from public view. The disappearance had focused public attention on FuTek, and the company had done little to dispel the speculation with its bland press release stating that Curry had "discontinued his active management role." A shareholder lawsuit five years ago, alleging that Curry was dead, had been settled out of court.

Since then, Dennis Curry had become a figure only slightly less elusive than Elvis, and Curry sightings had become a fixture in the tabloid media. None had been confirmed, although the most common theory held that the eccentric executive had gone off to Tibet, India, or some other Far Eastern destination in search of inner enlightenment. Meanwhile, a crack team of professional managers and attorneys ran FuTek, in which Curry still held a majority stake, and the company continued to grow and prosper.

Tori logged off the computer and let the conflicting theories, thoughts, and images swirl through her brain. Corman. FuTek. Kyle Jaworski. Scotty. Cindy. And Cindy again, in the most painful and persistent image of all, killing four people.

She jumped when the phone rang, fumbling with the receiver.

"Tori?"

"Yes?"

"This is Rick Percival."

"Rick—oh, yes."

He chuckled. "Yeah, the guy who damn near ran you down. How are you doing?"

"I'm—well, okay, I guess."

"Good. I was a little worried about you the other day. Listen, I really enjoyed meeting you, and I know it's a little spur of the moment, but I was wondering if you'd like to have dinner with me tonight."

"Oh, I don't know...."

Percival didn't respond.

Tori closed her eyes, listening to the emptiness of her house, to the sounds of silence and death. Why not, she thought, then realized she had said it aloud.

"Great," he replied. "Would you like me to pick you up? Or, I'd be happy to meet you somewhere."

"I live in the suburbs," she said. "I'll drive in and meet you."

"That's fine. Tell you what—you know where my office is, right? Would you mind dropping by here?"

"Sure."

"Around seven?"

"All right."

"Sounds good. Nothing fancy, now."

"Fine by me. See you then."

•

Tori turned south on Massachusetts Avenue. She had twice reached for her cell phone, determined to call Rick Percival to cancel. What on earth was she doing, having dinner with this man she had met once in a parking lot? She had no clear recollection of Percival now; she had been flustered and distracted at the time. But the main problem was not Percival, or even Ben; it was herself. She just wasn't ready for this.

Tori took the elevator to the fifth floor, emerging in the small anteroom of the national headquarters of Urban Hope. The room was darkened and vacant, and a sign directed after-hours visitors to ring a bell. She hesitated. It's only a friendly dinner, she thought. She pushed the button, and a loud buzzer sounded on the other side. Rick Percival emerged a half-minute later.

"Tori! Good to see you." They shook hands, and after a moment's scrutiny Tori realized that she must have been quite distracted at their first meeting. Rick Percival was a striking man, in appearance and in attitude. He was ruggedly handsome, lean and slightly bowlegged like a cowboy. His bearing and demeanor was open and friendly, but with a confidence that was unmistakably masculine. Her friendly dinner was already looking more complicated.

"Come on in," Percival said. "I need just a minute to finish things up here." She followed him back through a maze of cubes to an office with an exterior window. The room was small and cluttered, with book-lined floor-to-ceiling shelves and stacks of papers and files on the desk, floor, a chair, and a credenza. Another man, who rose to his feet when Percival and Tori entered, occupied a second chair.

"Tori McMillan, meet Myron Cooper," Percival said. Tori shook hands with a tall, fit man in his early thirties, with closely cropped blond hair. "Pleased to meet you, ma'am," said Cooper.

"Mike is our Director of Administration," Percival said. "He's the man who keeps things moving around here. And he keeps me organized—God knows that's a full-time job in itself."

"It's not so bad," Cooper said. "Rick is the only one here who puts in longer hours than I do." He spoke with the condescending, Southern-accented, slightly upward-lilting monotone common to military types, or to the state trooper who pulled you over for speeding.

"Well, I'm going to call it a day," said Percival, who had been tossing stacks of papers into a battered briefcase. "I want somebody to get on the Heartland Foundation's ass first thing tomorrow. We should have heard about that grant weeks ago."

"I'll do it myself," Cooper replied. He nodded to Tori as she and Percival left the room. "Nice to have met you."

Percival drove her to a small Italian restaurant on Pennsylvania Avenue SE, on the other side of Capitol Hill. When they were seated, Percival peered over the wine list, bantered with the waiter, and recommended a shrimp pasta dish.

When the wine arrived, Tori declined. "That's all right," Percival declared. "I hope you don't mind my indulging a bit after a long day."

"Of course not," Tori said.

Percival sipped the wine, twirled it in his glass, and sat back, looking at Tori. "I really appreciate your coming," he said. "You made my week."

"It's very sweet of you," Tori said, unable to take her gaze off him. His intense blue eyes were gentle, even saintly. His nose, strangely incongruent, was slightly but noticeably crooked, like a boxer's. He looked relaxed, composed, supremely self-confident but without arrogance. "I get so tired of nagging people and begging for money all day; you can't imagine what a treat this is—a quiet dinner with an interesting woman."

The compliment hadn't been extravagant, but Tori felt herself blushing anyway. "I'm afraid I won't be great company—I'm sort of preoccupied these days."

"Nonsense," Percival said. "I think we're always more interesting during the rough times. The barriers tend to come down."

Exactly what I was afraid of, Tori thought. She changed the subject. "How long have you been with Urban Hope?"

"Let's see—nine and a half years now."

"When did you become Executive Director?"

Percival smiled. "I suppose I started calling myself that a couple of years later. But at the beginning, it was only me."

"You mean you founded Urban Hope?"

He chuckled. "Yeah, and I sure didn't know what the hell I was getting myself into."

"But that's remarkable," she said. "You're a nationally known organization. You must have branches all over the country."

"Yes, we've grown," he said without elaboration.

"Maybe I'll try that wine after all," she said. Percival poured it for her. "How did you come to start the organization?"

"Oh, it was a standard mid-life crisis thing, I suppose."

"Mid-life? But you must have been—"

"I was only in my early thirties, yes. But everything had come quickly for me. I was in the corporate world and doing well. But I was coping with the deaths of some people close to me, and I got to thinking about what I'd really accomplished. Anyway, one night I was staying in Chicago—at a hotel up on the Gold Coast. I'd parked my rental car on the street, and I came down a little after midnight, and there was a kid trying to steal it. The kid couldn't have been more than thirteen. He tried to run, but I grabbed him. I asked why he was trying to steal the car, and he said he was running away. I asked him why."

Percival paused and sipped from his glass. Tori did likewise; the wine was an excellent, fruity white.

"I guess," he continued, "you shouldn't ask a question if you don't want to know the answer. We sat down in the car, and he told me a long story about how he'd watched gang members gun down his brother, how they were after him, how his father was gone and his mother was no help. He had nobody to turn to. A pretty typical story, unfortunately. Well, I wasn't about to turn the kid back out onto the streets, but I couldn't figure out what else to do with him, either. I spent all night and most of the next morning trying to find an agency or shelter to take him in, someplace he'd be safe, but I had a hell of a time. Finally I found a place, but the people were indifferent and the conditions were appalling. That's when I decided to give it a try myself."

Tori drained her glass, and Percival refilled it. "Let's eat," he said as their meals arrived. They ate in silence for several minutes; the food was excellent. "I've been doing all the talking," Percival said. "How are you doing?"

"Not bad," Tori replied. In fact, she felt more relaxed than she had in weeks.

"Where do you work?" he asked.

"At the moment, nowhere." She explained about her termination from Sattex.

His response was more resigned than indignant. "It happens, I suppose. You know, you could sue them for a hell of a lot of money."

She nodded. "I don't need the money. But most of all, I don't need the aggravation. I'll just take their severance package."

"That's an uncommonly mature attitude," he said. "But it still stinks. They're taking advantage of you during a vulnerable time. And it throws your entire career off track."

Tori squirmed. Why not be honest? she asked herself. Why not tell him the truth, that she had ceased caring about her career ever since she had met Ben? She had been on the fast track once, starting with her computer training in the army and a computer sciences degree in college, a law degree and big-firm experience, then steady advancement after her return to Sattex. Then she had hit the glass ceiling, passed over in favor of Max Tuten. But she hadn't been able to care about any of it; since the encounter five years ago at a water spigot on the C & O Canal, her career had been a sideshow.

It would not look good to admit, as a smart and capable woman in a world that finally honored and rewarded smart and capable women, that in becoming Mrs. Ben McMillan she may have achieved her life's highest purpose. Still, why should she care what Percival thought?

She looked at the man across the table from her, felt a little catch in her throat, and realized she did care.

"I'll be okay," she said.

Rick Percival smiled, and with no self-consciousness or hesitation, covered her hand with his across the table. "I'm sure you will."

Tori felt giddy, from the wine and the swirling thoughts and the lack of sleep and, most of all, from Rick Percival's enveloping presence. She needed to bring herself down, to regain her footing.

After dinner they walked out onto Pennsylvania Avenue, breathing in the humid air. Tori started across the street toward the car, but Percival stopped her. "Let's walk," he said. They strolled westward toward the Capitol.

"Tori," Percival said at last, "I'm no psychologist. But I'd like to think I'm a friend."

He paused, and they stopped to wait for the light at North Capitol Street. She turned toward him, meeting his eyes again.

"If you'd like to talk about your husband, I'm listening," he said.

They crossed North Capitol, then Pennsylvania, and sauntered across the grounds of the illuminated Capitol. Tori had no stores of resistance remaining. She told him the entire story, beginning with the diagnosis of Ben's lymphoma more than a year ago; the horrible ordeal of chemotherapy; the repeated hospitalizations; his wasting, deteriorating appearance; and finally his death at home. She told about the grinding exhaustion, not only from attending to Ben's physical needs, but from all the side battles she'd fought: with Ben's callous law partners; with his well-meaning but intrusive family members; with a stonewalling insurance company. And she told how every aspect of her own life had slowly died along with Ben: her career; her friendships; all of her hopes for a family and a future.

Finally she was done. They had walked all the way down the south side of Capitol Hill, then back up the north side, and now stood in front of the Supreme Court. They walked in silence across East Capitol, then paused.

"Let's sit down," Percival said. They sat down on the steps of the Library of Congress. The wind had turned chilly, and he took her hand again. After several moments of silence he said, "Tori, I don't know what to say. For what it's worth, I lost my wife a number of years ago, so I have at least some idea what you're going through."

"I'm sorry," she said, feeling helpless. "You've been so kind to me, and here I am, unloading onto you."

He shook his head. "I'm flattered, that you would share such personal thoughts with me."

They returned to the car, and Percival drove them back to Tori's vehicle, parked behind the Urban Hope building.

They looked at each other. Now came the awkward moment she had been dreading. Would they shake hands, kiss, or something more?

"What do we do?" she whispered.

"That's entirely up to you. All I'll say is that I find you very attractive, Tori. I'm a responsible adult with no diseases and nothing to fear from Megan's Law."

Tori looked away, out the car window at the darkened parking deck, knowing there was really no choice. This man, this relative stranger, knew her secrets. By revealing her neediness, her dependence, she had placed herself in his hands. And yet the revelations had seemed irrelevant.

Somehow, he had already known.

•

Kyle Jaworski sat in his car half a block away, watching Tori get into the Taurus registered to a Richard Percival. As he had watched them in the restaurant, it hadn't seemed as if they'd known each other well. But now they were apparently going to spend the night together.

That Tori's questions presented a danger to him he had no doubt. His hope lay in finding Cindy Stevens and closing the Sattex murder case as quickly and quietly as possible. But as much as Jaworski feared Tori, he was afraid for her as well. She had no idea what kind of evil she had brushed up against, what kind of danger her persistent questioning presented to herself and others.

He tried to ignore the flush of anger that passed through him as he watched Richard Percival kiss her. He would have to check Percival out; Tori was alone, vulnerable, and unwittingly involved in a dangerous murder case. The Taurus drove away, and Jaworski willed himself to stay where he was. His justification for the stakeout, done on his own time, was already dubious, based on the possibility that Cindy Stevens might try to contact her. And if the reason for watching her didn't hold up, if he had to acknowledge the true reason, from his deepest heart, he was no longer a cop on a stakeout.

He was an obsessed stalker.

CHAPTER 7

Jim Traeger settled into the jump seat of the limousine with President Roark Harris for the drive to the Pentagon, where the President was scheduled to take part in a war game simulation.

Harris stared out the window at a touch football game on the Ellipse. "So what've we got this morning, Jim?"

Traeger glanced at the list he had compiled during the morning staff meeting. Over the years he and the President had adopted the practice, in all but the most compelling cases, of considering matters of state before those items that qualified as purely political. It was a small concession to Harris' conscience; Traeger thought it was silly, coming from a man who wouldn't scratch his ass without taking a poll.

In planning for an upcoming Middle East summit, the President decided to ease off on the Israelis. He was always easing off on the Israelis. They agreed to fire a shot across the Fed's bow, expressing concern about the effect of any interest rate hike. Traeger and the Secretary of Labor would meet with Congressional leaders in two days to discuss a threatened rail strike.

Traeger leaned back in his seat and relaxed slightly. It was their normal signal that political discussion could begin. The President also seemed to relax, but his face was troubled. "Jim," he began, "I am still seriously pissed at you about this succession thing."

Traeger said nothing.

"I still don't understand it, and I still find it hard to believe. I just wish you and Roger could get together on this." He hated it when his advisors disagreed.

"That will be hard to do unless Roger takes a Hokanson candidacy seriously, sir. He's done no real polling or analysis on it."

Harris nodded reluctantly. "But you have to admit Amy is right," he said. "We'd be starting late."

"Maybe a little," Traeger acknowledged.

Harris looked out the window again as they rounded the Lincoln Memorial to cross the bridge to Arlington. "Why do I need this, Jim? Why tip over the shithouse and create a big stink?"

Traeger knew this was the real question troubling the President. His innate conservatism on matters of policy carried over into his political decisions as well, translating into a deep suspicion of unnecessary change or risk.

"Mr. President, you've got only a little over a year in office. What are you conserving your political capital for? What good is all your popularity and high approval ratings if you don't use it for something? Why not make your mark on history?"

Traeger could not see, but could well imagine, the doubt in the President's eyes. He didn't give a flea's fart about history. For him, popularity was a good enough end in itself; he liked being liked. After a long minute of silence Harris said, "I can't split the party."

"I doubt there will be a split," Traeger replied patiently. "Norm Whitelaw is a fine person. He's been loyal. But he simply isn't the best person to carry out your agenda. And regardless of his other good points, I seriously doubt he has the stomach for an open split with you."

"But if he does...."

"Believe me, Mr. President. You can handle Whitelaw. You can handle this situation." Traeger knew his boss could pull it off. He'd go on TV, tell about all the agonizing he'd done, what a great friend Whitelaw was and he hoped the Vice President would play an important role in the new administration, but now he had to put personal considerations aside, blah, blah, blah. People would see him as a statesman, not a treacherous turncoat.

The President stared straight ahead. "I don't know about you, Jim. I just don't know." He turned back toward Traeger. "I just can't do it. That's my decision."

Traeger felt his heart pounding loudly. "Mr. President, please. Don't do this now. Wait and consider your options."

"I don't want to hear it. I've already decided."

Traeger leaned forward, elbows on knees, and took a breath. "If that's your decision, sir, your decision, sir, I'll be submitting my resignation."

The President looked as if someone had shot him. "You can't be serious."

"I'm afraid I am, sir."

The limo had pulled into the tunnel and now stopped at the entrance. Harris signaled to the Secret Service agents to wait before opening the door. "What on God's green earth is going on here, Jim? You've worked for me forever. Doesn't that mean anything?"

"It means a lot. This is the hardest decision I've ever made. I know you value loyalty, sir. Loyalty from me, and from the Vice President. But we're talking about the most powerful office in the world. That is bigger than the personal relationship between any two people. Your legacy-your policies—have outgrown even you. And I'm committed to seeing that your true legacy is implemented."

The President's eyes narrowed. "You're committed."

"Yes."

"That means you'd do more than just quit. You wouldn't go quietly."

"No, I wouldn't."

Roark Harris's features tightened. He dreaded asking the next question, but knew he had to. "So what would you do?"

Traeger answered without hesitation. "I would create a national committee of concerned moderates to focus attention on the Vice President's extremist social agenda. I would go to Senator Hokanson and persuade him to run. I would manage his campaign."

"And I'm supposed to feel threatened by that?"

"Mr. President, nobody should feel—"

"I asked you a question, Jim."

Traeger nodded briefly, as if to himself. "Yes, sir, you should feel threatened. Milt Hokanson is a better candidate than Norm Whitelaw. He would make a better President. He would be running as your true successor. And he would win."

The two men stared at each other for a long moment. Traeger hadn't mentioned his own role in the scenario, but Harris knew that all of his own popularity, all his prestige, and all his purported ability to name his own successor, had to be balanced against a simple fact: Jim Traeger was a political genius.

He might be able to pull it off.

Roark Harris looked more sad than angry. "God, Jim. I can't believe

I'm hearing this. After all these years; after all we've been through."

Traeger remained silent.

"And," Harris added, "it's hard to believe you'd risk so much. Your whole future and reputation. You'd always be known as the man who split the party—divided the nation."

And now, Traeger wondered, who was supposed to feel threatened? "It's not a decision I've made lightly, sir."

The President leaned back in his seat and stared into space with a look that combined disgust, anger, and fear. "You know, Jim, if you could look me in the eye and tell me honestly why you're doing this, I just might do it." He slowly directed his gaze at Traeger. "But you can't."

•

That night, on the way home, Traeger told his driver to pull in at a convenience store. In the back of the store, Traeger dropped coins into a pay phone, waited for his party to answer, then heard the familiar clicks and buzzes.

"Temple here," said the whispery voice that, while electronically distorted, somehow sounded kind and understanding to Traeger.

"This is Traeger. It's not working. I've pulled out all the stops."

A pause. "I know you have, Jim. And I know how much we're asking of you. But this has to be done. We will have to prepare for more drastic measures."

"But as I've said, I've done all—"

"There are ways, Jim. You'll receive further instructions within twenty-four hours."

CHAPTER 8

It was one in the afternoon when Tori woke up, feeling groggy and exhausted despite twelve hours' sleep. She looked around Rick Percival's bedroom, a small, neat place with one brick wall. The stillness was total. She showered, put her clothes back on, and made herself as presentable as possible, while looking in the mirror as little as possible.

She walked out to the kitchen; the coffee maker was set up and ready to go, and she pushed the button. Percival lived in the lower level of a townhouse on gentrified Southeast Capitol Hill. Tori wandered through the house while the coffee dripped into the carafe. There was a small dining area between the kitchen and the living room, which was lined with bookshelves containing titles of every description. The bedroom was located at the rear of the house, next to another room with a closed door. Tori tried the door; it was locked. Aside from the books, the house was impersonal; she could see no photographs or mementos.

Tori sat at the small dining room table, drinking her coffee, feeling that she should get out and get going, but remembering once again, with a pang of unpleasant emptiness, that she had nothing to do and nowhere to go.

She set her coffee cup down and wept for a long time. Her shame was complete, and it went beyond the reasons that would normally apply in a situation like this, that with Ben gone less than a month, she had slept with a strange man she had met in a parking lot, who could be infected with AIDS or moonlighting as a serial killer.

She reminded herself that she hadn't had normal relations with a man in nearly a year; that Rick had been kind, considerate, and gentlemanly; that the experience itself—the warmth, the closeness—had been wonderful. But it didn't matter. She'd had to run for help.

She had failed herself, and failed Cindy.

Tori finished her coffee, took a last look around, then left. She retrieved her car from its parking spot on 5th Street SE, then headed slowly across town toward Maryland. She didn't want to go home to a dark, empty house. But there was nowhere else to go. She found herself wanting to call Rick.

At home she went through the motions. Paying bills. Cleaning the house. Running to the bank and the supermarket. Picking up the mail.

She walked across the shaggy lawn from the mailbox back to the house, flipping through credit card offers, home equity loan offers, catalogs, bills, and...a postcard.

She froze, studying the plain white card that had been mailed in Washington, D.C. and postmarked four days earlier. How long had it been sitting in her mailbox?

Cindy's familiar scrawl yielded two lines:

Please forgive me. I saw Scotty in Denver. C.

They met at a Starbucks coffee shop on Rockville Pike, just down the road from White Flint Mall. Tori was opening the door when Jaworski arrived in his Mercedes. He shut the engine off, and for a moment the sound of classical music floated across the parking lot.

"Pretty cultured for a cop," she said as he walked up, although the detective looked oddly at home in the world of classical music and elegant cars.

"My mother was a piano teacher."

"Pretty ostentatious, too."

"Give me some credit. Most civil servants wouldn't even try to keep up with the Joneses." He glanced at her Audi. "Or the McMillans."

"My taxes are paying for your luxury."

"Don't worry—I'm underpaid. I've just got nothing else to spend my meager salary on."

Inside, Jaworski bought a large cup of coffee and drank it black. Tori ordered a skim latte. The detective settled into the flimsy wooden chair across the small table from her. "You're getting to be a pest," he said. "But you know what? I'm glad you called anyway. Is that strange?"

"I hope not. I'm sorry about the disagreement we had last time. Maybe we could sort of start over again."

"Sounds good to me."

"Any word on Cindy?"

"Not yet," he said. "How are you coping?"

"That isn't exactly a standard police question."

"I'm trying to be friendly here."

"Point taken."

He blew on his coffee and sipped it. "You've had two terrible shocks in less than a month. Your best friend is gone. Do you have any family around for support?"

"Not really. My parents are alive. They're retired down in Texas."

"Did they come to your husband's funeral?"

"I didn't tell them Ben had died. Or even that he'd been sick."

"I take it you're estranged."

"Seriously. My brother came. He's a diplomat, and he traveled all the way from Brasilia. He's called a couple of times."

An uncomfortable silence followed. Tori drank some more coffee. "What about you, Sergeant?"

"Why don't you call me Kyle. You mean family?"

"Since we're getting personal here."

"My father is dead. My mother is in a nursing home in Baltimore and doesn't recognize me. I have two older sisters, in California and North Carolina. I send gifts to their kids at Christmas."

"No wife?"

"I was engaged once."

"What happened?" she asked.

"I called it off. It was about five years ago. I woke up and realized I knew too many cops with ex-wives and not enough with wives. I suppose a shrink would say I have trouble with risk-taking and commitment."

"You were a chickenshit."

"Basically."

Tori looked out the window. Waves of heat rose from the asphalt. "I know you don't want to hear this. I know you don't want to get into the psychology of why Cindy did it. I know it's not part of your job. But I hope you understand what the unanswered questions mean for me. It's very hard. Since we're using psychobabble here, let's just say that there's no closure for me."

"Go on."

"I'd just like to satisfy my own curiosity, as long as it doesn't interfere with your work."

"How?"

"Cindy and I pretty much lost touch over the past few months. I really don't know what she was doing, that might have led up to this. I thought maybe if I looked at her appointment calendar something might stand out, that would look unusual or jog my memory somehow."

Jaworski leaned back in his chair and took a large gulp from his cup. "That's not an unreasonable idea, I guess. Why, then, do I have this suspicion that you're not telling me something?"

Tori said nothing.

"If I went by the book," Jaworski said, "I would very politely assure you the case has been solved and thank you for your time. And it might get me into a bit of trouble, turning evidence over to a civilian."

Again, Tori remained silent.

"I'll bring it over tonight," he said.

She looked up. "No questions? Just like that?"

He shrugged. "Sorry for not giving you a hard time."

Tori stood up. "Well, thanks, then." She hesitated.

He remained seated. "Something bothering you?"

"I appreciate your helping me."

"But?"

She slowly sat down. "You haven't been too receptive to my questions about Cindy. In fact, you've been a little patronizing where the case is concerned. But on a personal level, you've been very friendly."

"Guilty on all counts."

"I think we have a little game going on here, called Guess the Agenda."

"And you're wondering what mine is."

She nodded.

"Pretty simple," he said. "I'm a cop trying to solve a case."

"I meant personal agenda."

"I know you did." He glanced out at the heat and the traffic, then down at his coffee. "All right," he said. "Now that the case is over, I just may have in the back of my mind, in a few weeks, when your nerves have settled and your grief subsided, to give you a call, on a personal basis. Low-key. No pressure. Just friendly. There, you forced it out of me."

Tori studied the detective. He was confident, intelligent, breezy, funny, and probably exactly what she needed right now.

"I'm sorry," she said. "I don't think so."

He nodded. "No problem. I'm just a task-oriented, narrow-minded bureaucrat, anyway."

Tori smiled. "Do I still get the calendar?"

•

Jim Traeger stood up from the dinner table. "I'm going out tonight."

Pam, her face already buried in a magazine, barely reacted. She was all too used to her husband's absences—on foreign trips, speaking tours, and trips to Roark Harris's ranch near Flagstaff, Arizona, now known as the Western White House. The girls were already upstairs, and Traeger felt a pang of guilt. He was not spending enough time with Caitlin. Not nearly enough.

He drove his Lexus across the Potomac, took the Tyson's Corner exit, and made his way to a parking garage, attached to an office building on the north side of the shopping mall. As he had been directed, he proceeded down to the second level and to the rear, on the side away from the elevators. He backed his car into a slot, shut off the engine, and waited.

Five minutes passed. Ten minutes. Traeger was starting to sweat, and thought about turning the engine on to run the air conditioning. But he had been told to leave it off. His conflict with the President was at a standoff. Roark Harris had not budged, and Traeger had not resigned. Neither had mentioned the succession issue since their confrontation in the Presidential limousine.

The headlights came into view quickly, and appeared to belong to a large vehicle, probably a pickup truck or SUV. The vehicle, its license plates hidden, came to a halt directly opposite him. Traeger slowly got out of the car, shielding his eyes from the headlights. The vehicle was still running.

The driver's door opened, and a figure got out, staying in the shadow of the headlights.

"It was hot last week," a man's voice said.

"It was worse last year."

The man appeared to relax. "All right. I guess we're both who we're supposed to be."

"Who are you?" Traeger asked.

The man ignored the question. "I have something for you. It's kind of foolproof." He sounded loose—even flippant.

"What is it?" Traeger began to step forward.

"Stay back, please." The man's rebuke was instantaneous and firm. Traeger stayed. He couldn't see the man's face.

"What is it?" Traeger asked again.

"'It' is a heart attack."

"A what?"

"A foolproof, untraceable heart attack. Should be suitable for your man—he's had a bypass and an angioplasty. Likes omelets a lot, too."

Traeger's mouth felt dry. He had suspected it was coming. More drastic measures—it had to have been something like this. But to be presented with it like this, in such a matter-of-fact way....

"Are you certain it will work?" Traeger asked.

"Oh, sure. We've used it plenty of times—no problems. We usually try to get somebody to do the job openly-you know, some opposition political figure, in a coup or something. But if we can't, well—there's always this."

Traeger knew better than to ask who "we" might be. "All right, then, I guess. How long does it take to...you know...."

"To kill him? Oh, usually twelve to fourteen hours. Well after it's been administered. And the stuff will have broken down completely in his system. It's undetectable. Any other questions?"

"I guess not."

"Fine. Good luck, then." The man got back into the vehicle, which was visible now as a sport-utility.

Traeger walked over to where the man had parked. Sitting on the greasy concrete, near a pillar, was a small vial. So this was what it had come down to. Another life, taken. An assassination.

He slipped the vial into his pocket. He would not hesitate. It needed to be done.

CHAPTER 9

Tori walked through the parking ramp toward the shopping center on the 16th Street Mall in downtown Denver, clutching a photocopy of Cindy Stevens' date book. Cindy's last business trip to Denver had been three months earlier, in late May. Cindy, then a sales manager for Sattex, had accompanied Polly Kendrick, a local sales representative, on several sales calls to customers in the Denver area. Tori couldn't remember exactly when Cindy had actually quit her job, but she knew it must have been shortly after the Denver trip.

Her suspicions about Kyle Jaworski had been correct; the detective had ulterior motives, and his judgment was questionable. But he had given her the calendar without pressing her about her reason for wanting it. He had not wanted to know, Tori thought. At least he'd been willing to accept rejection gracefully.

Which was just as well, since she felt guilty enough about Rick Percival. She had been prepared to break it off with Rick, but hadn't been able to do so when he had called her the previous evening. They had chatted easily, and she had thanked him for the flowers he'd sent her. She had found herself wanting to see him again, badly, but had dodged the issue by explaining that she would be out of town for a couple of days. When she got back, they would talk again and she would extricate herself gracefully.

She had made a copy of Cindy's postcard, then put the original in her safe deposit box at the bank. She could not have articulated exactly what made her conceal the existence of the postcard, even from Kyle Jaworski, but the omission was undoubtedly illegal. Thanks to the FBI's involvement, it was probably a Federal offense as well. Yet she couldn't ignore the implications.

It seemed incredible now that she'd taken so little notice when Cindy had drifted away from her during the months before Ben's death. Tori had been preoccupied, of course, and on one level, it had seemed natural enough that Cindy would disengage rather than bear the full brunt of another traumatic loss. But on another level, the loss should have brought them closer together, and loss or no, the friend Tori had known would have been there to support her. It seemed obvious now that something more had been going on in Cindy's life.

She had known all along that it had to be about Scotty. She knew Cindy Stevens, and there was only one thing that could have pushed her over the edge, made her a killer.

Tori entered the multilevel mall, ascended an escalator, and located the small Chinese restaurant across from a food court. Polly Kendrick, a round, middle-aged woman, waited at a corner table. She stood up as Tori approached, and they embraced.

"It's been a long time," Polly said as they sat down.

"More than a year, I think."

"You flew out for that call up at Boulder." Polly scrunched up her face to move her round glasses up on her round nose.

"Standard dog-and-pony show," Tori recalled.

"Hey, we got the business." They ordered, chatted, and examined photographs of Polly's children until their meals arrived. They ate slowly, exchanging Sattex gossip, carefully avoiding two sensitive topics.

It was not until they had cracked their fortune cookies open that Polly said, "I was so sorry to hear about your husband, Tori."

"Thank you."

"It must have been...so hard."

Tori nodded. In such conversations there was always a long version and a short version. She didn't think she could handle the long version now. "At least it wasn't unexpected," she said. "With Cindy, well...."

Polly scrunched up her face again. "No kidding. I heard you were actually there. Is that true?"

Tori nodded. "But I can't really add anything to what you've heard. It was all very straightforward and totally unbelievable. It was all over in less than a minute."

Polly shook her head sadly. "I knew Cindy for more than ten years. She was my boss for more than three. I've talked to dozens of people in the company and the industry, and nobody knows how on earth she could have done it."

"I don't know, either." Tori was relieved that Polly didn't seem to have the voyeuristic hunger for details about the shootings.

"Have they...found her yet?"

"No."

Polly looked surprised. "They don't think she's alive, do they?"

"No." Tori thought she saw relief on Polly's face. "Polly," she said, "do you remember the last time Cindy was out here?"

"Sure. It was in the spring—May, I think. She went with me to make the rounds of the major accounts. It was something we usually did once a year."

"Did anything unusual happen?"

"No, not that I can remember."

"Did—"

"Wait. Now that you mention it, she ended the trip kind of abruptly."

"How do you mean?"

"Well, let me think. It was on the second day. We'd just been down at Englewood to see Adams, Sartell, then we'd come up here to see Castle & Drinkwater...and then...." She scrunched up her face. "You know what? It was right here in this building. We came over here for lunch—this is my favorite place, and I always take people here. And then—hey, why don't I just show you?"

They fought over the check, with Tori winning. Then Polly led her out into the mall. They walked slowly, looking out over the seven-story open atrium.

Polly stopped in front of a Banana Republic store. "Okay. It was right about here. We were strolling along after lunch, looking around, just like you and I are now. And then Cindy stopped suddenly—right here by this bench, I think. She just stood there for a minute, looking—at something, I don't know what. Then she turned toward me, looking all pale and sick. She said, 'I'm really sorry, Polly. But something I ate just didn't agree with me, and I'm not feeling well. You can handle the next call, can't you?'

"So I said sure, I guess so—we were supposed to meet with Castle that afternoon, and that was the last call—so then she just rushes off."

"Where did she rush off to?" Tori asked, her tone urgent.

"Well, I don't know," Polly said, her tone defensive. "I mean, I was a little bit put out. I go to the China Garden all the time, and nobody I know has ever gotten sick from eating there. And she didn't get back to me until a few days later, when she was back in Washington, and she asked how the Castle call went. Even then, she didn't seem much interested in it. In fact, I didn't talk to her again at all. Somebody told me later she'd quit."

"Polly," Tori said patiently. "You said she was looking around. Where, exactly, was she looking?"

"I don't really remember. Why do you ask?"

"Let's assume for a moment that she didn't get sick from eating at the restaurant. Let's say she saw something that disturbed her."

"Like what?"

"I'm not sure," Tori lied.

Polly scrunched up her face. "Well, I don't really know what it could have been. She was just looking around. Actually, she was sort of looking up, like she was checking out how tall the atrium was."

"Up," Tori said. "In any particular direction?"

"I just don't remember."

"When you left her, where did she go?"

"I assume she went back to the hotel, but she left so abruptly, I'm not really sure."

"Which way is the hotel?"

"Straight ahead, the way we're going now. I didn't stick around to see where she went. I turned back the opposite way, past the restaurant to the parking garage. Tori, what is this all about?"

Tori took a breath, then put on a sheepish smile. "Nothing, really. I'm just searching for any kind of explanation. Obviously, at some point before the killings, she became disturbed, and went off the deep end. I've got some time now, so I'm just talking to some people who knew her, to try to get some kind of clue as to what might have set her off."

"I'm sorry," Polly said. "I wish I could help you. I know you two were close, and seeing her...kill people...my God."

The two women embraced, saying an emotional goodbye and promising to keep in touch.

Tori, after watching Polly descend an elevator to the ground level and exit to the street, walked back to the bench where Cindy had abruptly taken her leave of Polly. She assumed Cindy had been looking up when she had seen Scotty. If she had been looking down, she would have reversed course and headed for the down escalator, rather than forward, toward the elevators, stairs, and up escalator.

Tori looked up. There were two levels of stores above her, plus two levels of what looked like offices above that. The office levels did not appear to be connected by escalator to the shopping levels. She backed up slightly, then sauntered in the direction Cindy and Polly had been walking. Facing in the same direction, roughly two-thirds of the shopping mall was behind her; that portion could be eliminated. Facing forward and to the side, there was a fairly limited area in which a person's head could be seen above the railings. But that area encompassed four levels.

Tori sat down on the bench. Of course Cindy had not actually seen Scotty. The coincidence would have been incredible—astronomical, in fact. One first had to suppose that Scotty was still alive after seven years, that he had been abducted and taken to another part of the country. That was unlikely enough. Then for Cindy—who, to be fair, did travel extensively around the country—to have seen and accurately identified him, now that he was seven years older...

Yet here she was in Denver. However unlikely the scenario, she had to proceed on three assumptions: one, that Cindy thought she had seen Scotty; two, that she had followed him; and three, that whatever she had learned thereafter had been the reason she had killed four people, plus herself, three months later.

Tori looked back at the atrium. What would a fourteen-year-old boy have been doing at this mall? Hanging out with his friends? Playing hooky from school? Tori glanced at the stores that were visible: a couple of women's clothing stores; a General Nutrition store; a shoe store; a Waldenbooks; a Victoria's Secret; an Orange Julius shop. There were a couple of possibilities among them, but Tori didn't think any of them likely for a fourteen-year-old boy.

She took the elevator to the sixth level. There were four doors visible from where Cindy had stood: a public relations agency, a law firm, a graphic design firm, and an unmarked door. She went back and took the stairwell down to the fifth level. There were five possible doors here, two of them unmarked. The other three doors belonged to a dentist, an orthodontist, and a podiatrist.

She took the elevator down to the street level and walked out onto 16th Street. A couple of blocks away, she found a Walgreen's drug store and bought a cheap pair of wire-rimmed reading glasses and a plastic case. Then she returned to the mall and rode the elevator back up to the fifth level. She paused in front of the orthodontist's door, took a deep breath, and went in.

A perky young receptionist with bleached hair and a diamond stud in her nose looked up. A nameplate identified her as Amber. "Can I help you?"

Tori smiled. "I hope so. I have kind of a strange problem. You see, I was next door at Dr. Sheffler's office back in May. There was a teenage boy who came out of your office at the same time I was coming out, and he dropped his glasses." She held up the case containing the reading glasses. "I ran after him," Tori continued, "but the elevator door was just closing, and I couldn't catch up with him."

Tori looked embarrassed. "I should have come right back here, I know, but I was already late in getting back to work. I was in such a hurry, I figured I'd just come back here during my lunch hour the next day and leave them here, but wouldn't you know, I forgot all about it. I left the glasses sitting at the bottom of my bag until I discovered them yesterday, and I feel terrible about it. I mean, I feel so stupid."

Amber did not contradict her. "I don't remember anyone asking about a pair of glasses," she said.

"Well, it has been a long time."

"We do have a drawer here where we put things people leave behind."

"Listen," Tori said. "Would it be too much trouble just to check your calendar—see who was here on May 18th?"

The bleached receptionist hesitated.

"I'll take responsibility for sending it back," Tori said.

"We're not allowed to give out patient information," came the quick reply.

"I'll pay the postage."

"I don't know...."

"I'll bring in a paid mailer. All you'd have to do is put on a label and send it."

Amber stared at her. She was starting to become curious about Tori's interest.

"All right," Tori said abruptly, slapping the glasses down on the desk. "Just stick it in your drawer and forget about it." She turned on her heel.

"All right, hang on," Amber muttered. She let out a long sigh and swiveled the computer screen toward her. She entered some information, then stared at the screen, hitting the scroll button several times. "How old did you say the kid was?"

"Maybe fourteen or fifteen. The appointment would have been late morning or around noon."

More staring. More scrolls. The Bleached One looked up. "I think this must be the one. Jacob Hawes."

Tori, her heart pounding, nodded. "Thanks. Let me go get one of those thick envelopes for you."

"Wait a minute," Amber said, lowering her voice. "It's just a general delivery address. Maybe I'll just give it to you. Anybody could look it up in the phone book, anyway."

"That would be nice," said Tori, who had been wondering how to distract Amber long enough to sneak a glance at the mailing label, or intercept the office mail.

"It just says General Delivery, Dunston, Colorado."

Tori thanked the receptionist, then stepped out into the mall, wiping sweat from her face.

Jacob Hawes.

Scotty Stevens.

CHAPTER 10

Tori drove her rental car west off I-25 for a short distance, south on state route 105, and then west again on a county road toward the small town of Dunston. From the map, the town appeared to be only about forty minutes from the Denver exurbs. The more futile and farfetched her quest seemed, the more she kept reminding herself that it didn't matter. Her time was unlimited, her life without goals.

And yet that was really no longer true. Improbable as it seemed, she had now acquired a purpose. She knew this was her job, here and now, to find out why Cindy had killed four people, then herself. It was not just a matter of distrusting the police to find out, although they would not. It was simply an acknowledgment that this was now her function in life.

More than just a function, the quest was her duty to Cindy, especially now that she realized why Cindy had drifted away from her. It seemed incredible now that she had seen Scotty and not told her about it. But with Ben dying, she had chosen to carry the burden herself rather than dumping it on Tori. How could Tori refuse to take up the task now?

Having a purpose activated her deepest fears. It felt dangerous to care again, to risk losing again, whether the object was Rick Percival or the prospect of finding whatever it was that turned her best friend into a killer.

At the same time, her new quest had begun to reawaken the person she used to be, at least the person the world had seen. The same description had flowed forth from everyone she'd encountered after Ben's death. Capable. Strong. Resourceful. Efficient. Practical. Down-to-earth. You'll be okay, Tori. She was sick to death of hearing it. For the past five years she'd also fit the only adjective that really mattered. Happy. She would not fit it again.

Tori glanced again at her map; Dunston was about ten miles west from state route 105. She was in a valley now, with towering mountains on both sides. The rented Ford labored in the altitude, and she swallowed to pop her ears. It may have been dangerous to care, but at least she had the consolation of knowing that she would never care about anything or anyone as she had cared for Ben.

He had been loose, funny, and loathe to take himself or anything too seriously. Those qualities had provided a perfect foil for her serious demeanor and Type A personality. And the same qualities, she thought, had been what had made him such a good attorney. He had been able to look at his clients, their predicaments, and his opponents with uncommon detachment, to see their absurdity. Yet his seeming aloofness had hidden an inner core of commitment, integrity, and substance.

She could spend a long time listing Ben's good qualities. But the ways and means of attraction had, of course, defied such easy explanation. The fact was, simply, that she had loved him—adored him, been addicted to him—with all her being. And, miraculously, he had returned her love. They seemed to need nothing more than to be in each other's company. To be sure, they had led an active life, enjoying the outdoors and movies and plays. But all the activity was superfluous; they'd had each other.

The Kiwanis club, via a battered sign, welcomed her to Dunston, a town of 2,014, spread out for several miles along a creek, through the narrow valley. She drove past several clusters of buildings until she came to what appeared to be the main business district. A U.S. flag sprouted from a small brick building on her left, and Tori pulled into a diagonal parking space in front of the post office. She got out of the car, pulling her jacket around herself to keep out the suddenly chilly mountain air.

The clerk in the post office, a youngish guy with a scraggly beard and a duck-ass haircut, didn't seem very busy. He discreetly shoved a magazine under a scale when Tori approached the counter.

"Mornin'," the clerk said. "Can I help you?"

"Good morning," Tori said. "I'm from out of town, and I'm looking for a local family. The only address I have for them is General Delivery here in Dunston. The name is Hawes."

Tori wished she had been watching the clerk's expression more closely. The look that passed quickly across his face, then vanished—was it in reaction to the mention of the Hawes name, or to the General Delivery designation?

The clerk seemed to stiffen slightly. "I'm sorry, ma'am. We're not allowed to give out that information."

Tori had more or less expected this, even though she wasn't sure if postal regulations actually forbade such disclosures. "I'd really appreciate it if you could help somehow," she said. "You see, I'm just passing though Colorado, and Mr. Hawes is a distant relative of mine, and—"

The clerk shook his head firmly. "I'm sorry. We just can't do that."

Tori nodded and thanked him. Outside, the sun had gone under the clouds, and she shivered in the stiff mountain breeze. Two blocks further down the street, she found what appeared to be the town cafe, which was now filling up with the lunch crowd. She opened the door and was greeted by a blast of warm air, pungent with the smells of smoke and frying food. She felt eyes on her as she took a seat at the far end of a counter that ran perpendicular to the street, next to two middle-aged women, one of whom wore a nurse's uniform.

A woman in her fifties, wearing an old-fashioned waitress uniform, came up and poured coffee without asking whether Tori wanted any. "Howya doin'?" she asked.

"Fine."

"Visiting?" the waitress asked as she wiped the counter. She had a puffy face and dyed brown hair.

Tori nodded.

"What can I get for you?"

"How about a tuna sandwich?"

"Sure."

Tori glanced around the restaurant as she sipped her coffee. There were farmers wearing soiled baseball caps, a couple of Rotarians wearing polyester sport coats, and other people who defied classification. It was probably her imagination, but she thought she felt eyes on her again.

The sandwich arrived. Tori chewed listlessly on the stale white bread.

"Whereya from?"

Tori glanced up. The waitress was piling dirty dishes onto a tray. "Texas," she said without knowing why.

"Visiting relatives?"

"I'm trying to. I'm looking for a family named Hawes. Sort of a shirttail relation, I guess. The only address I have is for General Delivery, and they're not in the phone book."

Tori studied the waitress. As with the postal clerk, a look combining apprehension and recognition briefly crossed her face, which then returned to friendly and noncommittal. "'Fraid I can't help you there."

Tori nodded. "Thanks, anyway," she said, wondering what the hell was going on. She finished her sandwich, paid, and returned to Main Street. She wandered back toward her car, looking in store windows and wondering where to go next.

"Ma'am?"

She looked up to see a large man wearing a uniform. The sheriff.

"Can I help you?" he asked in a scratchy, high-pitched voice.

Tori fought off panic. "I don't think so," she said. Instinct told her this man was trouble.

"You've been asking questions around town." He was young, blond, and pudgy, wearing a heavy nylon jacket, Stetson, and tinted teardrop glasses.

Tori didn't respond.

"I said you've been asking questions around town," he repeated. His tone, while striving for authoritative, sounded merely unfriendly.

"Yes?"

"What do you want with the Hawes family?"

Anger was slowly replacing her apprehension. "I'm sorry, Sheriff. Is there a problem with what I've been doing here?"

The sheriff took a step closer to her, using his bulk to intimidate. "You're not answering my questions, Ma'am. That is a problem."

She sized him up, hoping she was judging him correctly. "I'm sorry," she said. "Until you demonstrate some kind of basis for questioning me, I'm afraid that will have to remain your problem."

"That's about enough," he snapped, his face turning red. "Let's see some i.d."

Tori stood her ground, drawing herself up to her full five-foot-three height. "Sheriff," she said, "I'm going back to my car now, and I'm willing to forget this encounter took place. You can stop me if you want, but you might want to consider whether you and your county can afford a multimillion-dollar civil rights lawsuit, plus more bad publicity than it really wants." She smiled, turned, and walked back toward the car.

Tori kept walking, willing herself not to look back. The sheriff would have to force the action now.

The car was about half a block away. She made it past one building.

Two buildings. She reached the car, unlocked it, and turned around. There was no sign of the sheriff. Like most bullies, he had backed down when someone stood up to him.

Inside the car, she started the engine, turned up the heat, and sat for several minutes, shivering uncontrollably. What on God's earth had she gotten herself into?

She jumped. Someone was rapping on her window. She fumbled with the buttons, finally succeeding in rolling down the electric window. A woman wearing a bowling jacket stood next to the car; looking more closely, Tori could see a nurse's uniform under the jacket.

"Hi," the woman said. She looked to be in her thirties, with hazel eyes and a bad complexion. "I saw Rod hassling you."

Tori nodded.

"He's an asshole. Anyway, I also sat next to you at the cafe, and I heard you asking Aggie about the Hawes family. They have a General Delivery address, right?"

"Right."

The woman glanced around nervously. Her jacket was partially unzipped, and Tori spotted a nametag identifying her as Pat. "I don't know these Hawes people. But when it's a GD address, and people start acting nervous and weird about it, you can tell what's going on."

Tori felt her heartbeat accelerate. "And what's that?"

"They're from the Belke community."

The name sounded familiar to Tori, but she couldn't place it.

"You know," Pat prompted. "Harlan Belke. He's got two or three of these communities. One here, one in Idaho—I don't know where the others are. But you know what they're like: They hate blacks, Jews—just about everybody except themselves."

And now Tori remembered. Harlan Belke was a white separatist leader, whose followers lived in fortified communities in rural areas. The group's views were a combination of racism, militia-like antigovernment extremism, and conservative, pseudo-Christian social beliefs. "There's a Belke community here?" Tori said.

"Right. We don't see much of them—they hardly ever come into town. Once in a while we see a reporter or somebody looking for a son or daughter who ran away—that kind of thing."

"So where is this place?"

Pat wrinkled up her acne-scarred face. "You don't want to go there. The place is like a prison camp—fences, dogs—the whole works. They wouldn't let you in, anyway. It's a good place to stay away from."

"Where is it?" Tori repeated.

Pat shrugged. "You go through town. After about three miles there's a tar road that goes off to the right. That turns into gravel in about a mile, and about five-six miles after that, they have a checkpoint. That's where the fence starts, too. Don't go there."

Tori pretended to think about it. "I guess I probably won't. But thanks."

Pat nodded and left, leaving Tori to marvel at the courage it must have taken to approach her openly on Main Street. Tori waited until Pat had climbed into a pickup truck several slots away and driven off before pulling out of her own parking space. Then she proceeded through town, glancing at her odometer, determined to find the unmarked paved road.

The paved surface gave out just as the level ground was doing likewise. Tori's rented car protested and downshifted as it climbed the steady grade along the side of the mountain. The road, while not paved, was fairly wide and well maintained. After a long mile, Tori stopped at the top of a rise, swallowing to equalize the pressure on her ears. Peering through a gap between the pines, she could see that the state highway had veered to the left once it left Dunston, winding between a gap in the mountains. The road on which she now drove continued through the original valley, along the creek. She still couldn't see any sign of the camp.

She continued down the mountain, then along the creek. She slowed down considerably after the four-mile mark, watching carefully for the camp and observing carefully the topography on both sides of the road.

The checkpoint appeared suddenly around a bend. Tori stopped the car abruptly, sliding on the gravel, then threw it into reverse. When the car was back around the bend, she got out and walked forward, moving from tree to tree, finally catching a glimpse of the community's entrance. It was indeed protected by a razor-wire fence, which ran out of sight, into the woods in both directions. Two guard huts flanked an electric gate, but no guards were visible at the moment. Also out of sight were the com-pound's buildings.

Tori returned to the car and sat motionless for several minutes. She looked at the beautiful, peaceful scene around her; the thought of violent, hateful people living here seemed impossible. But then again, so was the thought of Cindy Stevens killing four people. She did a careful U-turn and drove back toward Dunston.

CHAPTER 11

It was after dark the following day when Tori returned to Dunston, driving a rented Jeep 4x4 SUV. She wore warm, rugged clothing, and on the seat beside her sat a pack carrying food, a canteen, a compass, binoculars, a geological survey map, a flashlight, a camera, and night-vision goggles. She had purchased all of the items in Denver that morning, investing more than a thousand dollars, and spent most of the afternoon studying the map and making plans.

Dunston was quiet when she drove through at nine, keeping a watchful eye out for the sheriff. She nearly missed the turnoff on the other side of town, but eventually found her way up the side of the mountain on the paved, then gravel, road. She slowed down a mile from the top of the rise, killing her headlights. Then she cut the engine, pulled the jeep over to the side of the road, and walked the last mile up the rise.

If the Belke community were serious about security, it would post someone at this point, which commanded the valley in both directions, toward the camp and back toward Dunston. Tori doubted they were serious; what genuine security threat would such a community face? If they really did expect an invasion from the evil, omnipotent Federal government, they could no doubt put up a decent fight. But even a camp based on a mountaintop would be vulnerable to an assault by black helicopters. And they couldn't defeat the entire U.S. Army.

Tori was breathing hard as she hiked along the road, trying not to crunch too loudly on the gravel with her newly-purchased high-top athletic shoes. She approached the summit cautiously, stopping to listen every few yards. Then she froze.

In the dim moonlight she could see lights, then the faint outline of a vehicle. Then she heard voices. She couldn't make out what the voices were saying, and had no intention of getting close enough to do so. Dismayed, she made her way back down the hill toward the jeep. This was going to be more difficult than she had hoped.

Tori pulled the jeep off the road, engaged the four-wheel drive, and climbed a steep grade, bumping over the uneven terrain. She had remembered this small opening in the forest from her reconnaissance yesterday. She proceeded at a crawl, maneuvering around trees, until she couldn't go any further.

Tori stopped the jeep and got out. The night was black around her; the trees blocked even the faint moonlight. She hoped the jeep wouldn't be visible from the road. The air smelled of pine needles; crickets and the hiss of the wind through the trees provided the only sound. She found the night-vision goggles, turned them on, and pulled them over her head. Instantly, the night lit up in an eerie, greenish glow. Then she pulled the pack from the back seat, slung it over her shoulder, and set out along the side of the mountain.

The geological survey map, now more than twenty years old, had shown a logging road proceeding higher up along the mountainside, splitting off from the main road, which ran down to the creek and through the valley to the camp. She had parked in a semi-cleared area which was all that remained of the road's beginning; now she followed what remained of the rest of the abandoned road, which was visible only as a less-dense swath through the forest. She stopped frequently to listen and check the compass, which assured her that she was proceeding in a general southerly direction.

It had been many years since she had practiced this kind of thing in the army, and then she hadn't had to do it alone. She was still in good shape, but the altitude, plus the rough terrain—not to mention the late hour and the stress—conspired to drain her energy quickly. Her path continued uphill along the side of the mountain, generally parallel to the creek and the main road below. She stopped to rest after an hour, calculating that she had probably covered about a mile. Another hour and a half should do it, she calculated.

It took two and a half hours, including three rest stops. Tori was really winded now, and it took all her concentration to stay on course. Several times she had fallen heavily, tripping over a stump or a rock. Branches lacerated her face and hands. The wind seemed to be coming up the mountain from the valley, which would be helpful if the community really was using guard dogs. Here and there, breaks through the trees gave her a view down into the valley.

Finally, at about one in the morning, she spotted the compound, a clearing with dark block shapes that had to be buildings. She began to look for a vantage point, and found one several minutes later, behind a fallen log and a clump of bushes. Then, exhausted, she pulled out an inflatable pillow, blew air into it, and settled back against the log.

•

The daylight woke her up, and the sun felt surprisingly warm on her clammy skin. She stood up slowly, careful to stay hidden, trying to stretch her stiff muscles. It was past six, and the community below bustled with activity. She had an excellent view of the compound, which consisted of eight large prefab buildings arranged in a square, plus two Quonset huts, and two rough wooden buildings, situated away from the others, that appeared to house animals. Large vegetable gardens spread out beyond the square, toward the creek. Two huge fuel-oil tanks sat next to one of the huts. And in the main square, a group of perhaps seventy men had mustered for reveille.

She sipped water from her canteen and munched on some of the freeze-dried food she had brought, then took out the binoculars. The would-be soldiers were well-equipped, with semiautomatic rifles, and well-dressed, with pressed khaki uniforms. Most appeared to be young men, from their late teens to mid twenties, but a few looked as old as forty. The drill lasted half an hour, after which the men disappeared into the buildings. The square was quiet for another twenty minutes, at which time children carrying books began to appear, shouting, playing, and roughhousing until a bell rang at seven-thirty. At that point they filed into one of the buildings, which had a cross perched atop its roof.

Traffic in the square was sparse for the next half-hour. Two carloads of men went out of the main gate and down the road. Others—men and women—drifted back toward the barns and gardens for their day's work. Promptly at eight a small bus, about the size of a hotel shuttle vehicle, came in through the main gate. The bus turned onto a road behind one row of buildings, continued toward the creek, then took a left, stopping at a building Tori had not noticed before. The building, unlike the others in the compound, was made of brick, and was twice as large as the largest of the wooden structures. It was set back into the trees along the creek, barely visible from where Tori sat.

At least a dozen people got off the bus. They were dressed as if for a casual Friday at a large corporation, with khaki slacks, loafers, oxford shirts and blouses, and sweaters. They chatted easily, some carrying brown bags. Co-workers, ready for another day's toil. The bus stopped beside the building and parked. Tori moved to her right, trying to get a better view of the brick building. But tall pines blocked her view of all but the front door and a back corner.

At nine another bugle sounded, and people again began to assemble in the square. This time the men, now changed into work clothes, were joined by women and children. After a few minutes two uniformed men came out from behind one of the buildings, escorting a third man between them. Tori focused the binoculars on the prisoner, who was young, scared, and shirtless. He was tied to a wooden post in the square.

After a brief pause a very large man came out of what Tori had identified as an administration building. The man was huge and muscular with close-cropped hair, a blond version of the Incredible Hulk. He walked and carried himself with crisp efficiency, carrying a large whip. He stopped in front of the gathering and pulled a pair of wire-rimmed reading glasses from his breast pocket.

One of the two guards handed the Hulk a clipboard, from which he read, talking through a bullhorn. Tori could make out only a few words, including "dereliction," "unacceptable," and "example." Hulk handed the clipboard back, then slowly approached the young man, caressing the whip lovingly. Then, unexpectedly, amazingly, his face broke out in a huge, crooked-toothed grin, which vanished as quickly as it had appeared. He folded the spectacles and returned them to his pocket.

Then the whipping began. The young man flinched and writhed, his screams and pleas for mercy filling the air along with the rhythmic cracks. Tori found herself unconsciously counting. Ten lashes. Twenty. The Hulk performed his work with efficiency and, Tori thought, rather more enthusiasm than necessary. His face was contorted with fury as he cracked the whip again and again across the bloody back of the young man.

Tori couldn't watch any more. She found herself looking at the entranced faces of the assembled crowd. As she scanned the scene she noticed a man, standing in the open doorway of the administration building, arms folded, surveying the scene. A short, crewcut man with a small, weird grin, his face combining confidence and satisfaction with—what? An imbalance or madness of some kind, Tori thought. It was a face she had seen in magazine and television profiles. Harlan Belke.

After thirty lashes the punishment ended. The young man, hanging unconscious on the wooden post, was removed and dragged behind a building. The crowd dispersed with quiet murmurs, and the day's business proceeded. The schoolchildren studied and played. The soldiers practiced. The farmers farmed. The housewives toiled. And the people who had come on the bus did...something. By mid-afternoon Tori had estimated that the camp held about two hundred people, excepting those who had come on the bus. Several times, people went back and forth between the compound and the brick building. The visitor was usually a child, always accompanied by an adult.

It was nearly four when she saw Scotty. He was a tall, bespectacled boy who participated enthusiastically in a pickup basketball game. He had Cindy's blond hair, along with Larry's large nose, flat ears, and prominent jaw. And, having inherited Cindy's bad teeth, he wore braces. She followed him with the binoculars, back and forth in front of the basket as he played, waiting until the six players stopped for a drink of water. Then Tori reached for the camera with the telephoto lens, quickly snapping off three pictures. She had already photographed the camp in detail.

Her photography completed, Tori watched him for a long time. Whether the boy was Scotty Stevens, Jacob Hawes, or someone else, it didn't matter. The resemblance was more than enough to convince Cindy she had found her son. Tori herself simply wasn't sure. No one could be sure from appearance alone, not after seven years of growth and change.

Tori re-stowed her gear. There was no point in waiting around further, and she wanted to reach the jeep by nightfall. After one last glance at the boy, she set off on her return trip. The going was much easier in daylight. Not only was it easier to follow the remains of the logging road, but she was able to glance down and use the creek and road as references for staying on course.

She reached the jeep with a half-hour of daylight to spare, and cached her gear, not wanting to risk being caught with it. She spent the next hour resting, eating, and thinking. Had Cindy traced Scotty/Jacob here? If she had, it wasn't impossible to imagine that she had seen something, or someone—possibly the boy—that she wasn't supposed to see, and that she had run afoul of some violent, fanatical people. But that was not what had happened. Instead, Cindy herself had become violent, and target number one had been Larry.

She washed half a bag of potato chips down with water from a bottle, pondering an unpleasant thought she could no longer avoid: that Larry had somehow been involved in Scotty's disappearance. The thought seemed absurd, given Larry's gentle demeanor, rock-solid alibi, and the complete lack of any motivation Tori could think of. Even assuming Larry had harmed the boy—due to abuse, or punishment getting out of hand—the usual outcome would be murder, not abduction, and particularly not abduction by white separatists half a continent away. Still, two facts remained: 1) Cindy thought she had seen Scotty, and 2) She had killed Larry. There was no use pretending those two facts were unrelated.

Tori's thoughts and theories about Cindy, Scotty, and Larry were troubling enough. But as she put the jeep in gear and began to reverse back toward the road, an even more disturbing question kept working its way into her consciousness: What was going on in the brick building?

She had to back the jeep all the way to the road; there was nowhere to turn around. When the jeep's tires finally hit gravel, Tori let out a long sigh of relief, then disengaged the four-wheel drive and set out toward the main road.

She saw headlights almost immediately.

There would be no avoiding the vehicle. By now, they would have seen her headlights as well. A dozen scenarios, of confrontation and escape, raced through her mind as she took deep breaths, pulling over to the side and hoping the other vehicle would pass on the narrow road.

It was not to be. The other vehicle, a larger 4x4, pulled in front of her at an angle, cutting off her escape. A spotlight blinded her, and she ducked under the dashboard.

"Get out slowly with your hands in the air!" a male voice shouted.

Tori glanced up. There was no way out. She complied.

The voice had been shouted from behind an opened door of the other vehicle. She felt the spotlight on her again, and turned to the side to avoid its blinding effect.

"Hands on the car roof! Do it now!" The voice was young but authoritative.

Tori assumed the position. In her peripheral line of vision, she could see two figures come out from around the opened doors. One of them, a guy with a pointed face like a weasel's, patted her down roughly, while the other, a huge man, opened the rear door of the jeep.

"Clean here, partner," said Weasel after patting her down.

"No weapon here—just some trash," said the large man, whom Tori, with a sinking feeling, recognized as the Incredible Hulk. He continued rifling through her belongings.

"If you're the police, show me some identification and tell me the charge," Tori said.

"Shut up," said one of the men.

Tori glanced around. Both Hulk and Weasel were dressed in fatigues and appeared to carry only pistols. Their vehicle, a Suburban, had its dome lights on, which provided a view of a rack holding various long guns.

Hulk, now wearing his reading glasses, completed his search of the vehicle, including her purse. "What were you doing out there, Lady?"

"Looking for a place to hike tomorrow."

"At night?"

"It got dark a little sooner than I expected."

He replaced his glasses. "Let's see some i.d."

"I left it back at the motel." In fact, her driver's license, along with the roll of film, was wedged in against the spare tire.

"Which motel?"

"The El Rancho." Tori remembered seeing a motel of that name on the north side of town.

"What's your name?" Hulk demanded.

"Jane Doe."

Weasel said, "Don't fuck with us, Sister. Now what the hell are you doing here?"

"I told you. Looking for a good place to hike. Also minding my own business, which you seem to have a problem with. Where do you get off, holding a citizen at gunpoint on a public road?"

After a few seconds of tense silence, Weasel said, "Turn around slowly."

She complied. Instantly, Weasel's open palm came hard across her face, knocking her to the ground. "I hate a bitch with a smart mouth," he growled.

Tori, face stinging and head spinning, picked herself up, and Weasel shoved her back against the jeep.

"Backup will be here in a few minutes," Hulk said. "Might as well have her ready," he continued. "We'll let them take her in—I'll drive ours and you take hers."

Weasel nodded. In the dim light, he looked to be in his early twenties, moon-faced, with a pencil mustache. He glanced into the jeep, then back at Tori. "Where's the key?"

"In my bra."

He gave her a put-out look. "Pull it out carefully."

"Why don't you do it yourself?"

Weasel glanced at the Hulk, who smiled, showing crooked front teeth. "Why not?" he said. Tori, her hands still in the air, watched him as he stepped closer. She slowly turned sideways, perpendicular to the jeep, her hands still in the air. Weasel stepped around to the side, momentarily shielding her from Hulk.

Tori watched Weasel's right hand, which held the pistol, carefully, waiting for the exact moment he would transfer the gun to his left hand. Presumably he would retrieve the key with his right.

He stood over her for a long moment, then his left hand came up for the gun. Tori waited for the exact moment...

Now. Her hands still in the air, she pivoted and drove her knee up into Weasel's groin with the general idea of ramming his testicles up into his throat.

Weasel screamed. Somehow he held onto the gun with his left hand, but it was a simple matter for Tori to grab it from him. She put her arm around his neck and held the gun to his ear. "Drop it, or I shoot him!" she yelled.

The Hulk hesitated. His view had been partly obscured by Weasel, and Tori's hands had remained in the air, delaying his reaction briefly. Now he stepped forward.

"Freeze and drop it!" Tori repeated.

Hulk stopped but didn't drop his pistol. Tori thought she heard a vehicle approaching. The backup.

The pistol was an automatic, not unlike those she had used in the military. She felt with her thumb to make sure the safety was off, chambered a round, then aimed carefully at Weasel's foot and fired.

The roar of the gun and Weasel's agonizing scream were nearly simultaneous. Hulk started forward, then stopped himself.

"She shot me," Weasel wailed, disbelieving.

"Drop it!" Tori shouted.

"For Christ's sake do it," Weasel cried.

Tori aimed the gun at Weasel's other foot.

"All right, all right," Hulk shouted. He dropped the gun and raised his hands. "You're gonna pay, bitch!"

"Kick it into the woods," Tori commanded. When he had done so she said, "Lie down on the road. Face down." Again, the large man grudgingly obeyed, his face contorted with hate.

"You, too," Tori told Weasel, who was kneeling on the ground, holding his foot. When he didn't react immediately she shoved him in the back with her foot. He went down, howling in pain.

Tori retrieved the jeep's key from her bra, then got in. "I'm leaving now," she said. "If either of you moves, I'll run you down, then shoot you." She quickly shut the door and started the engine. Neither man had moved. She could now see headlights in her rearview mirror. She backed up, then jammed the shift lever into drive. Then she maneuvered the jeep carefully around the Suburban and floored the accelerator, showering the two prone men with gravel just as the backup vehicle was arriving.

She rounded a bend, and couldn't tell if the backup vehicle was giving chase. She simply kept driving as fast as she could, frequently checking her mirror. Either no one was following her, or she had outrun them.

She turned south, away from Dunston, both to do the unexpected and to avoid the town's sheriff who, for all she knew, might be an ally of the Belke community. She drove and drove, faster than was really safe, out of the mountains and onto the desolate high plains, encountering only two small towns along the way. Finally, as the fuel gauge hovered near empty and her concentration began to wander, she pulled over onto a gravel side road and stopped.

Tori glanced at her watch. She had been driving for more than two hours. She must have crossed I-25 at some point, but couldn't remember doing so. For the first time, she dared to release her grip on the steering wheel. Her hands still shook. She got out of the jeep, and the surprisingly cold wind cut through her sweat-soaked clothing. A sudden wave of nausea passed over her, and she retched convulsively into the ditch at the side of the road. She wiped her mouth, and was instantly thirsty. But her pack, along with the canteen, had been left near the camp, where she had shot the young man she had called Weasel.

The memory made her vomit again. And again, her thirst was overpowering. But she looked around and could see only prairie and stars;

there was no sign of civilization. She had, in fact, no idea where she was. She would have to find a town, to find food, water, directions, a motel. But for now, she could think only of Cindy and Scotty and the camp and the gun and Weasel....

She gripped the door of the jeep to steady herself. There had to be a limit, she told herself. How much could one person handle? It seemed impossible that she could live with the memories of Ben's death, the Sattex murders, and Cindy's suicide, much less a fresh supply of horrors and fears.

But she would. Somehow, for better or worse, and in drastically altered form, she was, for the first time in months, alive again.

CHAPTER 12

Jim Traeger was sitting up in bed, reading a memo about the need for a more coordinated strategy to fight the drug war, when the phone rang. He picked it up quickly, trying to avoid waking Pam, who lay motionless beside him.

"Traeger."

"Jim. Have you gone crazy?" It was Amy Burke.

"Hang on." Traeger took the cordless phone with him into the study across the hall and shut the door. He sat down behind his desk. "What's the problem, Amy?"

"Problem? Is that what you call going off half-cocked and threatening to quit? I've never seen him this pissed off—never."

"Sorry to hear that," he said noncommittally.

"Why are you doing this?" she said, pleading with him. "You have a future in this town—why are you throwing it away?"

"I appreciate your concern about my future," he said mildly. "But something tells me you might have other concerns as well."

"You really are a cold son of a bitch," she said, her voice biting. "Even if you don't care about me, I care about myself. And about Whitelaw, and the party, and the country," she said, her voice rising.

"You don't think the Republic will survive with Milt Hokanson as President?"

"You are missing the point—deliberately, in all likelihood."

Again, Traeger did not respond.

"You know what?" she said. "I think this is the final stage in your development. You're the smartest political operative this town has seen in a generation. And now you've added the final weapon to your arsenal of skills: unpredictability."

"Well, thanks, I guess."

"It wasn't a compliment. You're supposed to be unpredictable to your enemies. Your friends have to know they can count on you."

Traeger thought about Temple, and about the four other people who had come to mean so much to him over the past year and a half.

"They can count on me, Amy. And they are."

Traeger hung up the phone. He was at peace.

●

Tori stepped off the shuttle bus into the darkness and the driving rain. She ran through the remote parking lot at Dulles airport, dragging her suitcase, looking for the Audi. It took her perhaps five minutes to find her vehicle, and by that time tears mingled with the raindrops on her face. She tossed her bag into the trunk, then got in. She sat behind the wheel for several minutes—exhausted, stressed out, frightened to death, soaked to the skin, and feeling more alone than she had in her entire life.

After only the briefest of internal deliberations, she did what she had to do. She grabbed her purse and fumbled through it, eventually retrieving the slip of paper containing the seven digits. She pulled the cell phone from the glove box and punched in the number.

"Hi, this is Tori. I...need to see you."

●

Tori left the parking lot, not noticing the government sedan that sat idling near the exit. Inside the sedan a man reached for a radio.

"Unit two, subject is leaving the parking area. Over."

"Roger. We've got her onto the access road."

"I'll be reporting in, then joining you on the freeway."

"Roger and out."

The agent replaced the radio and picked up a cellular phone, punching in the number. "This is Toles," he said when his party answered.

"Status?" inquired the voice at the other end.

"She arrived as scheduled."

"Was she met?"

"No."

"Was she followed?"

"We don't think so."

"Well, stay on her and make sure."

"Yes, sir," said Toles.

A pause. Then, "We still have forty-eight hours not accounted for?"

"Basically."

"Unbelievable. Denver saw her heading south on I-25, and just let her go?"

"They claimed they had no orders to follow her out of the city."

"That's total bullshit," the voice said.

"I know. We do have some more news, though. Later that first day, she used her credit card to make purchases over a thousand dollars at three different stores in downtown Denver."

"In Denver. Then she couldn't have gone far."

"If it was actually her—we're trying to verify that. And we still don't know what the purchases were—we're checking on that, too."

"Do that. Then get on Denver's ass. I want this Polly Kendrick woman and that orthodontist checked out head to toe. I want to find out what the hell she was doing in Denver."

At the other end of the line, Special Agent Nolan Bertelson hung up the phone. His mission had changed abruptly; the Stevens woman was no longer a consideration. Now he was supposed to find out what Tori McMillan was up to. And he was failing, badly.

He couldn't fail Temple.

•

"Do you want to tell me about it?" Rick Percival asked.

"I don't know," Tori replied. "There's not much to tell." She sat on the sofa in his apartment, dressed in an old robe, sipping hot tea, soaking up the warmth from the apartment.

Rick had met Tori at the door, stared at her wordlessly for a long moment, then returned with a blanket. Now he sat across from her, legs crossed, sipping a scotch. He gave her a wry smile. "Just another evening out, right? Except you're exhausted, soaked, your face and hands are lacerated, and nobody knows where you've been for two days."

She looked up sharply, and he said, "I was worried about you. I'm sorry for checking up on you. Now that you're safe you can tell me about it if you want, but you don't have to."

She sighed and looked down at her tea. She owed him the truth, but where would she even begin?

Rick twirled the scotch in his glass. "Would it help if I told you I know you were Cindy Stevens' best friend?"

Her mouth dropped open.

"Again, I'm sorry for snooping," he said. "But it isn't hard to find things out, especially when they're in the newspapers." He put his drink down and leaned forward, elbows on knees. "You should have told me, Tori. No one should have to carry that kind of burden alone."

Tori felt the heat rise in her face. She felt guilty and defensive, for no real reason. "But I...."

"Barely know me, I know. And didn't want to dump on me—I know that, too. That's the kind of person you are. Considerate. Giving. But everyone has a limit. The death of a spouse might have been enough to push a lot of people over the edge. But to witness a mass killing, and then to lose your best friend...I was worried about you. I still am. I'll give you another chance to tell me if you want, and then I won't ask you again."

She pulled the robe tightly around her. "It's just...embarrassing, that's all. I went out hiking, not really knowing why or what I was looking for. I wasn't well prepared for a rainstorm. It's no big deal."

Rick nodded, apparently satisfied with her answer, which had contained a lot more truth than Tori had intended. He rose from his chair, came over and sat down next to her on the couch. "As far as the shootings go," he said, "that's up to you, too."

She nodded briefly. She was ready now.

Tori kept pushing herself, telling the entire story, detail by painful detail. After a while no internal prodding was needed. The story of the shock, the horror, the sense of betrayal, and the awful aftermath came spilling out of its own accord. She was exhausted, beyond self-consciousness or shame, as the tears fell like raindrops onto her lap. Percival remained motionless, his gaze fixed, as she completed the ordeal.

Now, saying nothing, he put his arm around her. She met his extraordinary eyes, and could discern no sadness—only layers of complexity.

They sat silently for a long time, perhaps twenty minutes. Rick looked comfortable and at ease. Tori shifted on the couch; his mere presence was making her feel tingly and warm.

"As long as I'm spilling my guts," she said at last, "I might as well try to do it right. I'm not sure I can tell you everything. You might question my sanity. You may already be doing that. But I have to find out what happened."

"You mean why Cindy did it," he said.

"Yes. And somehow, it has to do with her son."

She told him about Scotty, without mentioning the post card or her trip to Colorado.

"Cindy meant that much to you," he commented.

"Yes, she did."

After another minute or two of silence she said, "It's not only Cindy and Scotty. It's—well...."

"Well?"

"I guess it's mostly about me." Slowly, haltingly, she explained to him why Cindy's story, more than anyone could imagine, was Tori's own story, and why everything she did, she did for herself.

•

Cindy Stevens' child had been figuratively, if not literally, wrenched from her arms. Tori had never told anyone, not even Ben, that the same had happened to her in a Dallas hospital room eighteen years ago.

There had been something quaint and ruthless about the way she had been withdrawn from the University in Austin, labeled a disgrace, and shipped off to an aunt's in Fort Worth. But she would have expected nothing less from Louise Saunders, the most rigid, judgmental, socially ambitious woman she had ever known.

It seemed incredible now, from a new millennium vantage point, that she had ceded control of her body, her life, and her child to this woman. She had been of legal age, living on her own. Yet at the time there had seemed to be no alternative. She would not terminate the pregnancy, and the thought of raising a child by herself, cut off from her family, was more than she could manage. And now, two decades later, she still wondered which source of shame had shredded her psyche more completely over the years. Was it her complete failure of will, her inability to stand up to the woman who had taken her child away? Or was it her sense of failure at having disgraced and disappointed the mother who had been such a pervasive, overpowering influence in her life?

It didn't matter. The shame and loss, experienced in that single moment in a hospital room, had defined her ever since—dulling her senses, flattening her emotions—causing her to sleep-walk through the motions of a normal life. She knew this washed-out version of herself, and not the vivacious, passionate woman who had lived five glorious years with Ben

McMillan, was the real Tori. She had returned to normal.

Unlike Cindy, she had known it was coming. Louise Saunders had made all the arrangements, even obtaining the unnecessary consent of the dull engineering student with whom she had conceived the child. Her mother, even more than her infantry-commander father, had always been a stickler for detail. And so the new parents—good people from good families, she had assured her—had been present and ready when, dazed and exhausted after a protracted labor, she had handed over the baby boy.

Had she been given the opportunity she would have named him Nicholas, after her maternal grandfather. She had, of course, no idea where the boy was now, or what his real name was, or what he did. For her, he had ceased to exist, just as completely as Scotty had for Cindy.

It had seemed only fitting that she and Ben had not been able to have children. They had waited two years before trying, until Ben had made partner at his law firm. Ben had insisted on the wait, wanting nothing to distract him from being a parent. She had felt fatalistic and deserving when, after a year of unsuccessful efforts, the doctor had told them they would never be able to have children. But then the doctor had told them why: Ben had cancer.

•

They were silent for a long time, listening to the hum of the air conditioner and the occasional car on the street outside. Rick simply held her, occasionally stroking her hair.

At last he said, "Stop punishing yourself, Tori. You feel weak and needy. For God's sake, it's all right. Let go of some of the burden—don't try to carry it all yourself."

Tori felt defeated and exposed, all the more so for being so transparent.

He placed his hands gently on each side of her face and turned her toward him. "Please," he said gently. "Have faith. Trust me. Forgive yourself." She looked into his face—the most open, yet controlled—the most complete face she had ever seen. He smiled. "We'll put you back together again." His hands moved down, pulling the robe off her shoulders, fondling her breasts, moving all over. Tori moaned and threw her arms around him, holding him tightly as her mouth covered his.

If I'm going to be weak and needy, she thought, I might as well do it right.

•

Kyle Jaworski watched in alarm as Tori parked her car and went into Rick Percival's house. Tori was causing problems faster than he could keep track of them. First going to Denver, for reasons unknown, and disappearing for a day and a half. Then coming home, looking to be in bad condition, and under surveillance by Bertelson and two of his men. And now, going back to see a man who....

A man who didn't exist. There was no point in telling himself he had a good reason for investigating Percival. He didn't. But he'd done it anyway, and what he had found was alarming. Percival had founded an organization called Urban Hope and built it up into one of the country's leading social service organizations. His record for the past eight years was spotless. But prior to eight years ago, he hadn't existed. There was simply no record of Richard Percival anywhere. Who the hell was this guy? And now he was sleeping with Tori.

Jaworski hadn't experienced much rejection from women, and when he had, he hadn't taken it personally. But this was different. Tori was different. He hadn't handled it well. She had shunned him in favor of a guy who, depending on your point of view, was either a saint or a sinister character with a shadowy past.

His grip tightened around the steering wheel. She was getting to him, pulling him deeper into all kinds of dangerous territories. And he was helpless to stop it.

He drove home, crossing the 14th Street Bridge to the Parkway, then up to the Beltway, then out on I-270 to Gaithersburg. He owned a place now, a townhouse. He'd bought it when he thought he was getting married. The place had been in foreclosure and he'd fixed it up; that was the only way he'd been able to handle the payments.

He walked in through the small garage, killed the alarm, found a beer, loosened his tie, and turned up the air conditioning. He sat in front of the TV, reached for the remote, stopped, and stared at the blank TV screen in the darkened room.

He drank Sam Adams from the bottle. What a week. It seemed as though every wound, every scar, every vulnerability, every fear he'd ever experienced, had come blasting to the surface in a few days' time. All the baggage he'd carried, stacks of it, set in front of him, delivered to his door, blocking the exit. And his ineptitude in handling it had brought back memories of every past failure, every moment of humiliation and shame.

Over the years he'd retreated more and more deeply into being a cop. Kyle the Cop. And it was all he had; Kyle the Man had disappeared years ago, along with Scotty Stevens. And even the cop identity was thin, mostly a creature of his own imagination. He knew his colleagues considered him something of an oddball and a loner, a guy who lived by himself, dated irregularly, listened to Mozart, and even had abstract art on the walls of his immaculate townhouse.

But no one disputed his skill as a detective; that part of the persona was accurate. For better or worse, the Cop was his entire being, the only real, solid part of himself to cling to, to rely on. Which is why he was now forced to listen to The Cop, to the powers of detection that told him there was no way out.

The demons would have to be faced.

CHAPTER 13

Tori turned from the Beltway onto Connecticut Avenue, feeling ambivalent about being alive. Last night had been a close call. As the feelings of desperation had closed in on her, gripping her, leaving her without an exit, she began to understand what Cindy must have felt when she had ended her life. It seemed to Tori as if the fates were toying with her, destroying most of her life, dumping her into deep, black waters, then throwing her a life preserver named Rick Percival. And yet she knew it was her trip to the edge, along with Percival's intervention, that had brought her back to life.

What else could she have asked of Rick? He had delivered no bromides or homilies. He had offered coffee, concern, and support. And, later, love, which she had needed most of all. Despite her plight, she felt sure he was not doing any of it out of pity, that he saw something in her—what, she couldn't imagine—that attracted him.

There was plenty to like about Rick. He was self-assured but spontaneous. He possessed a natural easygoing charm, but underlying it all was a certain dignified reserve—perhaps even shyness. And his apparent lack of self-consciousness made the animal attraction all the more compelling. She had driven to his house from the airport, telling herself she wasn't using him, that he was the type of man she would be attracted to in any event. And now, after last night, she knew it was true.

Her shame about the relationship wouldn't end, might never end. But it didn't really matter. She wouldn't have made it without him.

Tori's pulse rate shot up when she turned onto her street and saw the car parked in her driveway. Her relief was palpable, but only momentary, when she saw Kyle Jaworski sitting inside the vehicle. She didn't feel up to talking to anyone in the shape she was in. And what could she tell him?

Tori opened the car door, and the August heat washed over her. She walked over to the Mercedes.

Jaworski put down his coffee cup and sports section. "Have you been checking your messages?" he asked without preamble.

"As a matter of fact, I haven't," she said.

"Jesus Christ."

He was angry, she realized. "Hey, what's the problem?" she asked.

"What's the problem? Look, can we go inside?"

Tori unlocked the back door, and led him into the kitchen. She sank into a chair while Jaworski remained standing. "I've been trying for three days to get hold of you," he snapped.

"Why?"

"Why? You ask for Cindy Stevens' calendar, then you disappear on me."

"What concern is that of yours?"

"What the hell is this, some kind of game to you?" He walked toward her, then stopped abruptly, threw up his hands, and paced back across the kitchen.

"I should be asking that question of you," Tori said. "You're the one who can't be bothered with human motivations. You just clear cases and close files."

"There's still an ongoing investigation," he said evenly.

"So what? There's no suspect at large. Just a body to find and a report to file. Another day's work."

Jaworski stopped, took a deep breath, and walked over to the table. "They haven't found Cindy yet, much to the embarrassment of the D.C. police as well as every jurisdiction downriver."

"Even though they know where she jumped. Isn't that unusual?"

"It's not unheard of. They're looking further downstream now, too."

"But what if—I mean, no one saw her jump."

"You mean what if she didn't jump?"

Tori nodded.

He sat down. "Let's see," he said as if thinking about it for the first time. "There would be three possibilities. The first would be that she faked her own death. She's wanted for four murders, and it would be a clever way of throwing the police off the track. The problem is that her picture is all over the airwaves. It would be mighty tough to just disappear. And there's been absolutely no further trace of her."

Tori knew there was an even bigger problem—that Cindy Stevens, after committing four murders, would be in no shape emotionally to plan a clever escape. And if she was alive, and apparently believed Scotty was alive, why hadn't she tried to rescue him? On the other hand, why would she kill herself without making the effort?

"Possibility number two," Jaworski continued, "is that someone kidnapped Cindy and staged her suicide."

"Why would anyone do that?"

"I have no idea, nor do I know why anybody would do Number Three."

"Which is?"

"Somebody killed her, but staged her suicide."

Tori sat back, letting the implications sink in. "If someone killed her, what does that mean? Somebody was using her?"

"Or she had a falling-out with someone. But I don't like number three. If they wanted her dead, why go to all the trouble of staging her suicide?"

"Why not present us with the body?"

"Exactly."

"Gee," Tori said. "We're doing a lot of theorizing here. You might even say we're probing her soul. Have you changed your mind about this case, Kyle?"

Jaworski clasped his shaking hands together on the table and leaned forward. "All right, rub it in," he said. "You were right. The case stinks. It's time to get real and figure out what happened and why she did it. And it's no use pretending it could never have anything to do with Scotty."

Tori responded cautiously. "Then what do you think happened?"

"Let's not get ahead of ourselves. But I think we can assume for the time being that Cindy planned to kill all four of those people. Not any four who happened to be there, but those specific individuals."

"But why?" Tori asked. "The idea of her killing even Larry is a stretch. Why three others as well?"

"I don't know. But bear with me. First of all, understand that she had to have done some planning to begin with. The reception at the state park obviously wasn't part of Larry's regular schedule. She had to have learned about it from Larry himself, or someone he worked with."

"All right."

"But it's not just Larry. The other three were there as well. That means she didn't have to track them down where they worked or lived. Not only that, but there's no security there. It's a big crowd. But it's a confined area. No place to run or hide. All she had to do was walk through the crowd, pick them out, and kill them. In short, if she wanted to kill all four, it was the perfect time and place."

"But you said there's no connection among the four."

"That we know of." He stood up and leaned across the table, putting his face uncomfortably close to hers. "Why did you want Cindy's calendar, Tori?"

"It was nothing. I mean, just an idea."

"I sort of went out on a limb to get it," he said, his voice tight. "I was hoping you might be able to be more specific than that."

"I'm sorry. I can't." She wasn't ready to tell him about Dunston, or Scotty; she had nothing solid, anyway. She had no evidence that Scotty was being held by the Belke group, and no probable cause to search the camp. All she could give the detective was disconnected thoughts, theories, dozens of unanswered questions, and a generous helping of raw, animal terror, none of which Jaworski could do anything about.

But all these thoughts were rationalizations. The fact was, she simply was not buying Kyle Jaworski's sudden conversion from bureaucrat to gung-ho detective. It was Guess the Agenda time again, and she didn't have a clue what his was.

"Goddamnit, Tori, this is not a game. What were you doing in Denver?"

She felt anger rising inside her. "How did you know where I was?"

"You used a credit card, and I was worried about you."

"I do not need you checking up on me behind my back."

"And I don't need you sneaking around, playing amateur detective behind mine."

"What do you care?"

He examined his hands. "You've made your point. I should have cared about it sooner. But I do now. I've thought about it, and I don't like any of it. And until I feel right about it, I'm going to stay involved, whether the higher-ups like it or not."

"And whether I like it or not?"

"Oh, you like it, all right. You can spare me the indignant routine. You care, too."

"Don't tell me what I want or don't want," she snapped.

"Tori, who is Rick Percival?"

"You bastard! I can't believe you've been prying into my life. Have you been following me?"

"What do you really know about him, Tori? About his past?"

She jumped to her feet. "Get out of here! Just go!"

He stood up. "Fine. Do it your way. You want to play games, I can't stop you. But right now you're all I've got."

"Then you've got a problem, Kyle."

"Do I? All I know is that I can't do anything." He reached into his coat pocket, produced a large envelope, and tossed it onto the table. "Photocopied case files," he said. "Take a look. See if anything strikes you as out of the ordinary."

She looked down at the envelope, then back up at Jaworski. "Are you serious?"

"Yes, Tori, I'm reduced to this. Recruiting civilians. Giving them unauthorized information, which could end my career. Because I don't know what the fuck else to do. Enjoy." He walked out.

As Jaworski's Mercedes backed out of the driveway, Tori walked quickly out to the garage and removed her overnight bag from the back seat. She carried it up to her bedroom, knowing she didn't have much time. The Belke people could have moved Jacob/Scotty by now. True, they had no reason to know her visit was about Scotty. But they would still want to know why she had invaded their compound and escaped by shooting one of their soldiers. She had escaped only because of their sexism; they had not expected a woman to resist, nor would they have suspected that she received MP training in the army, before transferring to the Signal Corps. But she had resisted, and because she had, they would be doubly angry. She pulled dirty clothes from the suitcase and threw them onto the bed.

Tori knew that in going to Colorado, she had succeeded only in stirring up a hornet's nest, leaving nearly every essential question unanswered. What had Cindy done after seeing Scotty? Had she confronted the boy and the adults who must have been with him? Had she followed them to Dunston? Then what? What had she been doing for three months? And why, why had she killed Larry and three other people?

Tori paused, holding a pair of dirty socks, feeling paralyzed, guilty, and terrified. She had just driven away Kyle Jaworski, the only person who might be able to help her.

But would he?

Jaworski had not only admitted to personal motives in his dealings with

Tori, but was messing with her life, checking up on her. That she didn't need. The thought of a man with the motives of a Max Tuten and the powers of a policeman was frightening. And, what if he had still other hidden motives? Could he be manipulating her, trying to get to Cindy somehow? Or was he trying to drag Tori into some kind of rivalry with the FBI, or even with his own boss?

She paused, staring at her empty room. All these questions were perfectly valid, and made even more so by a single, disturbing fact: Kyle Jaworski, for all his detached smoothness, all his initial professions of indifference, was now exposed as an obsessed man. Was he haunted by his failure to find Scotty, willing to risk his career to vindicate himself? Or was he, as she increasingly feared, obsessed with her? Or both?

More than that, all these feelings—all these suspicions she had—were somehow connected with, yet peripheral to, a fact she had barely begun to acknowledge to herself: she might very well be falling in love with Rick Percival. And she hadn't even felt comfortable telling him everything.

But even if she could trust Jaworski, how could she even begin to explain the situation she had gotten herself into? She knew it was only a matter of time before the inhabitants of the Belke community traced her. They had her license plate number; it would be a simple matter to locate her through the rental agency at the Denver airport. And then what? Would they try to kill her, to protect the secret of Jacob/Scotty?

She stopped herself, removing a fingertip from her mouth. She was biting her fingernails. Biting her nails. She had never done that in her life. Jesus, what was she going to do next? Start smoking?

Abruptly, Tori stopped packing again, moved the suitcase aside, and sat down on the bed. She wasn't going anywhere. These racist, violent people wouldn't drive her from her own home. She wouldn't abandon Cindy, or Scotty.

She thought of the files Jaworski had left with her. She had gotten herself into this mess and somehow, for Cindy and Scotty, she had to get herself out of it.

CHAPTER 14

Traffic was light in late morning as Jaworski drove his rented sedan north from Lubbock on I-27. Vast, flat expanses extended to the horizon in all directions, filled up by grazing lands, cotton fields, oil derricks, and cattle. It was the space, he thought—the sheer scale—that defined America. He knew it even though he'd lived all his life in the relatively crowded East. But who really knew what was out here? What type of people were produced by harshness and isolation? And what were their secrets?

He took the Tulia exit and headed west for twenty miles, then north. Isolation was a relative concept nowadays. A lot of people had fantasies about disappearing into the vastness of America. But everyone had fingerprints, and a lot of them were stored in databases. Rick Percival was no exception. Over the years, Jaworski had learned how to lift fingerprints if the job wasn't too tricky, and taking Percival's from the door handle of his Taurus had not been difficult. Nor had it been hard to find a match; the prints belonged to a Percy Richards, who'd been in the military, and whose last known address, nearly a quarter century old, was in Culver, Texas. The hard part had been following up; by switching work days with another detective, he'd been able to get two consecutive days off, and had traveled out here on his own nickel. Obsessions could be expensive.

Culver, Texas boasted a population of 2,454, according to the sign at the edge of town. The cotton fields came right up to the edge of town, surrounding the agricultural businesses and the inevitable Wal-Mart that preceded the town itself. The town looked dusty and surprisingly old. The courthouse, located on Main Street in the center of town, was an impressive red brick structure that came right up to the street.

Jaworski parked in front of the building, and was enveloped instantly by intense heat as he got out of the car. On the first floor, just inside the entrance, he found the office of Sheriff Vernon Q. Johnson. Jaworski announced himself to a female dispatcher who looked about thirteen years old.

"He's out somewhere," she said. Jaworski hid a pained expression; "out" could be two hours away in this huge Texas county.

"Have a seat," she said. "I'll get him on the radio."

Vernon Q. Johnson, a casually dressed, baby-faced guy who didn't look much older than the dispatcher, appeared about ten minutes later. He strode forward to shake Jaworski's hand. "Sergeant Jaworski? Come on in. How y'all doin'?" Jaworski was surprised; he'd expected a big-bellied old fart with a Stetson and mirrored sunglasses.

"Coffee?" the sheriff asked.

"No, thanks." Jaworski felt like an alien with his dark suit and Eastern accent.

Johnson followed him into the large office, then leaned lightly against the edge of his desk. He clearly expected this to be a short meeting. "I checked out this guy y'all asked me about," he said. "Richards."

"Right."

"And what kind of case is this again?"

"Homicide, but Richards isn't a suspect. It's actually a very cold file."

"Brought you all the way out here, though."

Jaworski nodded.

"Well, a few people remembered him, but his folks are dead now, and he doesn't seem to have any relations around here any more. He went to the local high school, but that was before I was there."

Maybe before he was born, Jaworski thought.

"Anyway," Johnson continued, "I think your best bet would be to talk to old Mr. Redman. He was the superintendent of schools here forever and remembers everybody. Retired now, but still sharp as hell." He stood up, gesturing toward the dispatcher. "Jody can give you directions to his house."

The two men shook hands, and as quickly as he'd appeared, Vernon Q. Johnson disappeared back into Mayberry.

Arthur Redman's house was a two-story brick structure, partially hidden by huge trees, set back from the street in what had probably been

Culver's finest neighborhood. Jaworski welcomed the shade from the trees as he walked up the front sidewalk, feeling sticky in his dress shirt and tie. Before he could knock, the door opened to reveal not a stooped invalid but a very tall man, completely bald, looking surprisingly vigorous.

"You must be Sergeant Jaworski," the old man announced in a booming bass voice.

Jaworski nodded as they shook hands. "I'm Arthur Redman. Jody down at the courthouse told me you might be stopping by. Come on in. How about some lemonade?"

"No, thanks."

"How about something stronger?"

Jaworski smiled. "You know, that sounds good."

Redman showed him into a small study just inside the front door before leaving to fix the drinks. The room was lined, floor to ceiling, with hundreds of books. He studied the titles; all appeared to be on the subjects of geography and travel. And all had numbers neatly handwritten onto white tabs on the spines. So Redman was meticulous, well read, and interested in geography. And he'd apparently gotten a deal on old schoolbooks.

The old man reappeared with two whiskeys, and they took comfortable wing chairs. Redman gave the impression of a man who'd once been enormous, but who had thinned considerably. His red, crooked nose looked like that of a boxer.

Jaworski sipped his whiskey, which was excellent. "Thanks for making the time, Mr. Redman."

"No trouble at all. Since my wife died, all I've got is the books. But they keep me busy enough. So I hear you're asking about Percy Richards."

"That's right. Do you remember him?"

"Oh, sure. Very clearly. That would have been in the seventies. After school, though, he pretty much dropped off the face of the earth. Do you know where he is now?"

"Washington, D.C. He runs a large nonprofit agency."

The old man's face registered surprise. "Really? I might have thought Percy was headed for a business or scientific career. He was very ambitious. I'm glad to hear he's doing well."

"So he was a student at your school?"

"A student of mine, actually. As you can see, we're small. The administrators have to teach, too. Percy was in my history classes. I was also coach of the debate team, and had Percy on the team. We did quite well in those years."

"So Richards was a good student?"

"Oh, yes, in all subjects. Smart to the point of being brilliant, I'd say."

Jaworski sipped his whiskey and studied his host. The old man's enthusiasm seemed forced, as if he'd had to psych himself up to talk about Percy Richards. "What can you tell me about his family?" Jaworski asked.

"His father, Delbert, was the town druggist; his mother helped run the store. They did quite well for many years, until the new Wal-Mart opened up at the edge of town. Keeping the store going was really a struggle after that. Delbert lasted for another three or four years before finally closing it down. He died shortly afterward, from a stroke. The mother, Loretta, seemed to deteriorate, too, but she lived until a few years ago."

"What happened to Percy?"

"His family had run out of money for college, so he enlisted in the air force after high school. At about the same time, he married a local girl."

"Do you remember her name?"

"I believe her first name was April. I don't remember her last name."

Jaworski drained the rest of his glass, feeling for the first time that Redman had not told him the complete truth. He followed the old man's eyes toward the door, and saw a middle-aged woman standing in the doorway, holding a book.

"Did you find it?" Redman asked her.

"Yes," said the woman. "I just left the slip on the round table, if that's okay."

"Of course. See you soon."

The woman left.

Redman looked back at Jaworski. "Sometimes the books are a hassle, but I don't get too much business any more. I sort of welcome it, actually—it's a chance to see people."

"Books?"

The old man smiled. "No one told you about the books?"

"I guess not."

"Well, maybe you'd like to have a look."

"Sure," said Jaworski, who still didn't have the faintest idea what his host was talking about.

Redman led the way past a small kitchen and living room into a hall-way which, like the study, was lined floor-to-ceiling with hundreds of books.

"Quite a collection," Jaworski commented.

The old man looked back and smiled again. "Yes, it is." At the rear of the house he opened up a door, which led to another part of the house. He flipped on a light switch, gesturing for his guest to enter.

Jaworski stepped through the doorway into a veritable warehouse filled with books. A large addition had been built onto the house, and it was bigger than some school—or even public—libraries he had seen. Thousands of books lined a dozen long shelves. Like the collections in the main part of the house, each volume was meticulously numbered.

"This is your private collection?" Jaworski asked.

"Sixty years' worth. It is private, although for eight years during the oil recession, it functioned as the town library, too. The town was strapped for cash, and they had to let the librarian go. Of course, there was enough money for a state-of-the-art football facility for the school—this is Texas, after all—but nothing for the library. So people started to come here. I had more books, anyway. They finally reopened the public library in the mid-nineties, so I don't get as many visitors nowadays. And these books are a little out of fashion; people want celebrity biographies now, or romances or mysteries. Not literature or history or science or the arts."

They walked among the stacks, which were organized according to the Dewey Decimal system. "Where on earth did you get them all?"

The old man shrugged. "It's sort of an obsession with me, I guess. I've collected them all my life. My wife and I used to go to Lubbock or Amarillo on weekends and look at garage sales and second-hand book-shops. During the years the public library was closed, people donated quite a few volumes, too. The largest section is History, of course, since that's my subject. But I've got a pretty wide variety."

"How many of them have you actually read?"

"Over ninety percent. I intend to read all of them in the years I have left."

They reached the rear of the library, and Jaworski noticed a wall lined not with books, but with photographs. Many were old; some were black and white.

"Here," Redman gestured toward a photograph of himself, already bald, with two teenagers holding a large trophy. One of the teenagers was unquestionably Rick Percival, his curly hair longish in the seventies style. His partner was shorter and stouter, with neatly trimmed hair and a strange little smile. "We won the Texas state high school debate championship two years in a row. I told you, Percy was good."

"Who was his partner?"

"A very capable young man, too," said Redman, who abruptly began walking back through the stacks toward the main part of the house. Jaworski followed him all the way through the house to the front entrance. He was being shown the door.

The old man turned around. "It was nice to have met you, Sergeant."

"Mr. Redman, the reason I came—"

He felt the old man's hand clamp around his elbow. "I know," he said softly. "Percy's done something. I don't want to know what it is."

"You're not surprised?"

Arthur Redman looked him in the eye, and for the first time, he looked old and weary. "I knew Percy was different. Extremely intelligent, but not in the conventional sense. He thought differently. He saw the entire world as organized around his own needs and preferences. And he was worldly and sophisticated beyond his years. He was...dangerous." He looked away suddenly, and Jaworski realized the old man had been whispering.

"Who was his partner?"

The old man held up his hand. "Sergeant, please. I just...don't want to talk about it. Please." His tone was pleading.

Jaworski hesitated. "All right. Thank you for your time." He began to push open the screen door.

"Wait," Redman said. "Go see Jenny Haller. She may be able to help you." Jaworski jotted down the directions in his notebook.

"Thanks, Mr. Redman."

"Sergeant?"

"Yes?"

"Be careful."

•

Jenny Haller lived in a small, single-story rambler in a newer part of town. A battered Plymouth Acclaim sat in the crushed-rock driveway. The neighborhood was quiet except for the faint drone of construction equipment Jaworski couldn't see. He rapped on a side door.

The woman who answered looked to be in her late thirties, with a weathered face and bleached hair. She wore a white uniform, the front of which was speckled with blood and yellow matter. A dental hygienist, he guessed.

She scrutinized his credentials carefully. "Maryland?" she said, her accent so pronounced he had to concentrate carefully to understand her. "What brings you all the way out here?"

"Percy Richards."

She showed no reaction at all, but her hesitation told Jaworski he had pushed the right button. "What's he done now?" she said.

"You know him, then."

"What the hell is this about?"

"Could I come in?"

She didn't answer, but turned around and went into the house. Jaworski followed her to the small kitchen, where dirty dishes lined the counters. Jenny Haller took a seat at the table, then slouched backward, looking utterly exhausted.

Jaworski took a chair across from her. "I'm sorry I upset you, but it's important. Mr. Redman gave me your name, but he didn't say how you were acquainted with Richards."

She stared at the wall a long time before answering. "He was my brother-in-law, the scum. Married my sister, April."

Jaworski took out his notebook. "When was that?"

"Twenty-four years ago. June 18th. They'd both just graduated from high school. My sister was the prom queen, the prettiest girl in the school. But she came up a little short in the common sense department. She was taken in by him."

"What was wrong with him?"

"Wrong? To her, it didn't seem like nothing was wrong. He was a big, handsome guy, but didn't want to play football—that should've told her something, don't you think?"

Jaworski suppressed a smile.

"He was a big talker—full of bullshit," Jenny continued. "Thought he was too good for this town—too good for anybody except Percy Richards. He was always reading books. Told us he'd been accepted at SMU and Georgetown; maybe he was. But he didn't have no money; his folks' business was going broke. So he enlisted in the air force."

"What happened next?" Jaworski asked, taking notes.

"Well, he went off to basic training, and April stayed at home. Then he got stationed somewhere, but April didn't go off to live with him."

"Why not?"

She shrugged. "Who knows? He said there wasn't a decent place for them to live at his base. It was here in Texas somewhere, down by San Antonio, so he came home to see her pretty often. But the months went by, and she still didn't go to live with him. She claimed there was nothing wrong, that they were happy and all, but...."

Jaworski made no move to fill the silence, and eventually she resumed. "She believed every word he said. She thought Percy was her ticket out of here." Her voice quavered, and she struggled to maintain control. "God knows she had the right idea. What is there for anybody in this town?" She looked up at him with defiant tears. "You know what she wanted? She didn't want to end up like me, divorced with three kids in a shitty house, looking in people's mouths all day and putting up with their spit and snot and cavities and bullshit and...." She dissolved into tears.

Jaworski waited.

Jenny Haller was quiet again. She walked to the counter, retrieved a pack of cigarettes, and lit one, inhaling deeply as she sat down again. "So what's the deal with Percy? He kill somebody else?"

Jaworski felt chilled despite the house's weak air conditioning. "What do you mean, 'somebody else?'"

"They didn't tell you, huh?" She sat back again, exhaling a large cloud of smoke. "He killed my sister. They'd only been married ten months."

Jaworski took a breath. "How did he do it?"

"Took her camping in the mountains one weekend. He'd always been big on that. April hated camping, but she'd never complain to Percy about anything. He pushed her off the side of a cliff. Of course they said it was an accident. They had an investigation and everything, but when it came down to it, they couldn't prove she hadn't just fallen. And Percy—he was a model student, smooth talker, one of our boys in uniform, so they believed him. And he didn't seem to have any motive."

"Why do you think he did it?"

"Because he could. Just to get away with it. He'd gotten away from here, seen the world a little bit, and he didn't have any use for April any more. She was just another small town girl. To him, she was nothing. Just another bit player in his world."

Jaworski replaced his notebook and stood up. "I'm sorry to have upset you," he said. "Thanks for your help."

"I hope you get him," she said without conviction.

He started to open the door, then looked back. "Ms. Haller, Percy was a debater in high school."

"Yeah. Great at talking."

"Who was his partner?"

She gave him a curious, bitter smile. "They didn't tell you nothing, did they." She stubbed out her cigarette into a coffee cup. "His name was Harlan Belke."

CHAPTER 15

Special Agent Nolan Bertelson trudged down Tori McMillan's driveway and got back into his car. Trying to get information out of Tori had been a waste of time. He supposed he should have tried the soft sell. But he couldn't out good-guy Kyle Jaworski. He'd just have to keep the pressure on and hope for the best. But meanwhile, he had some explaining to do. He let out a long breath, then reached for the special cell phone.

"This is Temple," answered the distorted, whispery voice.

"Bertelson. I just visited the McMillan woman. No luck finding out about Colorado."

"None?" Temple sounded a bit put out.

"I'm sorry. We still have that time unaccounted for. I leaned on her hard, but...."

"But she stood her ground. Her husband was a prominent criminal defense attorney, and she's a lawyer as well. She knows her rights and won't be intimidated."

"Well, yes."

"Then methods other than intimidation should be employed."

"I'm doing the best I can," said Bertelson, his voice strained.

"What about Jaworski?"

"He still appears to be a free agent. A wild card."

"But is he investigating?"

"We believe he is, but we don't think he's getting anywhere."

"Do you know for sure?"

"No."

Temple's pause was ominous. "You're aware of how critical both of these inquiries are."

The FBI agent stood his ground, but felt moisture on his hand as he gripped the phone. "Fully. But we simply don't have the capability of monitoring Jaworski around the clock. Or McMillan, for that matter."

"How did the woman appear to be reacting to Jaworski?"

"It's hard to say for sure. She denied having any contact with him since the beginning of the case, but I'd bet she was lying; we know he was trying to contact her. Even so, I don't think she trusts him fully."

"It's imperative they do not join forces."

"Understood."

"Keep me informed." Temple broke the connection abruptly.

Bertelson looked at the phone in his hand. He was playing a dangerous game, withholding information from Temple. Since he had never met Temple, nor did he even understand Temple's exact position, power, or role, he had no way of knowing exactly how dangerous he could be. But he'd had no doubt, in the four years since he'd been Bound, that Temple, and the organization he represented, were playing for very high stakes.

He had seen no reason to tell Temple that he had bugged Tori McMillan's house and seen a transcript of yesterday's meeting between her and Kyle Jaworski. He knew both Jaworski and McMillan were determined to find the truth, and Bertelson was determined to be on the spot when it happened.

He wanted to know the truth about the Bound just as badly as they did.

●

Kyle Jaworski stood in front of the parking garage on 16th Street in Denver, wiping sweat from his face in the heat. Workers were venturing from their offices to visit the restaurants and stores in the multilevel mall next to the garage, and conventioneers emerged from the large hotel to take in downtown Denver. Jaworski had called in sick this morning; tomorrow was his day off. His repeated, urgent phone calls to Tori had gone unanswered. He had resisted the temptation to press Vernon Q. Johnson about information on the death of Richards' wife; there just wasn't time.

Tori had asked for a copy of Cindy's calendar, which showed appointments here in late May. She had quit her job three days later. Jaworski had then checked airline and hotel records, which showed that Cindy had come back to Denver for three more weeks. The obvious implication was that she had gotten a lead on Scotty.

He stared again at the garage, then up and down the busy street. What had happened to Cindy Stevens three months ago? And where had it happened? On this street? In this hotel? This shopping center? This garage?

Had she seen Scotty here?

Almost certainly not. Jaworski had long since given up hope for the boy. But Cindy, after years of obsession and grief, was probably seeing her son everywhere. Still, whatever had happened here in Denver seemed to have precipitated her abrupt resignation from Sattex, as well as a further three-week stay here. More important, it may have started her on the course that had led to four murders and a suicide.

"She stayed here?"

Jaworski turned to Evan Miller, the Denver PD homicide detective he had befriended at an FBI training course at Quantico some years before. "That's the hotel," Jaworski replied. "And your police report shows the incident in the garage that's attached."

"You want to try that woman again—what's her name?"

"Polly Kendrick. No, I left a message on her voicemail and said it was pretty urgent."

Miller, a short, heavyset man with thinning curly hair, joined Jaworski in looking up and down the street. "It all sounds pretty thin, Kyle. You know this other woman—what's her name...."

"Tori."

"Tori. You think she was trying to figure out what happened to the first woman."

"I know she was," Jaworski replied.

"And you think Tori might have met with the same sales rep the first woman was scheduled to meet with."

"I'm almost positive. I checked Tori's credit card records last night. She had lunch at a Chinese restaurant in the mall."

"The China Garden? Good place. So this Polly ought to know something, right?"

"I hope so."

"Why don't you just ask Tori?"

A good question, Jaworski thought. He felt a surge of anger at Tori; he had traveled halfway across the country to try to piece together what she could have told him in a few minutes. But if he were Tori, would he trust Kyle Jaworski?

Maybe not.

"I tried, Evan. The usual cop stuff doesn't work on her."

"Tough lady."

"Yeah."

"She good-looking?"

Jaworski gave him a sharp look.

"Hey, I was just asking. Speaking of which...." Miller nodded toward the curb, and the two men walked over to a District 6 squad car that had just pulled over.

Miller opened the passenger side door. "Hi, Jess." He squeezed into the front seat; Jaworski got into the back.

Miller said, "Sergeant Kyle Jaworski, meet Officer Jessica Pawloski. I feel like I'm in Warsaw." Jaworski shook hands over the seat with a uniformed young woman with short, blond hair.

Miller handed the woman a sheet of paper. "Sergeant Jaworski's from Washington, D.C.—Maryland, actually. He's investigating a disappearance, and we think this incident might have had something to do with it. Remember this report?"

Officer Pawloski scanned the single sheet. "Yes. It was in the spring."

"Tell us what happened."

"Well, Dispatch sent me to an altercation at...." she looked up. "This parking garage here. The garage attendant reported a confrontation between a woman and a man. They appeared to be arguing over a teenage boy. The woman appeared to be trying to prevent the man and the boy from leaving. The man shoved the woman away, and he and the boy left in a red sport utility vehicle. When they came to the cashier, the man shoved a validated ticket at the cashier and drove away."

Jaworski looked at Miller. "A validated ticket."

"Exactly."

Officer Pawloski looked up. "Did I miss something?"

Jaworski explained. "If we can find out who validated it, we might get a line on where they were and why. As it is, it's impossible to tell—the mall alone must have dozens of stores, and there are hundreds of offices and stores within a block of here. Did you see the woman?"

Pawloski shook her head. "She was gone by the time I got here. Everybody was. This is all from the attendant, a Michele Davis."

"What did she think about the incident?"

"She was pretty upset—enough so to call the cops, anyway. And enough to get the jeep's plate."

"A detective ran it," Miller said. "Later that day. It was a dead end. Registered to an untraceable dummy corporation with a phony address."

Jaworski felt chilled. "This is getting curioser." He looked again at his copy of the report. "A big blond guy with short hair and crooked front teeth. Well, I'll have a talk with this Michele Davis, show her Cindy Stevens' picture. We can at least confirm Cindy Stevens was here. Thanks, Officer."

The two detectives took Miller's unmarked back to police headquarters on Cherokee Street, where Jaworski had left his rental car. The attendant on duty at the parking ramp had confirmed that Michele Davis still worked there, but wasn't scheduled to come on duty until 5:00 p.m.

"How did you ever dig up that police report?" Jaworski asked. "All I gave you was a date and an incident involving a blond woman and a teenager in a public place."

Miller shrugged. "I've got a good computer guy. What if it was her, Kyle? Where do you go from there?"

"I'll try to pick up where your people left off."

"Our people?"

"I know this woman, Evan. If she was convinced she'd seen her son, she didn't just drop it. In fact, she quit her job and came back here for three weeks. She would have contacted Denver PD to ask for help in tracing him. If we confirm it was her, I'm afraid we'll need the services of your computer guy."

"I'll start on it when we get back."

"Let's make sure. I've taken enough of your time already."

"No problem. You seem pretty uptight about this case."

Jaworski's features tightened. "I'm all right."

Miller gave him a long look. "Well, good luck then."

Jaworski picked up his rental car and headed south on I-25 toward Englewood, where Polly Kendrick, her husband, and daughter lived. Using his cell phone, Jaworski tried Kendrick again and got her voicemail again. He called Sattex, which confirmed that Kendrick still worked for the company, and had her office at home. Then he tried Michele Davis, the parking attendant. There was no answer. He tried Tori again, getting her voicemail again.

"Damnit, Tori, check your messages," he barked into the phone. "You've got to believe me—Percival is not what he seems. He's a killer, and I can prove it if you'll give me a chance...."

He clicked off the phone in frustration. He had only until tomorrow to complete his business here; he would be in serious trouble if his superiors learned he was tracking Cindy Stevens' movements.

In fact, he was already in serious trouble.

●

Tori sat down at the kitchen table with Jaworski's files on the four victims spread out in front of her. A fresh pot of coffee dripped into the carafe on the counter. She got up, checked the house's security system, then returned to her seat. She looked at the files. Then she got up again, went to the counter, and returned with her coffee, along with the cordless phone, which she kept within easy reach. She had ignored the voicemail message light on her phone; more bad news was something she couldn't handle now.

Tori took a sip of coffee, drew a deep breath, and opened the first file.

She first skimmed all the files, which consisted almost entirely of notes of interviews with friends, family, and employers. Four different detectives, including Jaworski, had taken the interviews, and all were fairly cursory. She reminded herself that brevity was to be expected. In fact, a case could have been made for not conducting such interviews at all, given the lack of any doubt about the killer's identity. The motive—anger at an ex-husband—seemed obvious enough to require little further investigation, even if a motive was needed.

The victims' lives seemed unremarkable; an account of her own would have read much the same way. They were normal people with normal families and jobs, observing the usual milestones. Marriages, divorces, deaths, graduations, job changes. But in reading the accounts more deeply, Tori was struck by similarities in the descriptions of the victims: A neat person, fun to be around. Happy—very happy. Really seemed content and doing well. These descriptions seemed to Tori to go beyond the usual tendency to speak well of the dead, as well as to heighten the tragedy of their deaths.

After skimming each file, Tori began to focus on the only common thread she'd been able to discern so far, triggered by Kyle Jaworski's comment about the victims: all upstanding citizens, volunteer in the community....

The volunteer comment was literally true. Each of the four victims was an active volunteer, and surprisingly, Jaworski had asked the details of each of their activities. Ron O'Hara from IBM was on the governing board of the National Bone Marrow Connection. Lori Haas from Borland worked for the National Runaway Registry. Michele Tanaka, as Tori had already learned, volunteered for an agency called Friendship House. And Larry Stevens volunteered for....

Tori dropped her cup, spilling coffee onto the table and floor. She fought off nausea, silently formulating a dozen excuses, rationalizations, and coincidences, while trying to fathom Larry's work for an agency called Urban Hope.

She gripped the sides of the kitchen table. Either the explanation was totally innocent or totally sinister. Either Larry Stevens just happened to volunteer for an organization headed by Rick Percival, which was entirely possible, or....

Or Percival was involved somehow in the murders.

Then another realization hit her with a physical jolt. My God, how had she been so oblivious? Cindy had been trying to see Percival when she'd been spotted by the homeless guy named Artie. She'd been seen next to Percival's building. How on earth had she missed the obvious? That was the entire reason Tori had gone down there. She'd missed the obvious because Percival had diverted her, quickly and completely. Yes, Cindy had been trying to see Percival—probably to kill him.

And afterward, Cindy had disappeared.

Feeling lightheaded, Tori eased herself down to the kitchen floor and lay there, motionless, as she pondered the latter possibility. Rick had seemed one of the most genuine, caring men she had ever met. And she had met him by accident. Or had she? Could Percival have been so calculating, so devious, that he had intentionally arranged the near-accident in the Urban Hope parking lot? Could all of his behavior, all of his expressed feelings for her, be a lie?

She couldn't face it. Not now. Not ever. She didn't want to know, couldn't bear the truth.

But she had to.

Tori wasn't sure how long she had been on the floor when she finally pulled herself to her feet. She wiped up the coffee she had spilled, walked carefully to the sink, and poured herself another cup. She set the cup on the table with shaking hands, looked at it for a long moment, then prayed.

She had prayed a lot when Ben had been dying, when it had been too late. Since then there had been nothing worth praying for—not her own life, not anyone else's. But now there was. For reasons she couldn't fathom, she desperately wanted now to survive and learn the truth. She hadn't yet completed her journey through hell, but she wanted to emerge on the other side, intact, ready to resume her life. For even if Rick Percival proved to be a sinister fraud, he had done her a service. He had awakened her will to live. And now her anger had been aroused as well. Tori found a blank sheet of paper and began making notes. Then she reached for the telephone.

It was mid afternoon when she hung up for the last time and pushed the phone aside. She glanced at the clock; it was past three in the afternoon, and she slumped back in her chair, exhausted. She stood up, stretched, and walked to the sink, where she splashed cold water onto her face. Then she took a can of diet soda from the refrigerator and returned to the kitchen table. She popped open the can, took a long drink, and then returned to her notes.

In three hours of inquiries about the victims' volunteer activities, she had failed in her primary task, that of disproving any link between Rick Percival and the victims, specifically Larry Stevens. But there was no evidence establishing a connection, either; Urban Hope was a large organization, and there was no reason its executive director would know about a specific volunteer. If Rick had known about Larry's involvement, he surely would have mentioned it.

Unless the involvement was not a coincidence.

What do you really know about him, Tori?

The details of the victims' activities had led her in a different direction. As she studied her notes, a clear pattern emerged: All four organizations in which the victims were involved—Urban Hope, the National Bone Marrow Connection, Friendship House, and the National Runaway Registry—held at least some of their meetings at the same venue. An organization called the Washington Area Nonprofit Resource Center (WANREC) maintained a conference center in Arlington. Tori rechecked her notes.

The Bone Marrow Connection, devoted to matching donors with recipients who needed transplants, had a governing board that met on the second and fourth Tuesdays of every month. The board of Friendship House met monthly, on the second Tuesday. So did the board of the National Runaway Registry. That meant three of the victims, assuming they attended meetings regularly, were in the same building at the same time every month. Larry Stevens had not been on the governing board of Urban Hope, which met on the third Monday of each month. But over the years he had been on several committees that held regular meetings, often using the WANREC facility. Tori hadn't been able to determine when these committees met.

Tori had likewise run into a dead end in trying to find out whether Ron O'Hara or Lori Haas had ever attended a Corman Seminar, and in learning whether Michele Tanaka and Larry Stevens had attended their Corman sessions at the same time and place.

Tori again found herself chewing on a fingernail. This time she didn't bother to stop herself. She looked at a calendar; the second Tuesday of the month had already passed; it would be weeks before the next set of intersecting meetings took place. But it was pointless, anyway; all the victims who had attended the meetings were dead.

She picked up the phone and punched in the number.

"Good afternoon. WANREC."

"Hi," Tori said. "I'm wondering what days a specific agency uses your facility."

"Let me transfer you to the facility scheduling director."

After a moment another voice answered. "Scheduling. This is Gail."

"Hi, Gail. I'm wondering if the governing board of Urban Hope uses your facility."

"The governing board."

"Yes."

"Okay, because a lot of committees use it, too. And yes, so does the board."

"And when are those meetings held?"

"On the third Thursday of the month."

"Thank you." Tori hung up. It wasn't much of a lead. But for once, luck seemed to be on her side. The third Thursday of the month was tomorrow.

•

Kyle Jaworski drove north on I-25, back toward downtown Denver. The visit to Polly Kendrick's house had been a waste of time; the teenager who answered the door had known nothing of her whereabouts. She had left at about eight that morning, presumably for sales calls. No one at home had talked to her since then, but there was nothing unusual about that. Polly was expected home shortly, but the detective didn't have time to wait for her. He had left his card and cell phone number.

It was now past five, and Jaworski found himself threading his way impatiently through traffic on the crowded freeway. He grabbed his phone and punched in the number of the parking garage where Michele Davis worked. The garage's manager, a man named Horvath, answered.

"Yeah, she's still scheduled to work at five," said Horvath in a gravelly voice. "But she's late. Hell, she's never late."

"Have you tried calling her?"

"No answer. Her bus must be running behind."

"This is Sergeant Jaworski from the police department. I'm wondering what you do with validated tickets that are turned in by your customers."

"You're the police?"

"Right."

"What is this, evidence or something?"

"It could be. Probably not."

"And you want to know what do we do with tickets validated by one of the businesses we have agreements with?"

"Right."

"As soon as the business pays us we toss them," Horvath said.

"How soon do you get your money?"

"A month. Two, tops."

"You wouldn't have any left from May," Jaworski said.

"Hell, no. I'd be out of business if I let them slide that long."

"Are there any records going back that far?"

"Just monthly totals by customer."

"I'd like a list of your customers from last May."

"Shit, we have over fifty."

"I'd like all of them."

Horvath hesitated. "I'll have to talk to my boss. We might need a court order for that."

"Thanks for nothing," Jaworski muttered, stabbing at the End button on his phone. He exited the freeway at Colfax and headed east toward Michele Davis's apartment. His next call was to Evan Miller.

"Hello, Kyle. I already found the file."

"That didn't take long."

"It's a short file. Cindy Stevens came in the following week and told us basically the story you've managed to piece together. She thought she saw her son at the mall with our big blond friend. He got away. She came to us for help the following week. The jeep was a dead end."

"What happened next?"

Miller sounded uncomfortable. "You've got to understand, Kyle. This thing must have sounded pretty farfetched. I know the detective who took the complaint—he's a good cop."

"Don't worry, I understand."

"Anyway, he called Montgomery County about it."

"He didn't talk to me," Jaworski said, seething.

"He talked to your good buddy and boss, Lieutenant Kandel, who said they had no leads or sightings related to Colorado. He also cast doubt on Cindy's credibility."

"Naturally."

"I'm sorry, Kyle. Our man felt his hands were tied. The jeep was a little fishy, but he didn't think there was enough evidence to warrant putting out a description of the boy."

"Don't sweat it, Evan. Thanks for your help."

He crawled east through the rush hour traffic on Colfax, then made his way to Martin Luther King Ave. Michele Davis lived in a shabby three-story building. The crumbling brick, the dirty windows, the graffiti—all announced that this structure's decline had been swift and angry, not slow and agreeable. Jaworski glanced at the mailboxes; M. Davis lived in apartment 302.

Jaworski started up the foul-smelling stairwell next to the front door. The building appeared to have four units on each floor; Michele Davis' apartment would be on his right at the rear.

He reached the third floor and pushed open the fire door. A very large man stood at the right rear door. He jerked his head quickly toward Jaworski, allowing the detective the briefest glimpse of crooked front teeth.

Shit. He'd brought no gun to Denver with him. Too much hassle, he'd told himself.

The blond man reached under his jacket. Jaworski dived at him, grabbing his right hand. The man shook him off like an irritating pest, slamming him into the wall on the opposite side of the hallway. Jaworski rammed his shoulder into the assailant's midsection, pushing him back against the door. His opponent grunted, then hit Jaworski on the shoulder blade. The detective felt his left arm go numb. He kicked viciously at the man's leg, knocking him momentarily off balance.

Jaworski used the delay to dart through the open stairwell doorway. Two silenced gunshots ripped into the heavy wooden door.

Jaworski scrambled down the stairs to the second floor, then glanced up. No one appeared in the stairwell above him. He cracked the door to the second floor. The hallway was empty. From somewhere he heard the thump of a heavy door closing.

Jaworski sprinted down the hallway and jerked open the door to a rear stairwell. He looked up and down, seeing nothing, then ran down the last flight of stairs. He pushed open a heavy exterior door, which looked out onto a shabby alley.

A red jeep, spinning its tires, sped away.

Jaworski ran back up to Michele Davis' apartment. It was foolishness to go in, unarmed and alone, but he couldn't help himself.

The living room, kitchen, and dinette were visible at a glance. They were empty. He trotted across the room and down a short hallway to an open door, then looked inside. Empty.

He wheeled around. There was another open doorway behind him; the room behind it was dark. He fumbled with the light switch, finally succeeding in illuminating the bathroom.

Jaworski jumped backwards. A figure knelt in front of the toilet. He walked slowly forward. It was a woman, presumably Michele Davis. Her arms extended out to the sides, as if she was going to embrace the toilet. One wrist had been duct-taped to a towel rack, the other to the sink's faucet.

She slumped forward. Jaworski knelt beside her. Her face and head were bruised, her mouth taped shut. He felt her neck for the pulse he knew would not be there, then stood up slowly.

He fumbled for the cell phone in his pocket, managing on the third try to enter the proper number.

"Evan? It's Kyle. I'm at Michele Davis' apartment. Our blond friend with the crooked teeth was here. Yes, I saw him. He drowned her in the toilet."

•

"What do you think, Jim?" The question had been asked by Cole Spencer, the Vice President's new chief of staff, replacing Amy Burke. The guy looked about twenty years old.

Traeger shifted his attention back to the meeting. He hadn't really been listening, but this was the type of meeting where only half his attention was required.

"I don't think he should meet with the opposition groups," Traeger answered. "The human rights people will beat up on us anyway."

"The Vice President needs to reach out to all kinds of constituencies," said Amy Burke, who sat at the other end of the table. Especially since he's running for President, she might have added.

The eyes around the table shifted to Vice President Norman Whitelaw, who sat next to Traeger. The purpose of the meeting was to plan his upcoming trip to Latin America. Besides Traeger, Amy, Spencer, and Whitelaw, representatives from State, Treasury, CIA, and the Drug Enforcement Agency were in attendance.

"I think Jim is right," Whitelaw said. "Garcia is one of the best friends we've got down there."

"There will be problems on the Hill," State warned. "They want us to lean on this regime."

"The President's policy is to support Garcia," Traeger snapped. In fact, it was pretty much always the President's policy to support right-wing dictators.

"Let's take a break," Treasury suggested.

The other participants gratefully agreed. State had been talking in circles, as usual, and the meeting had been going on forever. The Vice President stood up and left the room, and Traeger found himself eyeing Whitelaw's coffee cup, which sat right next to his own.

It would be a simple matter. The Vice President drank coffee constantly. Traeger fingered the vial in his pocket. No one would see him.

He couldn't wait much longer. It had to be this week, Temple had said. And Traeger's resignation took effect Monday. There might be one more opportunity after today, a meeting Friday to begin planning next year's State of the Union address.

"Still here?"

He glanced up, startled; the voice belonged to Amy Burke.

"Yeah, I'm still here."

"Sorry to scare you."

Traeger managed a smile. "You don't scare me, Amy."

"I don't suppose you've given up this insane quest of yours." She spoke quietly; the DEA man hadn't left the room.

"No."

"So when are you leaving?"

"Monday. I've given my notice."

"Hokanson still has no idea what you're doing."

"Not from me, he doesn't."

"What the hell are you up to," she hissed. "How can you be pushing him on the President if he hasn't even agreed to run?"

"I don't want the President mad at him. This is my idea."

"You seem awfully sure of yourself."

Traeger glanced at the coffee cup. "Do I?"

•

Tori pulled into the library parking lot, glancing again behind her to see if she was being followed. The research she needed to do probably could have been done at home by phone and computer. But she needed to get out of the house. If nothing else, she would now be a moving target rather than a sitting duck. For the eightieth time that week, she wished she could call Cindy. She needed someone to bring her down to earth, to keep her fears from getting out of hand, to tell her to quit thinking about her mother....

Louise Saunders. A woman for whom private sins did not exist. An offense appeared on her judgmental radar only if it threatened, however remotely, her standing in the suffocating, clique-ridden social pecking order of military wives. But when the blip was detected, her response was ferocious.

With the benefit of nearly two decades, Tori recognized her enlistment in the army, only a few weeks after her son's birth, as an act of defiance. Her refusal to go away, to stay on as an irritant, a reminder, a constant threat to misbehave, was the only form of protest she could muster. The army was a massive organization. Still, she could always run into people who knew her parents, and Tori hoped she would. That was her function, her goal—to be an embarrassment. And the army had provided a respite from decisions, uncertainty, and most of all from thinking through the implications of her failure of will.

Her father felt bad about the whole thing, he said. He eventually let it be known he'd be willing to communicate with his daughter on the sly, but Tori had refused. Though clearly torn, Major Saunders had, as always, ended up following the party line, and Tori didn't particularly care that he did it out of weakness rather than malevolence.

She walked into the library, glancing around again, and sat down at a terminal.

The first subject of her research was Harlan Belke. A magazine profile contained a photograph of a short, crewcut, bespectacled man, smiling a weird, smug grin. His racist organization maintained fortified compounds in the mountains of Virginia and Idaho as well as in Dunston. His empire included not only the camps, but a foundation (denied tax-exempt status by the IRS), short-wave radio stations, Internet sites, magazines, and an extensive direct mail operation.

Hate had been good business for the forty-five-year-old father of eight. After college, Belke had spent seven years as an accountant and salesman before quitting his day job to devote full time to racism. He was said to have a genius-level I.Q. Tori looked at a dozen articles about Belke, but could find no hint of how Scotty Stevens might have ended up in one of his camps, if in fact he had. Many people who met Belke found him so affable that they refused to believe his racist views were sincere. In a well publicized episode three years earlier, the managers of a suburban Denver shopping mall discovered to their horror that for years Belke had, under an assumed name, been employed by the mall as a Santa Claus every December.

Tori next set out to research the Washington Area Nonprofit Resource Center. Half an hour later, the facts looked as disturbing as ever. WAN-REC was owned by a nonprofit corporation. The incorporator was R.T. Percival, who still served as Chairman. Also on the board was Myron Cooper, Urban Hope's director of administration. Among the other board members were the Secretary of Defense, and a prominent Senator, Milton Hokanson from Florida. Despite the VIP cast of directors, it appeared that Urban Hope was more than a mere tenant of the nonprofit center; Percival had been WANREC's founder and driving force.

Tori shifted her research from corporate records to newspaper and magazine accounts of WANREC's development. The center had been announced with a fair amount of publicity, and was designed to offer a myriad of services to nonprofit agencies in the Washington area. The articles monitored fundraising, siting, land purchase, construction, and opening.

She now advanced the microfilm, scanning the *Washington Post* article reporting on the center's grand opening, some five years earlier. Rick Percival was featured in a large photograph, shaking hands with Senator

Milt Hokanson. There were extensive quotes from speeches by Percival and Hokanson. She looked at the final paragraph and froze.

"The people and organizations to be thanked are far too numerous to mention today," Percival had said, "but we cannot let this occasion pass without recognizing our chief corporate sponsor, FuTek, Inc."

Tori sat back and stared at the screen. Percival. Urban Hope. FuTek. Corman Seminars. WANREC.

And four murder victims.

CHAPTER 16

Jim Traeger risked another discreet glance at his watch. He was already five minutes late for the meeting. He willed himself not to finger the capsule in his pocket, as he had been doing for a week.

He could wait no longer. He stood up, straightened his tie, and walked out of his office, down the corridor to the Roosevelt Room. Everyone else was already there. Meetings in the Harris Administration usually started on time, mostly because of the insistence of Jim Traeger. Vice President Norman Whitelaw was already in the room, along with Amy Burke, pollster Roger Clayton, and various other speechwriters and aides. Traeger nodded to the group and took a seat near Whitelaw. Amy was chairing the meeting. "We were just talking about themes, Jim," she said. "The millennium thing's past and has been done to death, but it's hard to see how we can avoid it."

"We can work it in without making it the main theme," Roger Clayton contended.

Norman Whitelaw listened with interest. Ideally, he wanted the theme of the President's State of the Union address, still months away, to coincide with his own campaign theme.

The meeting went on for more than an hour until Amy called for a break. Traeger stood up but didn't leave the room. He eyed Whitelaw's coffee cup and glanced around. Two people remained in the room, but were preoccupied with an animated discussion. Traeger, shielding the table with his body, reached for his own coffee cup, which he would switch with the Vice President's. He had already emptied the capsule into his own cup.

"Mr. Traeger?"

Traeger's head jerked up. An aide stood in the doorway.

"The President would like to see you, sir."

Traeger felt panicky. This might be his last chance. He was set to resign Monday; today was Friday. But he couldn't switch the cups now. And there was no question of his not answering the President's summons.

Traeger forced a smile. "Be right there."

The aide did not leave. Traeger hesitated, grabbed his coffee cup and left for the Oval Office.

●

Outside the Starbucks coffee shop in Rockville, angry clouds had given way to white, diffused sunshine. Jaworski munched on a large muffin. "No donuts and two bucks for coffee," he muttered. "This is no place for a cop."

"But they're playing Mozart," Tori said. "Look, I'm sorry I got angry with you last time."

Jaworski looked relieved. "I'm sorry, too. I'm glad you called."

"So what have you been up to?"

"I took a little trip. To Texas. And then to Denver." The detective studied her reaction. "Some interesting things happened there." He sipped from his coffee. "I'm going to tell you everything."

"All right."

"No, I mean everything. Starting seven years ago. Normally cops don't have to explain themselves. They ask the questions, and the citizen cooperates. Except in this case, you're not cooperating."

Tori started to protest, but Jaworski cut her off. "I know. I should know better than anybody why you don't trust me. Your caution is justified; I've behaved like a jackass, not a professional. And, this case stinks to high heaven." He paused. "No, more than that. It scares me to death. It always has."

Tori found she was holding her breath.

Jaworski went up to the counter, ordered a fresh cup of coffee, and brought it back to the table. "Story time," he said. "It's a story about a young detective assigned to handle the Scotty Stevens kidnapping."

"You."

"None other. Anyway, the Bureau was quickly brought in, of course, as they always are in this type of case, and Bertelson handled it for them. He's an old-line agent—capable enough, I suppose. He tried to freeze me out of most of the decisions and the information, but there's nothing sinister about that—you expect that from the Feds. Bertelson ran a textbook investigation—did all the things you're supposed to do—to find Scotty. But it was wrong, Tori. All wrong."

"How so?"

"Well, this is where you have to decide whether I'm for real or not. Because I cannot point to a single, solitary shred of evidence supporting what I'm about to say. My feeling about this case is just that, as my superiors, led by the redoubtable Lieutenant Kandel, have never ceased to remind me. But I know it, just as certainly as I know you and I are sitting here, as certain as I've ever known anything."

"Know what?" Tori asked in a small voice.

"Everything on the surface was as it should be. Bertelson's investigation was textbook, like I said. But I'm telling you his heart wasn't in it— he wasn't really trying to find Scotty."

Tori gasped. "How do you know that?"

"It was a feeling, and that's all it was. No proof; no single action that looked suspicious. But it was a damned strong feeling. Some things you just know, and I know that Nolan Bertelson was dirty."

Tori suddenly felt short of breath.

"It's still an open file," Jaworski continued, "and we still get a couple of leads a year. But it's the most baffling case I've ever had. Normally you get some kind of feel for what might have happened, even if you don't find the bad guy. But in this case, zilch."

"That's when you and Bertelson came to blows."

Jaworski nodded. "And they decided at the same time I needed to dry out. So I got sent to a nice place out in the Virginia hunt country to write my life's story and sit in circles, talking to drunks who like to smoke." He sat back and took a deep breath, and Tori suddenly realized how painful he found it to recount the distant events.

"I survived," he continued. "I survived by being a chickenshit. By not asking embarrassing questions. By not bucking the system."

"By not probing the souls of murder victims," Tori said.

"Exactly. But somewhere in the back of this Polish brain, I always knew the Stevens case would come back to haunt me. I knew there was something seriously wrong, and some day I'd have to face it."

"What about your boss?" Tori asked. "Lieutenant Kandel. He's one of the things that's wrong?"

Jaworski looked away. "That's one of the questions I saw absolutely no profit in asking," he said, his voice unexpectedly bitter. "Hell, when the Sattex shootings occurred, it was my worst nightmare. If I'd pressed the issue seven years ago, been more persistent—"

"You would have been fired."

"Maybe. I'll never know. But I do know this: I've been a fool ever since Cindy shot those people. Why in hell did I think I could continue to look the other way? Kandel basically told me to take a nap, but what kind of idiot could ignore the obvious questions this time? Christ, if Larry was her only target, why didn't she just shoot him at home, or even at the office? Why track him down at this event off in the middle of nowhere? And why didn't Cindy just shoot herself right there? That's what usually happens in these domestic cases. Why flee from the scene, then commit suicide later?"

Tori nodded, exhaling. Jaworski looked out the window. It was her turn.

She gripped the sides of the small wooden table. "I'm trusting you. I hope to hell you're for real."

"You've got a lot of things to worry about, Tori. I'm not one of them."

She nodded, leaned back, and told him about the post card and Colorado. He reacted, as she had known he would, with a combination of alarm and disgust. His face darkened as she told him about her encounter with the guards at the Belke community.

"Jesus Christ!" he exploded. "They could be coming for you any time."

"I know."

"And you're—God, you're hopeless."

"I'm desperate," she said quietly. "And...and you were right about Percival." She told him about the victims, WANREC, and Rick Percival, omitting only the fact that the Urban Hope board met that evening. "I fell for it all," she said. "The 'accident' next to his building. His 'uncanny insights' that I was widowed, and grew up in Texas. It was all a crock."

He stared into space for a moment after she had finished. Then his gray eyes locked onto hers. "Tell me about the boy," he said, his voice nearly a whisper. "Describe him. Every detail."

Tori pulled the three photographs from her purse and laid them on the table in front of him.

"My God," he whispered. He examined them for another five minutes, moving them around, studying them from every angle. Then he sat back. "What do you think? You saw him in person. Was it Scotty?"

"I honestly don't know. I never met him personally; I've only seen photographs. But I don't have any doubt that Cindy thought he was."

Jaworski nodded, then gave her an uncomfortable look. "We need to talk about Percival."

Tori's features tightened, but she said nothing.

Jaworski told her about his conversations with Arthur Redman and Jenny Haller. When he had finished, he watched her for several minutes, her eyes watery, struggling for control, looking at nothing.

Finally she snapped out of it. "I was blind to the obvious," she said.

Jaworski nodded.

"No, you don't understand. I told you, you were right about him. Cindy was trying to get to Percival when she was spotted down on Massachusetts. And afterward she disappeared."

The detective sat back, tossing his napkin onto the table in disgust. "Jesus, I'm getting senile. You, at least, had a good excuse—you were going out with the guy. I'm supposed to notice these things." He pulled his chair back up to the table. "As long as we're on the subject, I think you need to know what kind of people you're dealing with." He hesitated, then said, "The big man who administered the whipping—the guy you called the Incredible Hulk—he killed a parking attendant who saw him with Scotty."

Tori felt the blood freeze in her veins.

"More than killed," Jaworski continued. "He tortured her to death, dunking her head under water repeatedly. I suppose he did it to find out what she'd told the police, but I'd guess it was mostly gratuitous. She'd already given them his description. Scotty's, too. She might have been able to remember that it was the orthodontist who validated the ticket, but they must know by now that's how you found them, anyway."

"My God," she said. "That means—"

"Yes. The receptionist at the orthodontist's office has been advised to leave town for a few days. And meanwhile, we have another problem: Polly Kendrick is missing."

"What do you mean, missing?"

"She had an appointment at a customer's office in Boulder yesterday morning. She never showed up. Her car was found on the street nearby. Nobody's seen her since."

Tori felt unable to move. Then the room began to tilt. In a moment, Jaworski was beside her, his arm around her, lifting a glass of water to her lips. "Take it easy," he said softly. "You'll be okay."

Slowly, she recovered. Jaworski sat down again. "It's too early to assume the worst about Polly," he said. "And frankly, the searchers' failure to find Cindy is starting to get pretty weird, too. Anyway, we've got half the cops in Denver looking for Polly and your friend with the crooked teeth. We know who he is, by the way, thanks to my time with the artist and mug books. Karl Steen, a four-time loser with a long history of violent assaults. He's rumored to be Belke's chief lieutenant."

"My God."

The detective sat up in his chair, looking decisive and impatient. "Time to face the truth: we've got no probable cause to go into the Belke compound to look for Steen, or Scotty. Of course, they've got three different compounds around the country and could have moved both of them by now. But the main problem is, these people are heavily armed. If we tried to execute a search warrant, there would be a bloodbath. Another Waco."

Tori nodded, trying to follow the detective's rapid thoughts.

"Even if you could execute a search warrant," he said, "I doubt if we could get one to begin with—insufficient grounds. They probably own the local judge anyway. And as far as searching illegally—well, we saw what happened with that. We know they've killed somebody now, but the whole thing would have been moot if he wasn't Scotty."

"But if he wasn't, why are they going to such lengths to cover up the sighting?"

"Because it was enough to start you and Cindy poking around. Maybe they're afraid you stumbled upon something else. Who knows, this might have nothing to do with Scotty. Now, we also have another decision to make: What do we do with you?"

"What do you mean?"

"You can't just stay at home. Not only will Belke find you, but Percival can do it even faster."

"Damnit, I won't let them drive me out of my own home."

"Look, there's a time for bravado and a time to take a stand. This is neither. It's time to stay alive. Do you have someplace you can stay tonight?"

She thought about it. "No."

"Why don't you go up to your in-laws in Pennsylvania?"

"No. I won't leave."

He sighed in exasperation, then wrote down an address on a sheet of his notepad, tore it off, and handed it to her. Then he dug into his pocket, producing a key.

"What's this for?" Tori asked.

"A house, belonging to a friend of mine. She travels a lot and is leaving for Japan this afternoon. You should be safe there."

"She?" Tori said.

"Her name is Susan. An old girlfriend—I'll clear it with her."

Tori, while infuriated at being driven from her home, secretly felt relieved. "All right, I'll do it."

Jaworski tore another sheet of notepaper from his pad and wrote down a phone number. "I can't watch you tonight," he said, sliding the number across the table to her. "Where's your cell phone?"

She patted her purse.

"Battery charged?"

"Yes."

"Promise me you'll program this number into the phone."

"All right."

"And give me the number," he said. She wrote it down for him. "Call me if you see or hear anything unusual. And for God's sake steer clear of Percival."

She promised.

He stood up. "Christ, I can't believe I'm just letting you go like this." He looked at his watch. "I'll check out WANREC and Percival as soon as I can. In the meantime, I've got to try to get some shut-eye. I'm now on the night watch."

"Why?"

He gave a short laugh. "Why? I'm damned lucky I didn't get canned. That little trip to Denver was nearly the last straw. I was able to justify it only because I did it at my own expense and because I hadn't been officially jerked from the Scotty Stevens case. That oversight has now been remedied. So I got off with a letter of reprimand and a transfer to nights. Good thing it's tough to fire a cop."

He walked to the door, then looked back. "Go to Susan's and stay there."

•

President Roark Harris, leaning back in his chair, didn't acknowledge Traeger when he walked in.

"Tell me again why you think we should do this," the President said.

Traeger, his heartbeat accelerating, sat down, put aside his legal pad, and went though all the familiar arguments, ending with the point about the President's place in history. "You could be known as the President who made the safe choice," he said. "Who did the obvious thing, who followed the course of least resistance. Or you could be known as the President who changed history, who took the bold course."

The President sucked in a breath. Changing history sounded all well and good, but being bold; going against a poll....

"And you really think we could pull this off," Harris said.

Traeger was nothing if not patient. "As I've said, Mr. President, there's nothing to 'pull off.' The people will go along with your choice. The party will go along. And, in the end, Norm Whitelaw will go along."

The President swiveled to look out over the South Lawn. Traeger felt a tingle of excitement. Harris was still thinking about it.

After three or four long minutes, the President swiveled back. "I talked to Roger again."

Jim Traeger waited.

"I asked him some of the questions you had about that succession poll. He didn't have very good answers."

Traeger nodded.

Harris looked Traeger in the eye. "All right, you win. I'm going to do it. I'm about to get a lot of people mad at me, and some will think I've gone crazy. But you've convinced me."

"You won't regret it, Mr. President."

"Hell, I probably will. But let me tell you why I'm doing this: You're right about doing the expected. For seven years all the media types have been saying I'm a patsy, that I'm disengaged, that I'm a tool of my advisors, a creation or a puppet of Roger Clayton or Jim Traeger or any of half a dozen other people. I don't give a shit if the *New York Times* writes that; everybody knows they hate me anyway. But I'll be damned if they write it in the history books. If I choose Milt, there can't be much argument that I'm doing what I want, not what everybody expects me to do."

"I appreciate your listening to my input, Mr. President," Traeger heard himself say.

Harris managed a smile. "I wish I could say I appreciated your giving it. In fact, it got me pissed off as hell. But, as usual, you're right." He leaned forward, hands clasped together on the desk. "Let's set up the announcement for about a week from now. You work with Nick on a speech, then tell Amy to get with Milt's people. Have them put a task list together. When we're done here, I'll call Milt and Roger and Amy."

"What about the Vice President?" Traeger asked.

Harris smiled sheepishly. "Norm will be in here at three. I want you here to hold my hand for that one."

Traeger began to stand up.

"Not so fast, Jim."

He sat down.

The President looked satisfied—smug, even. "You cooked up this idea," he said. "Now I expect you to make it work. You know what that means."

Traeger knew. It meant he would have to stay and run Hokanson's campaign, maybe even to serve in his Administration.

It would also mean the end of his marriage.

"There's a price for everything," Roark Harris said.

Traeger disappeared into the short corridor leading to his own office, stepped into a washroom, and emptied his coffee cup into the sink. He exhaled, looking down at his shaking hands and feeling his weak knees. There seemed no end to the costs he had incurred. Caitlin. Now Pam and Brianna.

But he had done it. That he had pulled off a coup of considerable political—even historical—importance, no one would doubt. But no one could know what he knew, that Roark Harris' decision had set off a process that would transform the planet, that would transcend any politician—indeed, any political system.

It might be the most important decision in the history of mankind.

CHAPTER 17

Tori parked her car on the street in front of the row house development in Takoma Park. The inner suburbs of Washington were filled with such places—sprawling, brick, and dingy. She walked slowly up to the door of Number 417, dodging a Frisbee thrown by an exuberant kid. Her knock was answered by a trim, middle-aged woman wearing what looked like a flight attendant's uniform.

"Hi," she said. "You must be Tori. I'm Susan Arkwright." She extended her hand. Tori shook it and followed her into the small house.

"Let me show you around," Susan said. She gave Tori a brief tour of the small, two-story townhouse, which appeared spotless if modestly furnished. They returned to the living room. "Something to drink?" Susan asked.

"How about a Coke?"

"Is Diet okay?"

"Preferable," Tori said. She felt overwhelmed by Susan's energy and perkiness.

Susan returned with two Diet Cokes, and took an easy chair across from Tori, pulling one leg up underneath her.

"I appreciate this," Tori said. "I don't know how much Kyle told you about my situation."

"All he said was that you were a friend who needed a place to stay for a few nights. That's good enough for me. And it's no trouble—I've been on the Asian routes for several years now, so I don't spend a lot of time here. One of the reasons this place doesn't have a lot of personality, I suppose."

"How long have you known Kyle?"

She smiled. "Since junior high school in Baltimore. More years ago than I'd like to think about. I always had a crush on him—he was so handsome, and he had this devil-may-care attitude."

He doesn't any more, Tori thought.

"He was the golden boy," Susan continued. "Star athlete—he was an all-state basketball player. He was at the top of the class, too, but I think he used charm more than hard work to achieve that. Still, becoming a cop was very much in character. His family was working class; his dad died early, and his mother gave piano lessons."

"He seems a little serious now," Tori commented.

Susan shifted in her chair, putting one leg on the floor and pulling the other up under her. "We're best friends," she said. "We have been forever. We tried dating in high school and that didn't work very well. But being friends—that's what's worked for us. We stayed in touch when I lived in Florida for eight years. He was there for me when I went through an abusive marriage and a divorce. I guess I know him as well as anybody. But that's not very well. He used to be more outgoing, to take more risks." She hesitated. "Sometime after he made detective, I lost him."

"What do you mean?" Tori asked.

"He just went into this shell. I'm not sure what happened. But he's not the same any more. He never used to take things very seriously. Now he takes everything seriously, or maybe nothing. He takes it all...equally."

"Hasn't anybody challenged him, tried to draw him out?"

Susan stiffened. "I accept him as he is, just as he does me. We don't dig into each other's pain."

Tori studied her, noticing for the first time the numerous strands of gray in her dark, shoulder-length hair. Tori guessed that Susan was a year or two older than Jaworski.

"He's an incredibly bright man with a good heart," Susan continued. "He's always had to fight some self-destructive tendencies, like his drinking and his temper. By and large, he's kept them in check, I think. But he's still got those demons down there somewhere." She smiled and shook her head. "He's gotten just a little too intense over the years, I guess. Too many layers."

"Does he like his job?" Tori asked.

"He'd never admit it, but he loves the job. That's why he's stuck with it even though he doesn't have much chance for advancement."

She stood up. "Well, I've got to be at the airport by seven. Nice to have met you. Make yourself at home." She collected her rain coat and rolling suitcase and left.

•

Shortly after seven that evening, Tori turned from the Beltway onto I-66 and headed east toward Arlington, armed with binoculars, a camera, and a thermos of coffee, as well as her cell phone.

Tori had said what she'd needed to say to get Kyle Jaworski to help her, while at the same time leaving her alone. On one level, she'd been massively relieved by the detective's turnabout. More than ever, she needed an ally, and he had said all the right things. But at a deeper level, she was still troubled by what Susan had called his demons. She wasn't ready to fully confide in him yet.

Staking out WANREC tonight was a very long shot, but the opportunity wouldn't arise again for another month, and Jaworski couldn't do it himself. And she knew if she stayed alone at Susan's, listening for things that go bump in the night and thinking about Scotty and Polly and Cindy, she might go mad.

Tori circled the WANREC building several times. Parking was scarce; the neighborhood was near the Metro station and had undergone high-density redevelopment. She finally settled on a parking ramp, attached to an office building half a block away. She took a ticket, drove up through the nearly deserted ramp to the second level, and settled back with her binoculars trained on the main entrance to WANREC.

The people entering the nondescript brick building parked in a small lot, on the side opposite Glebe Road. All used a key card to enter the lot, and again to enter the building. Perhaps two dozen people entered the building just before and after seven o'clock; another dozen came at about seven-thirty. Thirty-eight in all. The exterior was well lit, allowing Tori a good view of the people who entered. Most were well dressed, and looked like confident, successful professionals. Rick Percival was not among them, but Tori assumed it might not be mandatory that the executive director attend every Urban Hope board meeting.

Two or three of the participants looked vaguely familiar, and she identified one of them positively. He was Traeger Traeger, President Harris' chief of staff. Tori watched him with a hopeless feeling; Urban Hope seemed immensely powerful. A senator and a cabinet member had attended the building's dedication, and now a person often called the second most powerful in the world seemed to be involved as well.

Nothing much happened between seven-thirty and eight-thirty. Tori began to feel stiff and cold. She moved the car down a row to a better vantage point, then drank some coffee. People started coming out, singly and in twos and threes, shortly after eight-thirty. Tori didn't notice anything unusual about them, probably because she didn't know what she was looking for.

She jumped when her cell phone trilled.

"Hi, it's me," said Kyle Jaworski. "Everything okay?"

"All quiet," she said.

"You're not at Susan's, are you."

"Of course I am."

"Then why didn't you answer her phone? Tori, these people are serious."

"I'm perfectly safe," she asserted. In truth, she could not have given a good reason for sitting in front of WANREC at 9:00 p.m.

"You have to be the most thick-headed, stubborn woman I've ever met."

"Is there anything else?" she asked sweetly.

"Yes. Go back to Susan's, damnit." The line went dead.

Tori clicked the phone's Off button. Jaworski's charges of thick-headedness and stubbornness had at first shocked her. But now, reflecting on it, she was not displeased.

The next stream of departures came shortly after nine. Tori watched and resumed her count. By nine twenty, five people, including Jim Traeger, were still unaccounted for.

It was nearly ten before anyone else left. They departed separately, five people, spaced between thirty seconds and a minute apart. Jim Traeger was the last to leave, walking out briskly and climbing into a Lexus, the last car in the lot. The building was now dark and silent. If there was a watchman, he didn't have a car in the lot.

Tori, dreading the thought of going home, finished the coffee and waited. At ten thirty she started the car and began to back out of her parking stall. Then a movement caught her eye. A car had entered the parking lot.

Tori quickly shut off the engine and retrieved her binoculars. The car, a nondescript sedan, didn't take a parking stall, but pulled up right in front of the entrance. The driver killed the engine and got out. Tori didn't get a good look at his face, but there was no mistaking the ramrod posture and brisk, efficient movements of Myron Cooper, Urban Hope's director of administration.

Cooper inserted a card into the reader by the door, looked around, and went in. Tori watched the parking lot, expecting that someone would be arriving to meet with Cooper.

No one came. Cooper reappeared within five minutes, carrying something in his left hand. Tori quickly adjusted the binoculars; the object appeared to be about the size and shape of a paperback book. Slightly larger, perhaps. She squinted, trying to follow with the binoculars as Cooper walked around to the driver's side. Tori caught one last look; the object was a videotape.

Cooper had already pulled out of the lot when it occurred to Tori that she ought to follow him. Of course doing so could be a waste of time; Cooper might merely be going home. But, as always, it seemed, Tori had nowhere else to go.

She caught up with him at the I-66 entrance ramp. He turned east, toward Washington. Tori, while afraid of losing him, was even more afraid of being spotted. She allowed several cars to pull in between her and Cooper, doing her best to keep him in view. He turned off the freeway onto the George Washington Parkway just before the Roosevelt Bridge, then continued south, past the Pentagon. Then she followed him north, across the 14th Street Bridge and onto the Southwest Freeway. She assumed now that he must be going to the Urban Hope office.

But Cooper, instead of turning north onto I-395, continued east on the Southwest Freeway. It wasn't until he had exited at 6th Street SE that Tori realized where he was going. She dropped well back, letting him turn north and out of her line of vision. But there was no urgency, now that she knew his destination.

She stayed well back as she cruised the side streets up to 4th Street SE, then spotted Cooper's sedan, double-parked in front of Rick Percival's townhouse. He was in and out in a minute, returning without the videotape. Tori let him go; she didn't care where Cooper was going next. But she was very, very interested in what was on the tape.

CHAPTER 18

Tori willed her hands to stop shaking as she approached the house on 4th Street SE. She had spent all morning at Susan's house, trying to build up her nerve, and at noon had finally placed the call to Rick Percival, first blocking the caller I.D. feature on Susan's phone.

"Tori! Good to hear from you. I've tried you at home a couple of times."

"I know," she lied. She had not checked her answering machine, unable to stomach more messages from Max Tuten. "I've been pretty busy lately."

"That's good. How are you feeling?"

"Better. I'm really sorry for unloading on you the other night."

"Now don't get started on that," he said. "You know it was no trouble at all. Are you free for dinner tonight?"

"Actually I'm not. But I thought maybe—well, afterward...."

"Sure. You want to come over around eight?"

"Fine. See you then."

Tori found a parking spot a couple of blocks away, just off Seward Square, and walked toward the house. She hadn't told Jaworski about her stakeout of WANREC, or about the videotape. She had determined to trust the detective only to the extent necessary. And, she had no desire to look foolish; she couldn't have articulated any theory as to how Percival could be involved in the murders, or why the videotape might be significant, or how WANREC or Urban Hope provided any meaningful connection among the victims. But mostly, she admitted to herself, it was shame. Shame at being taken in and used by Percival; shame at her own weakness; shame at the fear she now felt. And shame because, even after all she had learned, she still wanted Rick Percival.

Percival greeted her at the door with a kiss on the lips. He was dressed in jeans and a sweater and seemed, as always, relaxed and friendly. "How about a drink?" he asked.

"Sure." She took a seat in the living room, which only a few nights earlier had seemed so cozy and inviting. Now it felt sterile and threatening.

He handed her a glass of white wine and sat down next to her on the sofa. They clinked glasses. "Glad you could make it," he said. "And I appreciate your coming down here; I know it's a long drive."

"I don't mind getting out of the house," she said truthfully.

"Good. What have you been up to the past few days?"

She studied his face, but could detect no hidden motive for asking the question. "Odds and ends," she replied. "Estate stuff. Cleaning. Shopping. Bill-paying. Fielding a few calls from work. It doesn't seem as though I've accomplished much, even though I've been busy. I'm sure I'll have time on my hands before long, though."

"Have you ever considered volunteering?" he asked. "We've got plenty of opportunities."

Tori panicked; what was he trying to get her into? "I haven't really thought about it."

Percival smiled. "Of course not. But you might want to think about it. You're a caring, capable person with spare time—" He laughed, shaking his head. "I'm sorry. Here I am, recruiting even during the evenings. I try hard to leave the job at the office, but...." He shrugged.

As they talked further, Tori found it harder to keep her mind on the flow of the conversation. Finally she felt his arm around her shoulder. She looked up at him; his smile was warm and knowing. "Some evenings just aren't meant for talking." He leaned down and kissed her.

Instantly, Tori felt the electricity flow through her body, as shame and awkwardness changed to passion, then to near-frenzy. My God, she thought. How utterly screwed up am I?

Afterward, she tossed fitfully for what seemed like hours, her desire and guilt having given way to cold fear. Percival, sleeping soundly next to her, barely moved. Finally the adrenaline subsided, exhaustion set in and she drifted off into a troubled sleep.

•

She woke up suddenly in a panic. Percival was gone, and she could hear water running. How long had he been in the shower? She threw on her clothes, then ran around to the other side of the bed. Percival's trousers were thrown over a chair. Hesitating briefly, she dug through the pockets and pulled out a key ring. It held more than a dozen keys.

Damn. Two were obviously car keys and could be eliminated. But that left ten more. She grabbed her purse and rushed out of the bedroom, turning to face the door of the locked room.

Key number one did not work.

The shower stopped.

She willed her hand to remain steady as she tried the second key, to no avail.

"Tori?"

Panicking, she dropped the keys. Oh, God. Where had she left off?

"Tori?"

The third one from the black car key. "I'm making coffee," she called toward the bedroom.

No response from Percival.

The fourth key did not work.

The fifth key worked. She quickly slid into the room, closing the door behind her. She felt for a light and flipped on the switch. The small room was lined with shelves, which seemed to contain mostly books and videotapes. There were hundreds.

"Tori?"

A small desk sat in the corner. On top of it were a small television, a VCR, and a videotape.

A videotape.

She picked up the tape; it was marked "Urban Hope," and bore yesterday's date. She grabbed the tape and swung open the door.

Where she came face to face with Rick Percival.

He stood there, hair wet, wearing a robe, and saw her with the tape. She tried to run past him, but felt a strong hand clamp around her arm. She let her purse strap slide down her other arm, into her hand, then swung the purse at his head with all the strength she could muster.

The purse connected solidly with the side of Percival's head. He grunted and let go of her arm, but in the process, she had lost the purse.

There was no time to retrieve it. She sprinted through the dining room and down the hallway. She lost precious seconds fumbling with the lock and chain, then threw open the heavy door.

She could feel Percival's breath as he caught up and grabbed at her arm. But he was unable to get completely through the door in time, and Tori shrugged off the arm and ran up the short flight of stairs to the street.

Tori ran down the brick sidewalk toward Seward Square. Then she went down, hard. Percival, still chasing her in his robe, had brought her down with a flying tackle. Half-crawling, she scrambled around a tree toward the street, screaming for help.

Just then, a car squealed to a stop in front of her. Tori got to her feet, only to be grabbed by Percival.

"Hey, what's going on?" a male voice from the car yelled.

Percival reached for the video; Tori tossed it onto the hood of the car, a black Honda sedan. Percival tried to move around her toward the car, but now Tori hung onto him, and bit him in the arm.

Percival, yelling in pain, reached back and hit her in the face. Tori went down, grabbing his ankle just above a bare foot, and again sinking her teeth into him.

Percival howled again, kicking at her. By this time the car's driver, a young black man, had come out of the car and taken the video.

"Help!" Tori screamed again.

"Hey, leave her alone!" the driver yelled. "I've called the cops on my cell phone!" He did not, however, step forward to take on Percival, who was taller and outweighed him by at least thirty pounds.

"Give me the tape," Percival demanded.

"We'll let the police sort it out," the man said, retreating to the side of the car, still holding the video.

"Just give it to me."

"Don't give it to him," Tori pleaded

Sirens interrupted Percival's advance toward the driver. Percival froze momentarily, looked around, then turned toward Tori. "Just return the tape, Tori. There'll be no reprisals. But if you don't return it by noon today...." He let the threat hang in the air. He turned on his heel and strode briskly back toward the house. "We can tell if it's been viewed or copied," he yelled without turning around.

"Are you all right?" the driver asked.

"Yes. Thank you so much."

The driver waved away the thanks and held out his hand. "William Graves. I was on my way to work, and—well, this situation just didn't look right."

Tori, tears streaming down her face, took his hand and said, "Thank you...that was the kindest thing."

"No problem. Do you know this guy?"

She nodded. "It's really embarrassing. I'd just as soon forget it."

Graves looked troubled. "The police will be here any minute." But in fact, the sirens had died out; the police apparently had bigger fish to fry than an attempted mugging on 4th Street.

"Please," she said. "My car is right around the corner. I'd just as soon go."

He nodded. "I understand. Let me give you a ride to your car. And I guess this belongs to you." He handed her the tape; Tori wasn't about to admit it didn't belong to her.

She was waving goodbye to William Graves when she realized her purse was still in Percival's house. With it were her money, credit cards, ATM card, cell phone, driver's license and, most importantly now, her keys.

Tori began walking briskly toward the Capitol. She found her way up to Pennsylvania Avenue, passing the restaurant where she'd had dinner with Percival. Finally, she ended up sitting down on the front steps of the Capitol, the most public venue she could think of, under the eyes of watchful security guards.

She tried to think; in adding up the damage, she had to assume the worst. She wasn't sure she could remember her VISA account number and, even if she did, she would have to assume her cards would be canceled shortly, or monitored for activity. Without money, she couldn't go anywhere. She couldn't get a locksmith to make her another key for the Audi, pay for a taxi, or even buy a fare card for the Metro. Her cell phone was gone; she didn't even have money for a phone call, and wasn't sure whom to call if she did. All she had was a videotape and the clothes on her back.

She went inside the Capitol and found a rest room. Surveying herself in a mirror, she didn't look too bad, although a bruise was beginning to form on her left cheek, where Percival had hit her. She washed up as best she could, cleaning the scraped skin from her palms and knees where she had hit the sidewalk. And then she noticed the watch.

Tori walked back outside, sat down again on the Capitol steps, and fingered the beautiful gold watch Ben had given her for their first anniversary. No way could she do it.

But she remembered the hatred she had seen on Percival's face. She thought about Cindy, and about a young parking attendant in Denver. Tears streamed down her face as she removed the watch.

Forgive me, Ben. It's life and death. I know you'd understand.

Then she found a phone kiosk, took out the Yellow Pages, and looked up the closest pawnshop.

•

Special Agent Nolan Bertelson was beginning to feel excited, the way he always did when a case neared resolution. He sat in his office, listlessly shuffling through accumulated paperwork. He hadn't felt this way since the early days after he'd become Bound, when his entire future had looked so different from the way he'd always imagined it. He'd been recruited at just the right time, a logical time, when he was becoming disillusioned with his Christian faith. The Bound had provided him with the same sense of community as had his church, but without the enforced conformity that had begun to seem stifling to him.

Even in those heady early days, in the midst of love and euphoria, he had felt sad, knowing that he would never again really approach the same level of well-being. Still, all the recent developments had made him realize that the Bound, whatever it really was, and his own involvement in it, were entering a new and final phase. What it would look like, he couldn't really say. And that excited him.

When the phone rang, Bertelson picked it up automatically.

"Temple here," said the familiar distorted voice.

Bertelson was shocked; Temple had never before called him "in the clear," over his normal phone line, at the office.

"What can I do for you?" the agent asked.

"We have a full-blown emergency. Victoria McMillan must be caught and eliminated. She has a videotape in her possession that must be retrieved. Anyone who may have seen the tape—especially Jaworski— must also be eliminated."

Bertelson was flabbergasted. "Elim—" He glanced self-consciously around the busy office; no one seemed to be taking any special interest in his conversation. "Do you know what you're asking?"

"Fully."

"Good Lord, this is just—"

The distorted voice hardened. "Nolan, you have never had a more important assignment in your life. You must accept our word that this is necessary and unavoidable. We need you. This must be done, at all costs."

Bertelson hesitated. "All right, then," he said decisively. "Does she know you're looking for her?"

"Yes."

"Then she probably won't go home; she hasn't been there for a couple of days, anyway. I'll keep a watch on the house, just in case. And we'll step up the surveillance on Jaworski."

"Good. Her vehicle is parked on the west side of Seward Square. She was last seen in that vicinity."

"Acknowledged." He lowered his voice, looking around again. "You know that if I really do what needs to be done here, I'll have to call in a lot of markers, and do some things that might be irrevocable. It might be the end of my career."

"We realize that fully, and we appreciate it. We're counting on you, Nolan."

•

Tori stood at the phone booth on 14th Street and punched in the number.

"Homicide."

"Sergeant Jaworski, please."

"He's not available right now. He'll be back in the office around three. Could someone else help you?"

"I don't think so."

"Well, then, if you'll give me your name and number...."

"There's no place he could return the call. Look, it's really important that I talk to him. If you could just put me through—"

"I'll have to get your name and number, ma'am—"

Tori hung up, cursing Percival. He had her cell phone, and with it Jaworski's direct phone number, programmed inside it. She took a deep breath, glanced up and down the block, and began walking south on 14th Street, toward the White House. Time for Plan B. The pawnbroker had given her only $50.00 for the watch. Not enough to flee. Enough for a few subway rides and a decent meal, if she was lucky. She had cash at home, but the house was undoubtedly under surveillance. So was her car, by now. It would be towed at four o'clock if she didn't move it. Even Susan's house might not be safe.

She pondered other alternatives. She could go back to her neighborhood and enlist the aid of one of her neighbors. But if her house was being watched she would still be caught. And she might get the neighbors in trouble. She could go out to the police station in Rockville and wait there for Kyle Jaworski. But what about the detective's boss, who was at the very least unsympathetic, and at worst might be working for the wrong side? Somehow, she had to hang in there until three o'clock. Without thinking she glanced at her wrist, checking the watch that was no longer there. It had to be somewhere around ten, she thought.

Tori got on the Metro at McPherson Square, then transferred to the Red Line at Metro Center. She rode out to Montgomery County. At least she could be closer to home. She got off at Dupont Circle, then took a bus out to the public library on Connecticut Avenue in north Chevy Chase. She felt silly and exposed, carrying the videotape and no purse. She walked into the library and approached a bored-looking clerk, an older woman, at the reference desk.

"Do you have a VCR here?"

"Sure. In the back."

The clerk went back with Tori and insisted on showing her all the details of how to run the machine. It was all Tori could do to keep from lashing out at her, telling her that she damn well knew how to run a VCR.

She waited patiently for the clerk to leave, then popped the tape into the machine, turned off the lights, and sat down to watch. The screen showed a group of people—five, she counted—sitting around in a circle. The gathering appeared to be illuminated only by candlelight.

A familiar-looking man was the last to take his seat. The five people held hands.

"May the bound be forever unbroken," said the man she recognized as Jim Traeger.

CHAPTER 19

From her vantage point, in the bushes up near the bridge, Tori could see Kyle Jaworski's unmarked car take an illegal parking spot down on Rock Creek Parkway, next to the softball field. The day was cold and windy, with thin sunlight poking intermittently through gray, threatening clouds. Jaworski got out of the car, looked around, and walked slowly over to a bench behind the field's wire backstop. Tori forced herself to wait several more minutes. Then, seeing no one, she scrambled down the hill to join him.

"Sorry to keep you waiting," she said, taking a seat next to him on the bench.

"It was unnecessary. Nobody's following me."

"I can see that."

He turned toward her suddenly, ripping off his sunglasses. "Goddamnit, Tori, you still just do not get this, do you."

She said nothing.

"You're off playing Lone Ranger again. You have no right to do this to me."

"What are you saying?" she shot back. "That you have some claim on me? Some interest in me? Well, you don't."

"What the hell do I have to do to convince you I'm for real?"

"I don't know."

Jaworski was, she noticed, keeping a constant watch up and down the parkway. "Presumably you're here for a reason. Presumably you want me, obsessed scumbag or no, to help you. You have to talk to me."

She handed him the videotape. "This is a meeting of the people who took Scotty," she said.

Jaworski found himself holding his breath. He recovered his senses and looked up and down the street. "You've seen this tape," he said. "So what is all this about?"

She handed him the video. "It's some kind of group—like a cult. It's called the Bound. There were five people at the meeting, but there are probably other groups. I recognized one of the participants. It was Jim Traeger."

"The President's chief of staff."

"Yes. And, this is really weird, but you can see it for yourself...He's giving up his daughter a week from now. Like a human sacrifice, or some kind of demonstration of loyalty. Her name is Caitlin. I don't know how it works, but he's doing it."

"Jesus."

"It gets worse."

"Make my day, Tori. Tell me what's worse than sacrificing children."

"Traeger has talked the President into dumping Norman Whitelaw. He's going to endorse Senator Milt Hokanson as his successor."

Jaworski shrugged. "Hokanson's a better candidate."

"You don't understand," Tori said, her voice urgent. "Hokanson is one of them. He's on the board of Urban Hope. He helped to raise money for WANREC. The next President of the United States is going to be part of this group. They're announcing that at the end of the month, too. That's only a week away."

Jaworski let out a breath. "Now we know why these folks are a little serious. Let's back up for a moment. Who are these people, besides Traeger?"

"The other people at the meeting sounded like government employees with fairly important jobs, but I don't know what they do. Their names are Ed, Tom, Joanne, and Tina. Apparently they all met, or were inducted, or whatever, at a Corman Seminar they went to down in Mexico. And they made a couple of references to a place called Sian Ka'an. I looked it up at the library—it's a big biosphere reserve south of Cancún—pretty much a rain forest, I guess."

"What else?" Jaworski asked.

"That's about all. There's so much we still don't know. What are this cult's beliefs? What holds them together? Somehow, it's a really tight-knit group. I mean, these people love each other—you can tell from the way they interact. But basically, we don't know how the Bound connects with anything else. Is this FBI agent, Bertelson, a member? And what about the murders? Did they have a group at Sattex? Was Larry a member? And Scotty—"

She looked up, and suddenly they both understood. "He might have been sacrificed, or given away, or whatever, just like this Caitlin," Jaworski said.

Tori's hand went involuntarily to her mouth. "My God."

"And," Jaworski continued, "maybe Cindy found out about it somehow, maybe in Colorado, and decided to take out the entire group. But hell, the questions just go on and on. I don't know what Bertelson's involvement is, either. And what about Harlan Belke? And Corman? Somehow, the FuTek Corporation is probably in on it, too. They own Corman and helped to finance WANREC."

"Any word on Polly Kendrick or Cindy?" she asked.

"No trace. And that is mighty weird." Jaworski pulled an envelope from his pocket. From a packet of papers inside he extracted a photograph, apparently from a magazine article. "Look familiar?" he asked.

"He looks about ten years younger, but it's Rick Percival," she said.

"He's the same guy," Jaworski agreed. "But his name is Percy Richards. He was an executive at FuTek, according to my research. Held a senior position at a very young age. That was about eight years ago, before he dropped off the map."

"Eight years," she said. "That's around the time Urban Hope was founded, and about the time Dennis Curry, FuTek's founder, disappeared."

Jaworski managed a smile. "Sheer coincidence, I'm sure. Anyway, I couldn't find out much about Richards. He was a research scientist at Merck, then at another pharmaceutical company, before taking the job as executive vice president of FuTek."

Tori said nothing.

"For what it's worth, I'm sorry about Percival," he said.

She nodded.

"Tori, you have to trust somebody. I know I behaved like a fool, blurting out my feelings for you. But we're talking about something bigger here."

Tori struggled for control. "You have to understand. The idea of just putting myself in someone's hands.... I mean, what if I'd trusted Bertelson? He's a duly appointed officer of the law, just like you...."

"I know. And you trusted Percival, too. I'm not telling you it's easy." More softly, he added, "I got into the confessional box and gave you a blow-by-blow on how I've behaved like an idiot for the past seven years, in order to try to make you understand me. I've done all I can do to connect with you."

Tori, swallowing hard, detailed how she'd gotten the videotape, starting with her stakeout of WANREC and ending with her escape from Percival's house that morning.

Jaworski, maintaining his watch up and down the parkway, was silent for several minutes after she had finished. At last he said, "What you did was incredibly foolish. And incredibly brave."

"But what do we do now? We have the tape, but where does that get us?"

"I don't know about you, but staying alive gets priority from me." Without moving his head, he said, "Tori, they're here. I want you to get out of here, the way you came, as fast as humanly possible. They might not have covered the slope yet."

"What? Have you lost your—"

"Tori," he said, his voice even, "Don't go to Susan's. Just stay out of sight, keep your head down, and call me."

"But—"

"Just fucking do it. Now."

Tori hesitated, then ran back up the slope, toward the bridge and Connecticut Avenue. Halfway up, she glanced back. At least three cars, unmarked sedans, had pulled up next to Jaworski's. Men in suits were running toward the softball diamond and the bench.

Jaworski knew there was no escape for him; he just had to hope Tori could get away. They had bugged his car, he now realized. How else would they have been able to track him? Then he felt the object in his hand. The video. He hadn't given it to Tori. Christ, how could he have been so stupid? It was too late; Tori was already halfway up the slope.

He looked around; FBI agents were approaching from three sides. He couldn't outrun them, and there was nowhere to ditch the tape.

Bertelson was part of the first group of three agents to reach him. He and two other men had drawn their guns. Jaworski raised his hands.

"Your piece, Sergeant," he said. "Carefully."

Jaworski withdrew his pistol from its shoulder holster and tossed it to the ground, where one of the agents retrieved it.

"Now your cell phone, please."

Shit. It was the only way Tori could reach him. He handed it over.

"And now the tape," Bertelson said.

"What tape?"

"Don't waste my time, Kyle. The one in your left raincoat pocket."

With despair creeping through every cell in his body, he gave Bertelson the tape.

•

Up at the bridge, Tori again looked back. Agents were headed up the slope, but they wouldn't catch her. They would, however, radio to other agents, who would soon be appearing at the top of the slope in vehicles. She saw Jaworski, his hands in the air, handing over the tape to a man in a suit, who must be Bertelson. She froze for a moment, then ran for the bus stop.

As soon as she was safely ensconced on an outbound bus, Tori began to think about her next move. Jaworski had been right; staying alive was her only real concern now. The tape, along with Jaworski himself, was in enemy hands. There was little hope of doing anything about Caitlin Traeger, or the President's endorsement of Milt Hokanson. As soon as she got a chance, she would place an anonymous call to the police, warning them that Caitlin was in danger, and might soon be killed or kidnapped. It wasn't much, but it was all she could do.

Staying alive may have been her top priority, but how to accomplish it was far from clear. She had $50.00 and the clothes on her back. She couldn't go home or to Susan's, and police everywhere were looking for her. That meant her neighbors, or people she used to work with, couldn't be contacted. Her brother in Brazil, with whom she maintained only sporadic contact, might be willing to send her money. But where would she receive it? The only other alternative seemed to be to contact her parents. With a couple of phone calls, Major Dwight T. Saunders would be able to have her whisked off to a place of safety, and would undoubtedly be glad to do it. But she knew she would never place the call.

She would rather die.

The bus continued up Connecticut in the early-evening darkness. She scanned the street, waiting for police to stop and search the bus. She was out of options.

Suddenly she pulled the signal cord, jumped up, and got off at the next intersection. Passing a street in the Friendship Heights neighborhood had triggered memories for her. Memories of numerous social gatherings at a home about a mile away, toward Wisconsin Avenue. She set out through the residential neighborhood, toward Max Tuten's house.

Tori had dutifully attended these functions at Max's house, events he had called team-building exercises. "It's a chance for me to get to know everybody on a personal level," he had always said with a smirk. "Especially you."

Good old Max. Always volunteering to help. Fine, he could damn well help now, with some money and transportation. And her neighbors and former co-workers, responding to police questioning, would inevitably describe Max as the last person she would ever visit. Of course he would turn her in if he deemed it expedient. But with any luck, he wouldn't know she was being hunted. She estimated it must be close to six o'clock. Max, never a workaholic, would be home shortly. And she was still a mile away. She hurried on through the neighborhood, keeping a wary eye out for police cars. None appeared.

She slowed down a block from Max's house, an undistinguished two-story brick colonial on Van Ness Street. There was a fair amount of traffic, from people arriving home from work. But no police. After hesitating briefly, she walked up the front sidewalk and rang the bell. No response. Two more tries likewise went unanswered.

She walked around to the garage. Max's BMW, his only car, was parked inside. She let herself in through a gate in the back fence and approached the back door. There were lights on inside the house.

She rapped on the back door. "Max?"

The door was open. She walked in.

"Max?" The kitchen was to her left; a small den to the right. And the next room on the right, with its light on, was....

A bathroom. Where Max knelt in front of the toilet, his chin resting on his chest, his wrists duct-taped to a window handle and a faucet. Tori fought back nausea as she quickly stepped back into the hallway.

And then it all fell into place. Jim Traeger's group consisted of five people. Cindy had killed four people at the picnic. Which meant someone in Larry's cell was missing: Max. Max, who had repeatedly asked who the victims were. Max, who kept exclaiming that it could have been him. Cindy had looked around briefly after killing the four victims; she had been looking for Max.

And now there was literally no one to turn to. All she could do was get away as quickly as possible. She ran toward the back door, nearly running into the person who stepped out of the kitchen. She looked up; the person was a large man, muscular and blond, with crooked front teeth. Karl Steen. The Incredible Hulk. He smiled.

Also smiling was the man who stepped out of the kitchen behind him. Rick Percival.

CHAPTER 20

Tori looked back and forth between the two men who now blocked her path to the back door. Percival gave her his composed, saintly look, which infuriated her. His act was wearing thin. "I guess we were entitled to a break," he said. "Your showing up here is most unexpected, but I'll take it. Our friend Bertelson is turning into a screwup—covering the high ground of a rendezvous point ought to be pretty basic in FBI training."

Tori had thought the same thing, but as with Percival, she had accepted the break. "You bastard," she said.

"You shouldn't be surprised, Tori. I guess we used each other."

Tori exploded. "You guess?" She bolted for the front door, but was stopped in her tracks by a vise-like grip on her arm. Steen yanked her roughly back into the kitchen.

Percival, following them into the kitchen, gave her a sad and mildly disapproving look. "Tori, please. You can hardly claim to be an innocent victim. In the beginning, perhaps. But not after all you've done since. Let's talk." Steen shoved her into a chair.

Percival leaned casually against the counter. "You shouldn't have gotten involved, Tori. You should have let it go."

"Where is Cindy? Is she alive?"

Percival thought about his answer. "You're better off to think of her as dead. She is not alive, in any meaningful sense."

"What is that supposed to mean?"

"It's difficult to explain. Just let her go. Let it all go. It's over. We have the tape. We'll have to determine what you may have told others, but it's over."

Tori swallowed her anger. "What is all this about? What is this organization of yours? And what about Scotty?"

Percival merely shook his head. "We need to learn some details from you, and we really don't have time for explanations. It's most important that you tell us everything that has happened today." He nodded to Steen, who handed him a small leather bag. From it Percival took a hypodermic syringe and a small jar filled with clear liquid.

"Oh, God," Tori exclaimed involuntarily.

"We have to be sure," Percival said, sounding apologetic. Steen stood directly behind her.

"When I'm done telling you everything, you're going to kill me, aren't you."

His expression looked genuinely remorseful. "You have to understand, Tori. No one regrets it more than I do. I...developed genuine feelings for you, despite myself. But there's a larger cause here. Much larger. If you've viewed the tape you must realize that." He pulled back the stopper, filling the syringe from the bottle.

Tori thought fast, trying to stall him. "Why did you kill Max?"

"Max was a disappointment. He was weak. We do our best to screen our people, but we're fallible." Percival squirted a small stream of liquid from the needle. "It's time, Tori. I'm truly sorry, and I promise you there will be no pain."

"So what happens after the drug? A bullet?"

"No, not at all. You won't exist any more as a person. But you will be making a contribution, an important one."

Tori moaned and leaned forward in the chair, her face nearly touching her knees. "I'm going to be sick," she said.

"Tori...."

She felt rather than saw Steen leaning over behind her, then sat up quickly, throwing her head back violently, butting him in the face. She felt his nose crack.

"Shit!" Steen grunted, and Tori felt warm blood from his nose falling on her neck. Almost simultaneously, she kicked Percival in the crotch. Reflexively, he dropped the needle onto the table, and Tori grabbed it, springing forward, out of the range of Steen, whose powerful punch just missed her head, knocking over the wooden kitchen chair she had been sitting in.

Tori wrapped an arm around Percival's neck, holding the syringe up to his right ear. "Freeze, both of you!" she yelled, "or I'll jam it into his brain!" Steen, ignoring her, advanced across the kitchen. Tori lightly jabbed the needle into Percival's eardrum. He flinched in pain and yelled, "Stop, Karl, for God's sake!"

Steen stopped.

Percival tentatively straightened up, bringing his hands up slowly from his crotch. Tori tightened her grip around his neck, digging her thumb into his Adam's apple. "Don't try it, Rick," she said quietly into his ear. "You know I'll do it; you're going to kill me anyway, and I'd love to take you with me. You've left me with nothing to lose."

Percival stiffened but said nothing.

"All right," Tori said. "Steen, move to your right and lie down on your stomach. Then put your hands on the back of your neck."

"Fuck you," Steen spat.

"I'm going to count to three," Tori said. "If you're not on the ground, I stick the needle in."

Steen, his features distorted by the same internal fury he had shown while whipping one of his compatriots, looked to Percival, who said nothing.

"One," Tori said.

Percival said, "Give it up, Tori. You kill me, he'll kill you."

"So what? You'll do it anyway. And your cherished cause will be dead along with us. Two."

Neither man moved nor said anything.

Tori trembled. She could feel sweat on Percival's neck and chin.

She closed her eyes and tightened her grip on the syringe.

Silence.

"All right," Percival said quickly. He moved his head slightly, nodding to Steen. Hesitating briefly, Steen lowered himself to the floor, still glowering. Tori turned Percival to keep him in between Steen and herself. Now, with her back to the door, she backed up slightly, pulling Percival with her. Using her left foot, she hooked the fallen kitchen chair, moving its back between her legs and Percival's.

"We're going to sit down now, and I'm going to call the police," she said. Then she jabbed the needle into Percival's neck, pushing the plunger down all the way. Percival yelled and yanked himself free. By then, Tori had already kicked the chair into his path and bolted for the front door. As she fumbled with the lock, she heard Percival fall over the chair, and heard Steen trying to get around or over his sprawled figure. Steen appeared behind her in the hallway.

She finally got the deadbolt unlocked and threw open the door.

Steen sprinted down the hallway, covering it in three long steps.

She backed out the door. Steen arrived an instant later, reaching through the door for her.

With all her might, Tori slammed the door on his wrist. She felt the bones give way, and Steen's scream was blood curdling. Tori sprinted for the street, then ran down toward Wisconsin Avenue. She had never run so fast. All that jogging, she thought. Comes in handy once in a while. Yet she didn't even need to look back to know that Karl Steen was close on her heels.

She looked around frantically; there was no traffic on the quiet residential streets. She could run for one of the houses, but Steen would catch her before anyone could let her inside. Steen had to have a broken wrist, but it obviously wasn't affecting his ability to run.

Tori darted in front of a parked car and ran between two houses. An eight-foot wooden privacy fence enclosed the back yard of the house on the right. Tori jumped, caught the top of the fence, and began to swing herself over. Then a hand caught her right ankle.

She kicked viciously, catching Steen in the shoulder, then yanked her foot free and clambered the rest of the way over. Steen might be strong, but he wouldn't be able to pull himself over one-handed. She began to run again, then tripped and fell face-first into a sandbox. She picked herself up and resumed running toward the rear of the yard. The lot's back border was enclosed only by a three-foot chain-link. She vaulted over it easily, then ran through another yard to the street on the other side.

Running toward Wisconsin Avenue, she risked a look backward. Steen was nowhere in sight, although she had no doubt the neighborhood would soon be crawling with FBI agents or D.C. police.

At last she reached Wisconsin Avenue. She didn't want to risk entering a Metro station. But after walking north for two blocks, she was able to hail a taxi. She collapsed into the back seat, and the driver turned around and asked where she wanted to go.

"Away," was all she was able to say.

She got out across from the Mazza Gallerie shopping mall, the only crowded public place she could think of. But before she could cross the street, two police cars pulled up slowly in front of the mall. She quickly hid her face, moving down the street, away from the mall. Officers were leaving the cars and moving up and down the sidewalks, questioning pedestrians.

Tori walked quickly inside an office building and took the stairway up to the second floor. All the offices on the floor appeared to be locked, as were the restrooms. She walked up to the third floor. Halfway down the hall she found an opthamologist's office, where several patients waited for their early-evening appointments. She took her jacket off, left it in the hallway, and walked in, trying not to look at the waiting patients. The front desk was unoccupied; Tori saw the restroom key on the counter, grabbed it, and left quickly.

Down the hall, she found the ladies' room, opened the door, and jammed her jacket into the doorway. Then she returned the key and went back to the restroom. Looking reluctantly into the mirror, she was horrified by what she saw. A dirty, disheveled woman with bloodshot eyes, looking scared to death. She cleaned herself up as best she could, then, sitting down in the rear stall, she simply waited, trying to hold herself together.

Without a watch, there was no way to judge how much time had passed. By what she guessed must be about eight o'clock, only one other person had used the bathroom. She got up, peered out into the hallway, and seeing nothing, took the stairs down to the lobby. The opthamologist's office closed at eight, and she hoped that by now the search would have lessened in intensity. She had earlier spotted a phone booth behind the bank of elevators. Hands trembling, she put the money in and dialed Kyle Jaworski's cell phone number.

The phone was answered, but no one spoke.

"Kyle?"

"Hello, Tori." It was Nolan Bertelson.

Tori gasped. "Where is Kyle?"

"He's fine. Now, where are you? We need to talk."

"Talk? Don't insult my intelligence."

"Listen to me," he said, his voice urgent. "You have nothing to fear from me. I am not Percival—please believe that. Your only hope is to cooperate."

"Cooperate? I—" She broke the connection abruptly. Jaworski's phone undoubtedly had caller I.D. They would trace her location within minutes. She walked quickly through the darkened lobby toward the door.

"Ma'am?"

She wheeled around. The voice had come from a security guard, who sat behind a desk, watching television.

"You need to sign out," said the guard, sounding bored.

Fighting off the urge to flee, she walked back and scribbled an illegible signature on a log sheet. Then she left quickly, glancing up and down Wisconsin Avenue. It was mostly dark outside. There was plenty of traffic, but no police visible. For the next hour she walked north on the residential streets that paralleled Wisconsin, reflecting idly that by walking across the District line into Maryland, she was guilty of interstate flight. As she neared downtown Bethesda and her own neighborhood, she began to look for a place to pass more time. She settled on a park, and took a seat in a wooded area near a swing set.

For the next couple of hours she shivered in the chilly, damp night. Once, she had flattened herself on the ground to avoid a spotlight, shined from a police car, apparently on routine patrol rounds. Finally, she began walking north and east, into her neighborhood. There was hardly any traffic on the quiet streets, and Tori hid behind one of the numerous large trees whenever a car approached.

Her heartbeat accelerated as she approached her own street. From two blocks away she easily spotted the car that sat in front of her house. Less obvious was a second car that sat around the corner on a side street. She reversed course, circled around, and came up to the street behind her house, crossing three blocks down to avoid being seen by the car that sat on the side street.

There were two parked cars on the street behind hers. Neither looked like an FBI sedan; one was a minivan and the other a smaller car. She would just have to hope they were what they appeared to be. Scooting from tree to tree, she approached the house behind hers, a large, lovely Cape Cod structure that appeared lifeless.

She darted to the corner of the Cape Cod, then glanced around to its back yard, which was enclosed by a chain link fence. Her own back yard, visible through the fence, was better lit than she had hoped; she had never noticed how close the street light was to her house. Peering between her house and the one next to it, she could see the unmarked car, with two figures sitting in the front seat.

Tori flattened herself against the house, then let herself through the gate and into the back yard as quietly as possible. Immediately, she dropped to the ground and slithered to her left, out of the watchers' line of sight.

Then she continued on her belly toward the back of the neighbors' lot.

This is stupid, she thought. But all the other options were even more so. She simply couldn't go anywhere without money and identification, and her house was the only place to obtain either. She reached the back fence, soaked and filthy. She felt something sticky on her stomach. Dog shit! Lovely.

She climbed quickly over the fence, then dropped to the ground again, crawling toward the back door, trying to rub the dog shit off her jacket. She reached the back of the house and, fumbling in the dark, retrieved the key from inside a phony rock placed along the border of her weedy, neglected garden. Then, flattening herself against the house, she quickly let herself in. Crawling on her hands and knees into the hallway, she disabled the security system, certain that the loud beeps could be heard in the street outside. Then, discarding her filthy jacket and stuffing it into the washing machine in the laundry room, she continued crawling to the front of the house and peeked through the front window. Two figures were now visible in the front seat of the car outside. One appeared to be dozing.

Tori crawled upstairs. She assumed her house had been searched. But she hoped they had not pried open the wall safe Ben had installed in his den. Still on her hands and knees, she groped her way across the room to Ben's desk. She rifled through the top drawer, finally locating a flashlight. Then she turned to the credenza behind the desk. She opened a door, moved aside some papers, and pried open a false back, revealing the safe.

Using the flashlight, she dialed the combination and opened the safe. Everything still appeared to be there. She removed an envelope containing five thousand dollars in cash, stashed there to prepare for the predicted collapse of the banking system when the Year 2000 had arrived. Then she removed another envelope containing her passport, as well as Ben's. She removed her own, re-stashed the envelope, and closed up the safe and credenza.

Next, Tori turned back to Ben's desk and opened a bottom file drawer. She located the file marked Credit Cards instantly, and after a minute of searching with the flashlight, took out a VISA card in the name of Victoria Lynn Saunders. She had twice asked the bank to change the name on the card to reflect her marriage, but it had never done so. She had given up on changing the name, but had kept the card active, thinking that with its large credit line, it might be useful in an emergency. Maybe this qualifies, she thought. Sometimes it paid to be an anal, responsible firstborn.

The next stop on her crawling tour was the bedroom, where she retrieved a clean sweatshirt and a vinyl waist pack, filling it with toiletries. Then she crept back downstairs, re-set the security system, and left the way she had come.

•

Kyle Jaworski drove from the District back to his office in Rockville, having completed his futile, unauthorized interviews of Max Tuten's neighbors. Had Bertelson gone mad? Sticking up a local officer and confiscating evidence showed either audacity or desperation on a level he had never seen from the FBI agent before. Yet he knew it would be pointless—more than that, dangerous—to file complaints through usual channels. He knew, as Bertelson undoubtedly had, that he could ill afford to draw attention to his own activities. Yet Bertelson had let him go, despite being in cahoots with people who hadn't hesitated to kill.

Which meant they wanted him alive. Jaworski glanced again at his rearview mirror; they must be hoping he would lead them to Tori. There was no danger of that, as long as he didn't know where Tori was. His conversation with the FBI agent had been short and one-way; Bertelson had warned him to stay out of it and, if he was really smart, to tell Bertelson what he knew. After Jaworski had told the agent to fuck himself, Bertelson had simply nodded and walked away. And why not, Jaworski thought. Without the video, Tori's uncorroborated word provided the only evidence of the cult's existence. That was apparently of no great concern to the firm of Percival, Bertelson & Belke. And now Tori, as with Polly Kendrick, seemed to have fallen off the face of the planet. Worse, she had no secure way to contact him.

He jumped when his pager went off. He shut it off, glanced at the number, and knew he was in trouble. Of course Bertelson would not simply walk away; Jaworski should have known his FBI nemesis would try to turn up the heat. He pulled over to a drive-up public phone at a gas station and called the number.

"Hello, Steve, it's Kyle."

Assistant U.S. Attorney Steve Wright spoke in a low voice. "Kyle, I don't know what the hell's going on, but you are in a shitload of trouble."

"Legal trouble?"

"Big time. Our office is preparing an indictment against you, and an arrest warrant to go with it."

"What are the charges?"

"RICO and obstruction of justice for sure. And maybe more—I haven't seen the whole thing."

"Make my day, Stevie. Tell me what else you know." He held his breath; he had always known Wright as a straight shooter, since the days when they had worked together on a drug task force.

"I don't know much," Wright confessed. "It's coming from the very top—I can tell you that much. And it's a rush job—we've got people scurrying around here to get it done. You'll probably have the Feebs on you in two or three hours, if not before."

Jaworski paused, letting the news sink in.

"One more thing," said Steve Wright. "Your own boss swore out one of the affidavits."

Jaworski thanked his friend and hung up. He watched the rush hour traffic crawl by on Rockville Pike, pondering this latest development. It wasn't just a matter of the game getting rougher—they were no longer even playing the same game. And without a game, there were no rules. The chances were excellent that he would be shot trying to escape the officers executing the warrant, but not before they would interrogate him, using any means necessary to learn what they wanted to know. Chances were also good that they had already done the same to Tori.

He sighed and restarted his car. His only hope was to elude capture, and to find Tori—if she was still alive.

CHAPTER 21

Tori turned from side to side on the lumpy hotel bed, trying unsuccessfully to sleep. Beyond the open balcony door, the Caribbean Sea lapped against the beach down below. In this peaceful, faraway setting, the unreality of the previous three days was now complete. Of course she didn't feel safe. But would she ever feel safe again?

She gave up on sleeping, put on flip-flops, and walked through the hotel lobby. A voice hailed her from behind the front desk.

"Is everything okay, Mrs. Saunders?"

"Everything's fine, Ramon. I'm just going for a walk on the beach."

The hotel's owner, a heavyset man with thick gray hair, nodded. "Enjoy your walk."

Tori shuffled through the sand as the sun set behind her. The hotel was newer, part of a small development that included a larger resort, plus time-share condominiums. Down at the beach, she pulled off her flip-flops and walked through the fine white sand as tame, shallow waves lapped at her ankles.

It was tempting to congratulate herself on a successful escape. But she couldn't stay down here forever, and she had little doubt that sooner or later they would find her. And her current safety was an illusion; as long as she was being hunted, she would feel no peace. To compound her anxiety, she had willingly traveled to within minutes of the place where she was sure she would find the answers to her questions about the massive, malevolent conspiracy she had stumbled upon. It seemed a logical place to look, and her serviceable, near-fluent Spanish might be of assistance.

After leaving her house, she had walked up to East-West Highway, then hitchhiked to Philadelphia. It had been early morning when she had arrived at the Philadelphia airport. There, she had found a charter flight to Cancún. She wasn't sure how record-keeping for charters worked; she'd had to show her passport, but didn't think her name would be entered into the worldwide databases used by the major airlines. After sleeping fitfully on the flight, she had bought some clothes at the Cancún airport, and had had to use the Victoria Saunders VISA card to rent a car. If the searchers were thorough and creative, they might pick up the transaction.

She had driven south along the coastal highway until she had been within a few miles of Tulúm, near the entrance to the Sian Ka'an park reserve. Then she had driven around the area until she'd located this small hotel with the friendly owner. Ramon had told her of several archeological sites and tour operations in the area. After catching up on sleep, she would start asking around to look for any connection with Corman Seminar participants.

Since boarding the plane in Philadelphia, her emotions had swung back and forth, convinced one minute that coming down here was the most foolish course imaginable, and the next that her only hope of achieving safety and peace lay in uncovering the truth about the Bound.

She trudged back up the beach to the hotel, then walked around, past a thatch-roofed restaurant, to the main entrance. Back at her room, she unlocked the door and walked in. The lights were on, and a man was standing by the window.

"Ramon?" she said.

His look combined relief and infinite sadness. "I am sorry, Señora."

Tori followed his eyes across the room to another figure, a short, stocky man with an abnormally large head. "Howdy," he said in a harsh Texas drawl, his face covered with a nasty smirk.

Harlan Belke.

CHAPTER 22

It took about twenty-five minutes to reach the encampment, driving westward from the hotel. Belke had brought two men with him, smaller but as tough looking as Karl Steen. After gathering up the few possessions she had brought, they took her out through a side door to a Land Rover, and tied her hands and ankles. One of the two enforcers took the front seat after putting Tori into the back with Belke. After a few minutes, Tori realized that the other man was following them in Tori's car.

The racist leader looked relaxed, puffing on a cigar as the Land Rover bumped along the rutted gravel road into the thick jungle. "Sorry about the ropes," he said. "But you've been an irritating little bitch. Getting away from us twice. Shooting one of my guys in the foot, then breaking poor Steen's wrist. Percy said you kicked him in the nuts and shot him up with his own truth drug." He laughed, emitting a short, mirthless bark. "But he said you were a good fuck, too. I suppose that's not too bad a trade-off."

Tori, flushed with anger, said nothing.

"I'd say Percy went above and beyond the call of duty on this one," Belke continued, looking her over with a leer. "But I can't blame him—you're a good piece."

"Shut up," she snapped.

He smiled, showing perfect false teeth, Tori thought. "Percy may have trouble keeping it zipped, and he gets a little soft-headed now and then. But the man is smart—I've known that ever since he was my high school debate partner back in Culver, Texas. He knew you'd turn up here. That worked out pretty well, since I was scheduled to be down here anyway."

They reached the encampment, a cleared area in the jungle. In the dim rays of the waning sunlight, she could see a trailer, a small cinder block building, and three tents off to the right side. The Land Rover turned to the left, and Tori could see what looked like two large trailers, several tents, and a large round wooden building with a thatched roof. The vehicle came to a stop. "In my office," Belke said shortly, and he disappeared into the trailer.

The man driving Tori's car joined the Land Rover's driver, and they pulled Tori out into the damp evening heat. Insects seemed to be swarming everywhere, their sound drowned out by the hum of a generator beside the trailer. The men pulled Tori out of the vehicle and sliced away the ropes binding her ankles. Then they led her up a makeshift wooden stairway into the trailer. Tori, still wearing shorts and T-shirt, was instantly chilled by the air-conditioned environment.

Most of the trailer appeared to consist of a large living room, equipped with homey, worn furniture, a small refrigerator, and an entertainment center with a large-screen television. They took her through a door to the left and into what appeared to be Belke's office. The cluttered room was equipped with bookshelves, filing cabinets, a computer, and a television. Belke, who sat behind his desk working at a laptop computer, didn't look up when they entered. He merely grunted and nodded to the two men, making a brief, vague head motion.

The two men grabbed Tori's still-bound wrists and swung them up over her head, fastening the ropes to a hook in the low ceiling. There was no slack; if the ropes had been any tighter, she would have been forced up onto her tiptoes. Then they retied her ankles. Belke nodded again, and they left the room.

It was perhaps twenty minutes before Belke looked up from his computer screen. Tori, exhausted and scared out of her wits, willed her mind to go blank. But she could not erase the mental image of Rick Percival with the hypodermic syringe, along with his enigmatic explanation. You won't exist any more as a person. It sounded similar to his living-death description of Cindy's fate. She is not alive, in any meaningful sense. This couldn't be it, Tori told herself. She couldn't die without learning what had happened. And yet she was still alive; she wondered what purpose they could have for keeping her around.

Belke provided the answer less than a minute later. He stood up and stretched, then walked lazily over to Tori. He grabbed a pair of scissors from the desk and, eyes clouded with lust, began methodically cutting off her T-shirt.

Tori turned away, trying to blink back the tears that streaked lazily down her face. "Why are you doing this?" she whispered.

He stopped work for a moment, then looked up at her as if he had never heard a more ridiculous question.

"Why? Why? Because I can. Because you're here. Because you have nice tits. Because I feel like it."

"Because you have the power."

"Sure," he said, sounding almost cheerful. He removed the last of her T-shirt, letting the cut-up strips fall onto the floor. He looked up. "Why fight me? I bet you liked it well enough when Percy did this."

"You son of a bitch!"

Belke laughed and cut away her bra. As he moved his hands lightly, lovingly, over her, Tori looked away, fighting off the urge to vomit. Meanwhile, Belke enjoyed himself, caressing, kneading, feeling with his callused, icy hands. "Why does anybody do things?" he said. "It's about power. It's always about power."

After feeling her for perhaps five minutes, he stepped back, his face reddened, breathing heavily. "Well, that got the old juices running," he said. Abruptly, he sat down behind his desk and glanced at his watch. Reaching into a desk drawer, he produced a television remote control and pointed it at the set against the wall. He sat back, waiting for the screen to flicker to life, then glanced back at Tori.

"Don't worry," he said. "I'm not going to fuck you—I'll let Percy handle that end of things. I've been married to the same woman for twenty-two years. But I still need to get revved up every now and then." He turned back to the television set, then glanced at Tori again. "Of course, when we're through with you, you still get Percy and his magic needle." He barked out a short laugh, then returned his attention to the screen.

Tori, half-naked, aching and freezing, felt even colder.

The image on the television screen was very faint. Tori, after staring at the picture for several minutes, was able to make out the outlines of five people, all apparently dressed in white robes. After a moment she saw a sixth person, a man whose skin was noticeably darker than the others. The group gathered around a circular pit, in which a glowing, translucent globe seemed to poke out of the earth.

"Good group," Belke murmured.

On the screen, the group bowed in unison. Then they began a chant, the words to which Tori could not understand. The chant seemed to last a long time. When it was over, the participants clasped hands in a circle, then bowed their heads, listening to what sounded like a recitation or prayer, uttered by the dark-skinned man. Then they placed their hands out in front of them, holding them over the shining globe.

By now Tori was in agony. Her wrists, back, and legs felt ready to explode. Her only consolation was that she might freeze to death first. Belke continued to watch the screen without comment.

On television, the six people were now exchanging hugs, long, warm, embraces, lasting a long time, with many pats on the back, rocking from side to side. And then it was apparently over. One by one, the group members walked out of the room, toward the camera, giving Belke and Tori a closer look at each of them. There were two men and three women, and their expressions went beyond contentment, or even happiness. Their faces showed pure joy.

Ecstasy.

Belke shut the set off and stood up. "Showtime's over," he said. He reached into the desk drawer and pulled out a roll of masking tape. Tearing off a strip, he walked toward Tori.

She twisted away. "Aren't you going to—"

Belke clamped the strip of tape over her mouth, pressing it down firmly.

"'Night," he said, shutting off the light, leaving the room, and closing the door.

•

They came for her about half an hour later. For Tori, time had ceased to exist. She had always been tied to the ceiling of this trailer, always would be. Several times she lapsed into near-unconsciousness, but managed to revive. The office door opened abruptly, and she was blinded by the overhead light. The two men untied the ropes from the hook, but left her wrists tied together. She collapsed and they caught her, half-dragging her out of the trailer and across the gravel yard to the small cinder-block building she had seen earlier.

Her wrists and ankles were quickly untied and the tape removed from her mouth. And then she was in the dark again, on a concrete floor. Though exhausted, she spent what seemed an eternity wiggling and rubbing her hands and feet, trying to restore feeling. After a while she stood up, walking with short steps, reaching out into the dark, exploring the cell. The enclosure appeared to be about six feet square, equipped with a small, license-plate-sized window near the ceiling, a bucket, mosquito netting, and a thin straw mat. Tori stumbled onto the mat, lay awake for a short time, and drifted off to sleep.

•

The heat, rather than the light, from the blazing sun woke her up. The room around her looked even worse in the daylight than she had imagined it the previous night—filthy, dark, and tiny. She was unable to see out the little window up near the ceiling. She still wore only a pair of shorts, and felt dirty, sweaty, and desperately thirsty. Her head pounded as she lay motionless, trying to ignore the heat that gradually turned the small room into a furnace. So much for her life as a suburban widow, she thought. The unreality of being captured, abused, and imprisoned in a faraway jungle seemed total. Any minute now, the charade should end, and she would be transported back to Chevy Chase.

Eventually Tori stood up, walked over to the heavy door, and pounded on it. The knocking produced only soft, dull thuds on the thick wood.

"Hey!" she shouted. "How about a drink of water? How about letting me out of here?"

There was no response. After perhaps two hours the door opened a crack and a tray slid through on the ground. Tori sprang up and hammered on the door, but it was already closed and locked. The tray held a cheese sandwich, a banana, and a large plastic cup of water. She consumed all of it greedily, then returned to the mat on the floor, sitting with her bare back propped up against the concrete wall.

It was like being in a steam room with a locked door. For hours she tried to remain still and think of nothing. But the nightmare images persisted stubbornly: Rick Percival with his hypodermic needle; the bruised, bloated face of Max Tuten as he knelt in front of the toilet; the evil face of Karl Steen; the lustful eyes of Harlan Belke as he fondled her.

Tori tried to shift her thoughts to more palatable topics. To Cindy, and most of all, to Ben. He would have found something witty to say about her current predicament. He would have kept his spirits up, somehow, as he had during the final months of his life. She ached for him, for his voice, his touch, for the humanity he had retained to the end.

Every time she heard a sound—a trailer door closing; vehicle tires crunching on the gravel outside; indistinct voices—her thoughts would snap back to the present. Why was she still here, still alive? So Belke could keep tying her up and abusing her? She knew it wouldn't last forever.

Of course, you'll still end up with Percy's magic needle, he had said.

Which meant death, or some form of it she dared not think about.

The hours dragged by. The heat was unbearable. Yet she had to bear it. She could sense the movement of the sun as the shadow moved across the cell. In what she thought was mid-afternoon, the door opened again, and she received another large cup of water.

Darkness seemed to provide no respite from the heat. She kept waiting for the door to open again; her whole existence had become the heat and the door and the concrete wall.

It had been dark for several hours when the door opened. Her heart pounded, and she shrank against the wall as the two men entered the room. Suddenly she was in no hurry to leave her tiny prison. It was one of the same two men who had been handling her since yesterday. Or was it the day before? No, it was yesterday. Yesterday morning she had been in Philadelphia.

The second man was new.

But not new. He was Karl Steen.

Tori felt faint as she eyed the large man, his left wrist in a cast, nose bruised and swollen, his mouth wrinkled in a smug grin. He studied her for a long minute, drinking in her terror. Then he walked up to her. "On your feet," he commanded.

She hesitated, then stood up slowly, keeping her back to the concrete wall. He reached out and grabbed her chin in a vice-like grip, then fondled her breasts. "Nice tits," he said. "Mr. Belke promised me an hour with you before they give you the needle." He grinned again, then motioned to the other man, who tied her wrists again.

They took her across the yard to Belke's trailer. Tori was unsteady on her feet, but grateful to escape the sauna-like prison. There was a slight breeze, which felt good on her bare torso but failed to keep the mosquitoes from buzzing around her.

Belke was seated behind his desk when they brought her in. Once again, her wrists were tied to the hook in the ceiling. Belke made a vague hand motion to the two men, and they loosened the rope a bit, allowing Tori to stand more comfortably. Then after a long, knowing look from

Steen, the jailers left, and Tori was alone with Belke. He spent about fifteen minutes reading and doing paperwork before standing up and walking over toward Tori.

Tori wanted to talk to him, to demand better treatment, to make him tell
her what all this was about before they killed her, but she felt too weak.
She would have spit at him, but couldn't work up enough saliva in her
mouth. She felt resigned and powerless; twenty-four hours in the concrete
hellhole had broken her.

This time, Belke made no move to touch her. After a few minutes, he
left his office, returning a moment later with a glass of water. He held it
up to her lips, and she drank it down. He returned to his chair.

Belke leaned back in his chair and simply stared at her. "God, you're
good," he said at last. "I can really see why Percy went for you. But as
usual, he was thinking with the wrong appendage. You've caused us one
hell of a lot of trouble, Tori McMillan. At least we're getting some good
use out of you. Me, Percy, Steen—we'll all get our share."

As he had on the previous evening, Belke took a remote control from
his desk and turned on the television. Once again, Tori recognized the circular pit and translucent globe. And again, the group of six white-robed
figures assembled around it. All exchanged embraces. Then five of the
figures sat cross-legged on floor cushions. The sixth man, the dark-
skinned one, began to address them.

"What you experienced last night was the true essence of the Bound—
the love, the connection among yourselves, and the link between yourselves and the universe. You experienced it with your heart and with your
soul." He hesitated. "That is as it should be. Frankly, there is no way to
fully explain this experience on a rational level. One could also argue that
there is no need. But we have found that years of linear thinking, years of
logic, years of functioning intellectually, with the soul squeezed out of us,
has created the unavoidable necessity of doing our best to understand the
cause to which you have willingly committed your lives."

There were nods around the circle. "The Bound," the man continued,
"embodies the true values of all major faiths—love, truth, faith, and one-
ness. As with all religions, we call on our followers to become better people, to seek out the best in themselves. However, we reject tribalism and
claims of exclusivity. We have no churches, no ministry, no creed, no
dogma. As you have learned, what we do have is love. Love, and something else no one can offer you: happiness—not just the promise of it in

the next world, but the reality of it in this one. We have answered the call of all major religions, a call most of them have long forgotten, to put love into practice, to change the world, to transform the lives of our brothers and sisters on this earth. This was the call understood by those Egyptian alchemists so many thousands of years ago. This is the legacy they've left us: the zest of life."

The dark-skinned man walked slowly, contemplatively, back and forth in front of the orb. "What we ask—what we require—in return, is a total, lifelong commitment. Only in this way can the gift of the Bound be given to others. Only in this way can the world be transformed." He paused. "What does this commitment mean?"

He leaned forward, hands resting on the circular pit. "Each of you will be called upon to work actively for our cause. Each of you will be called upon to make personal sacrifices. These sacrifices can be painful, even terrible, involving the loss or estrangement of your loved ones."

Tori, already cold in the air-conditioned room, suddenly felt frozen as the dark-skinned man continued. "You'll be asked to help prepare our world to receive what we have to offer. This may involve taking actions whose purpose may not immediately be clear to you—actions that may be secret, that may even seem wrong to you or appear to harm others. You'll be working with others in your group. They must be able to depend on you, totally and unquestioningly, just as the Bound will—"

The screen went blank. Tori looked over at Belke, who was returning the remote control to his desk drawer and standing up. She nearly gasped with frustration, coming so close to understanding and then....

"I've heard this shit too many times," Belke said, straightening the papers on his desk. "But hell, it works. Damn, that Nabib is good." Once again, he placed masking tape over her mouth and shut the lights off. "Have fun with Steen," he said and left the room.

CHAPTER 23

This time the door opened after only about ten minutes. But the light did not go on, and Tori sensed only a single figure enter the room. The figure clicked on a small penlight, pointing it at the ceiling above Tori's head. In the faint light, she saw the face of the dark-skinned man she had seen on the television screen only minutes earlier.

Without saying anything, the man named Nabib pulled a chair over beside Tori. He pushed at a ceiling tile, examined the hook to which Tori's hands were tied, and said, "Good. It's just hooked around this conduit. Looks like it used to be a plant hook." He grabbed the hook with both hands and gave it a violent yank. The hook came loose, and Tori collapsed to the floor. Nabib rummaged through the drawers of Belke's desk, producing a jackknife. Then he pulled her to a sitting position, slicing the ropes on her hands and ankles. That done, Nabib stood up, replaced the ceiling tile and chair, and returned the knife to the desk drawer. Walking across the room, he peeked through the blinds. "Still quiet," he said. "Belke's thugs shouldn't be here for another fifteen minutes."

Nabib walked over to a metal cabinet and, after peering inside with the penlight, produced a white T-shirt. "Here you go," he said, tossing it to her. "Courtesy of Corman Seminars." Tori put the T-shirt on, and Nabib handed her a small object. "The keys to your car," he said. He pulled a piece of paper from his pocket and pressed it into her hand. "Twenty dollars. It's all the cash I have—they don't have ATM's around here."

"Thank you," Tori whispered. "Why are you doing this?"

"It isn't right, the way they've treated you. Whatever else they're into here—at least it's not violence, not until now. Just get out of here and drive."

"But what is all this?"

"What these people feel for each other—what they've learned about themselves and about life—the love they've learned—it's very real. Still, it's...tainted."

Tori grabbed his arm. "What do you mean? What is this Bound all about?"

He shook his head. "I can't tell you that."

"Why not?"

"Just go."

"What about you?" Tori asked. "They'll kill you if they find out you let me go."

"I'll be all right," he said without conviction.

"You're welcome to go with me if you want."

He hesitated. "Let me get my wallet. I'll meet you outside in a minute."

Tori nodded, and Nabib slipped out of the trailer. Tori ran behind Belke's desk and opened the drawer. It took her about ten seconds to find the jackknife. Then she followed Nabib out the door.

The yard appeared deserted as she found the Land Rover, parked next to her rented Nissan, just outside. She produced the jackknife, slashing first one tire, then a second. Then she returned to the Nissan and got behind the wheel. Nabib appeared seconds later, climbing into the front seat beside her.

The windows were fogged with humidity as she turned the key. The engine roared to life, and the vehicle lurched forward, tires kicking up gravel. She could hear shouts and see lights behind her as she left the compound. She bumped along the narrow, twisting road—really only a dirt track—through the jungle. How long would it take them to change two tires? Ten minutes? Fifteen?

"Step on it," Nabib said, looking back every few seconds.

"I'm doing the best I can."

"You've got to be worn out. I can drive."

"Thanks. Let's get to the highway first. Where should we go?"

"Just head straight for the Cancún airport," he said. "We need to get out of Mexico."

"That's the first place they'll look. I'm going south, toward Belize. They won't expect that."

"You don't have a passport."

"I'll find some American tourists, or a policeman."

He hesitated. "All right. Look, I don't have any more money. Is there someone you can call for help back in the States?"

"Yes. A policeman."

"Great," Nabib said, looking relieved. "I do have a long distance credit card. I can place the call. I'm so relieved to be out of this nightmare. What's going on down here—it's incredible."

"You can tell me all about it," she said.

He nodded.

She continued bumping and swerving through the jungle, concentrating with all of her waning energy, several times nearly running off the road into the jungle. Still, no headlights appeared in her rearview mirror as they reached the main highway and turned south, away from Cancún.

Tori pulled over and stopped, leaving the engine running. "Could you drive now?" she asked, opening her car door.

"Of course." Nabib opened his own door and jumped out. Immediately, Tori closed her door and floored the accelerator, swerving back onto the highway. A hundred yards down the road she stopped, reached over, and closed the passenger side door. In the thin moonlight she could see Nabib sprinting up the road and yelling.

She resumed driving south for another few miles until she reached Tulúm, then pulled over again, consulting the car rental map in the glove box. After a minute's study, she continued south for another mile, then took a right turn on the Coba highway, proceeding north and west through the jungle.

There was still no sign of the Land Rover. She had to assume they had an extra spare. In fact, approaching the problem as Ben had in evaluating a criminal case, she had to assume the worst, that they would be only a few minutes behind. A worst-case analysis required further assumptions: that police along the way might be cooperating with Belke; that the Cancún airport would be watched; that further accomplices, like the hotel owner, might be enlisted to intercept her.

In suspecting—no, knowing—that Belke had deliberately let her go, she was making the ultimate worst-case assumption. But it all seemed painfully clear. They didn't have Jaworski, and they had hoped she would lead them to the detective, with a phone call, a rendezvous, a postcard— whatever. Why else would Nabib have told her to go to the Cancún airport, the most obvious destination? Nabib had to know how easy it would be for a Land Rover to overtake the Nissan, but hadn't suggested disabling the faster vehicle. And, in retrieving her keys, he had obviously gotten access to her purse. But all he had given her was the keys. Without money, credit cards, passport, or other identification, and Nabib with her at all times, it seemed extremely unlikely Tori would escape their surveillance, but very likely she would try to contact Jaworski.

Nabib had been good, supplying just the right amount of disarming candor; showing just the right amount of hesitancy; just the right amount of fear; maneuvering her into bringing him along. But he was also a good soldier; thus his eagerness to take over the driving, and to place an incriminating phone call.

She gripped the wheel with terror every time headlights appeared in her mirror. Several times, cars or trucks zoomed past her. She imagined it must be one or two in the morning. She drove as fast as safety permitted on the narrow highway, her headlights revealing only jungle, with an occasional clearing and, rarely, a light. At Coba there were more lights, structures, and roads, which gave out quickly as she proceeded north. She came to an intersection, giving her the choice of Cancún or Valladolid. She took the latter route, to the left.

Tori drove on through the night, fighting exhaustion and pain. At the very least, she thought, she had left Belke guessing as to her destination. Her objective now was not the obvious one—Cancún—nor the Belize border, but Mérida, the provincial capital and home to a U.S. consulate and an international airport. The problem was distance. From the map, Mérida appeared to be several hours from Belke's compound, and some of the route ran through remote country on questionable roads.

It was after daybreak when she was presented with another choice. There were two main road connecting Cancún and Mérida: one labeled cuota and the other libre. She took the latter, not sure if she had enough money for the toll road. The road was poor, but there was more traffic here, including, by mid-morning, buses bringing tourists from Cancún to the spectacular Mayan ruins at Chichen Itza. She stopped for gas at a Pemex station near the main entrance to the ruins, using some of the twenty dollars Nabib had given her. From nearby vendors she bought a large Coca-Cola, two bottles of water, and a croissant. She sat in the car and ate, watching the traffic go by. Hesitantly, Tori looked at herself in the rearview mirror and was horrified by the sight of a person she barely recognized, haggard and sunken-eyed. The sensible course would be to stop and sleep right then and there.

Hesitating briefly, she took a breath, started up the engine and pulled out onto the highway. She couldn't stay right on the highway, in plain sight. She needed the anonymity of a large city. She pressed on, toward Mérida.

It was late morning when she reached Mérida's outskirts. She crossed the loop road and drove on toward the city center, enduring some brief traffic jams, looking for a hotel. She was tempted to go straight to the consulate, but decided she would have to make a more careful approach. Belke might have the building watched, or even have someone working inside. She rejected the Holiday Inn and other American chain facilities, settling on a smaller place on Calle 57, just past the cathedral, the Parque Hidalgo, and Plaza de la Indepencia. Then, after making herself as presentable as possible, she walked in. Using most of her charm and all of her Spanish, she managed to check in using her VISA card number, recited from memory, with the last two digits changed. They didn't call to verify the number, but there was a decent chance they would do so later. It couldn't be helped. She would have to move quickly.

From her room, which seemed not to be air conditioned, she found the phone number for the U.S. consulate and called, not giving her name, and telling a story about having her purse fall overboard in Cozumél. A bored-sounding employee told her nothing could be done yet that day, and suggested she make an appointment for the following morning. She gave a false name and made an appointment for ten-thirty. Then she lay back on the bed and closed her eyes. One more call to go. She would contact Susan Arkwright. It was the logical place to leave a message for Jaworski. She would rest first, for just a few minutes....

•

A loud banging noise awakened her. Tori opened her eyes and sat up in a panic. The banging was actually knocking. She fought to wake up; what time was it? It was still light outside, but she knew she had slept through to the next day.

The knocking continued. She walked over toward the door; there was no peephole and no chain. What if it was Belke?

"Who is it?" she asked in Spanish.

The reply came in English, from a familiar male voice. "I'm from the Yucatan Damsel In Distress Rescue Service, ma'am."

Tori gasped, then opened the door.

"You could have at least sent a postcard," said Kyle Jaworski. "You know—wish you were here, enjoying the beach—that sort of thing."

He stepped forward, and she threw her arms tightly around him. They held each other a long time while Tori wept.

CHAPTER 24

They didn't talk until they were on the plane back to Washington. Jaworski, after paying a man fifty dollars to ditch Tori's rental car in the jungle, had taken her to the consulate, where they had quickly obtained a temporary passport. From there it was on to the airport, where an airline official had taken them past the counters and directly onto the plane. Tori, dazed and exhausted, had simply gone along with these maneuvers without question.

Now, as they reclined in their first class seats, with the Gulf of Mexico appearing beneath them, Tori finally asked what was going on.

"Good question, which I can't answer," Jaworski replied, sipping from a glass of Sam Adams. "Bertelson and his people are baffling the hell out of me—I can't figure out why they're just letting us travel around like this."

"What do you mean?" Tori asked.

"Let's not kid ourselves. With rare exceptions, when the FBI really wants to find people, they find them. With their connections and resources—their ability to throw manpower at a problem, they wouldn't have much trouble tracking down a couple of freelancers like us."

"You're saying they don't want to find us?" Tori asked, gulping her third glass of mineral water.

"No, just that they're not trying as hard as they could be."

"Why not?"

"There are a couple of possibilities. One is that Bertelson can't afford to go all-out on this one. Maybe he's afraid of calling too much attention to himself, or he's called in too many markers already. Maybe he can't justify the manpower for the shaky accusations against us. Or...."

"Or?"

"Or maybe he's not as deeply in the sack with these loonies as we thought."

Tori thought about it. "When I talked to Bertelson, he said 'I am not Percival—please believe that.'"

"He may not be Percival, but he's close enough for me. He took the videotape, put out a warrant for my arrest, and is coordinating the search for us. We'll just have to try to avoid him and hope for the best. Supposedly we're not on this flight; if we can get through customs at Dulles we should be okay for a while. Of course, I'm too much of an optimist to mention the most likely reason they're not looking very hard for us."

"Which is?"

"We're not worth the effort. Sure, it would be nice to capture us, to tie up all the loose ends. But the bottom line is, they don't think there's anything we can do to them, at least not without the videotape."

The words struck Tori with a powerful blow. Optimist or pessimist, Jaworski spoke the truth. "So how did you find me?" Tori asked at last.

"Too damned easily. Obviously you had to get out of Washington. But I knew you'd still want to keep digging. I figured you'd try either Mexico or Colorado—both places seem to have bases of operations for the Bound. So I called my buddy Evan Miller in Denver and had him keep an eye out for you. Then I called somebody I know in the Foreign Service, who in turn knows somebody in the consulate in Cancún, and asked them to keep an eye out for somebody meeting your description."

"Then what happened?"

"I get a call back telling me they got a mysterious-sounding call at the consulate—not in Cancún, but in Mérida. Of course we couldn't be sure it was you, but it sounded close enough, and to be honest, I was grasping at straws. And, I was getting restless sitting around Susan's apartment, and Mexico didn't sound half-bad. All this VIP treatment we're getting from the airline is courtesy of Susan, by the way. So I came right down. Meanwhile, my friend had already started calling hotels. When I got here, I showed your picture at a couple of the likely places and sure enough, here you were."

"That's amazing," Tori said.

"Not really. What's amazing is that Bertelson hasn't done the same thing. Nobody down here at the consulates had been alerted by the FBI.

As far as I know, they never picked up your flight or car rental down here, either. He must be keeping the entire search as low profile as possible. If he brought twenty agents into it, he might have a lot of explaining to do."

The flight attendant served lunch. Tori, despite Jaworski's encouragement, ate very little, while consuming yet another glass of water. After eating they were silent for a long time. Tori lay back and closed her eyes, but Jaworski knew she wasn't sleeping.

"Are you ready?" Jaworski asked.

"I'm not sure," she answered without opening her eyes.

"Better to get it over with, as soon as possible."

She opened her eyes, took a drink of water, and recounted everything that had happened after Rock Creek Park: her discovery of Max Tuten's body and her subsequent escape from Percival and Steen; her secret entry into her house; her hitching a ride to Philadelphia and flight to Mexico; her capture and abuse at the Bound's camp; and finally, her escape to Mérida.

When she had finished, Jaworski sat for a long time, making no comment.

"Well?" Tori said.

"Well, what?"

"Aren't you going to say anything? Tell me how stupid I was?"

Jaworski studied her, astonished. "You're serious."

Tori bristled. "What do you think, this is all a joke?"

Jaworski burst into laughter, which grew, feeding on itself, until he was wiping tears from his eyes.

Tori failed to see the humor. "What?" she said, feeling annoyed and defensive.

Jaworski finally calmed himself down, shaking his head. "You're a piece of work," he said at last. "You started out on the run, with no money or I.D. Yet you successfully skipped the country, endured a kidnapping and two days of sadistic abuse in a jungle hell hole, and twice escaped from killers. And here you are, beating yourself up, critiquing your performance."

"I had to be rescued."

"Bullshit. You put yourself in a position to get help. Let me tell you something: Not one in a hundred people would have realized Belke was intentionally letting you go."

"None of it helped us much."

"More bullshit. You learned an incredible amount. More than that, you lived to fight another day." He paused. "Tori, I don't know much about the meaning or purpose of life, but you know, living to fight another day sounds pretty good. For me, that's about as close as it gets."

After a moment she said, "Why are you looking at me like that?"

"Like what?"

"Like—I don't know."

"I guess I was just thinking that you're beautiful."

"Kyle...."

"I know, I know. That's not what you want to hear. But I was hoping maybe I'd earned the right to say it."

She took his hand. "Maybe you have," she said quietly.

Jaworski smiled, leaned back in the seat, and closed his eyes.

They cleared customs at Dulles without incident. Then, after taking a bus to Baltimore-Washington International Airport, they retrieved Susan Arkwright's car and started driving back toward D.C.

"Where are we going?" Tori asked.

"Back to Susan's."

"If they're looking for you, won't they check your friends' houses first?"

"Not Susan's. I don't talk about my friends to anyone, Tori. My private life is just that. Susan keeps a very low profile, anyway. She had to ditch an abusive ex-husband. That meant using her maiden name, staying out of the phone book, and being very careful about the people she associates with. She's out of the country a lot, anyway." He turned the Toyota from the Baltimore-Washington Parkway onto the Beltway. "No, staying at Susan's doesn't worry me. My main concern is, what are we going to do when we get there? We're chasing shadows; we just don't have a solid handle on these people."

"We do know one thing," Tori asserted.

"Which is?"

"In a couple of days they're going to kidnap Caitlin Traeger."

•

The argument started before they reached Susan's house. "We can't just let her be kidnapped," Tori maintained, following Jaworski up the sidewalk to the house. "She's just a child—I'm not sure exactly how old, but young enough not to have anything to do with the Bound."

"You're missing the point," Jaworski replied, opening the back door.

"All it would take is an anonymous phone call to warn the police. They would have to take seriously a threat against the daughter of a high public official."

"That's possible," he said. The house was stifling. Jaworski immediately turned up the air conditioning and retrieved two bottles of beer from the refrigerator. He offered one to Tori, who shook her head.

"Guess I'll have to drink both then," he said, sitting down at the kitchen table. "I know we haven't resolved anything, but first things first. You need sleep, or you won't be able to function."

Tori knew he was right.

"We won't do anything until you're awake and ready to go," he assured her.

Reluctantly, Tori went upstairs to the guestroom, threw off her clothes, and climbed into bed. She fell asleep almost instantly.

•

It was after eight in the morning when Tori woke up. She listened in vain for any sounds in the quiet house, then staggered to the shower, spending a long time washing off the accumulated grime and fatigue. Then she dressed and went downstairs, looking in vain for Jaworski. The detective was nowhere to be found. Tori found a bagel and some orange juice, and ate her breakfast with a growing sense of apprehension and anger. Had Jaworski double-crossed her, using the opportunity to handle the case his way?

He reappeared at nine-fifteen, wearing his suit and tie. "Good morning," he said. "You're looking about a hundred percent better."

"Thanks. And I was surprised to find you a hundred percent gone."

He shrugged, poured himself some orange juice, and sat down at the table.

"I thought we were a team," Tori said. "That means no secrets."

"I was just...out," he replied. "Nothing to do with the case."

She gave him a long look, then resumed eating.

"Any more of those bagels?" he asked. She gestured toward the refrigerator.

Jaworski pulled out a bagel, sliced it, and put both halves into the toaster. "All right," he said. "If you must know, I went to Mass."

She gave him a surprised look. "You...."

"Well, it is Sunday."

"It's all right," she said quickly. "It's just...well, I don't know."

He buttered the bagel slices. "I hadn't gone since high school, but I started again a few years ago. I'm not sure why, exactly. I suppose we're all looking for something bigger than ourselves. Something that transcends all the smallness and meanness I see out there."

"Did you find it?"

He sat down, took a large bite, and chewed thoughtfully. "Yeah, I guess I did. At least I've kept going back. I feel the need."

"Well, aren't you just one surprise after another. Good for you, I guess."

"I suppose we have business to discuss."

"Yes, we do. We have to warn the police about Caitlin."

Jaworski was unmoved. "First of all," he said, "a warning may not necessarily be effective. We don't know what kind of contacts the Bound has in the police department or Secret Service, that might be able to intercept the tip or manage it. Number two, the girl is in for a world of hurt, no matter what happens. We might be able to keep her from being kidnapped, but we can't keep her father from being implicated in any number of crimes and scandals."

"You're just rationalizing," Tori asserted.

"Maybe I am. Maybe I should come right out and admit that I'm willing to sacrifice the girl if we have to."

Tori was speechless. "You're...my God."

"We're up against a bunch of crazies who are about to choose the next President, and then do God knows what afterward. They've got a highly secret and presumably sinister agenda, and they have people planted everywhere. We will do everything in our power to make sure Caitlin is kept safe. But if we fail, we are talking about the life of one person against untold evil. It's a shitty tradeoff, but a necessary one."

"Spoken like a true churchgoer. That has to be the coldest—"

"If we successfully tip the police, we have absolutely no handle on these people. We're back to square one. Actually, that's not true. We're worse off than we were before, because Percival and company will know where the tip came from. They will know we are alive and well and in Washington. And they will turn up the pressure on us. And we will have eliminated any chance of stopping this thing."

"But—"

Jaworski stood up suddenly. "Tori, when was this disappearance supposed to occur? I mean exactly."

"Well, he said it was going to be the middle of this week."

"Today's Sunday. So we have to assume they meant Wednesday, or possibly Thursday."

"What are you getting at?"

"The end of the week. That's what Traeger was told by this Temple guy, right?"

"Yes."

Jaworski quickly left the room. A moment later he returned with the newspaper, retrieved from his overnight bag. He moved the breakfast dishes aside and spread the paper out over the kitchen table. He leafed through the pages quickly, scanning them column by column. A minute later he stopped, reading carefully. "Here it is," he said. "Harris is in Flagstaff until Thursday. Traeger is with him."

"So?"

He tossed the paper aside. "They're going to move early. They're going to take the girl before the date they gave Traeger."

"You mean they'll double-cross him?"

"Yes. I remember when Scotty disappeared. Larry was stunned. He was genuinely shocked and outraged. You just can't fake that kind of reaction. Now I know why. They'd told him Scotty would disappear a few days after he actually did. Larry was out of town when it happened. He knew Scotty would disappear, but he'd planned on being able to say goodbye, to spend a little more time with him. But they crossed him up. That's why he was so stunned and furious."

He sat down, reaching absently for his orange juice. "It's fucking brilliant," he said. "You produce in the guilty parent an absolutely authentic reaction. You reduce the chance that the parent will have second thoughts or act strangely around the child during those last few days. Plus, you give him a perfect alibi; he's out of town. And, in this case, you presumably do it to fake us out, too. We know it's going to happen, and they know we know." He looked up suddenly. "They're going after Caitlin early, Tori. Maybe even today." He grabbed his jacket. "I've got to get over there and stake the place out right away. Stay here."

"Stay here? You've got to be kidding." She stood up, following him out of the kitchen.

"These folks are serious, Tori. You know that better than anybody."

"And you said I've handled myself reasonably well."

"You've had some luck, too."

"You're not going without me."

He stopped and turned around. "Yes, I am."

"You leave me here and I'll call the police."

"Tori—"

"I will not be treated as some helpless, clinging female. I'm coming, and that is final. Now, do we do this the hard way or the easy way?"

The detective's features tightened. "You have to be the most stubborn, the most obstinate—"

"Skip the compliments," Tori said. "Let's go."

CHAPTER 25

As they drove toward Potomac, Tori reflected that Jaworski had probably outmaneuvered her. He had agreed to let her come along, but somehow the debate about tipping the police had been resolved in his favor. Still, she could not fault his logic. It seemed virtually certain that the Bound would move early.

"One thing I don't understand," she said, "is why Larry put up with being double-crossed like that. He had to have been furious at not being able to say goodbye to Scotty."

"He's a guy who sacrificed his son—his only child—to these people. Why wouldn't he put up with being jerked around a little about the particulars? They might have mollified him, too—let him make a secret visit out to the camp to see Scotty. Hand me that phone, will you?"

Tori took the cell phone from the glove box and gave it to Jaworski.

"This should be interesting," Jaworski said. "In the back of your mind, you always wonder who your friends are when things get sticky. Now I'll find out."

"How?"

"Basic police axiom: you always start with the dispatcher." He punched in the number. "Hey, Denise, what's happening? Serious heat, sure. Hell, my ass is always in a sling. You know that. What's Kandel like these days? Oh yeah? Then I must be doing something right. I need a favor, Denise. A small one...come on. They're always small...yeah. It's an address, a home address, of a VIP. Gotta keep it under your hat, okay? For Kandel, the Feds, Internal Affairs—it never happened, okay? All right. It's in Potomac. The name is Traeger. Yes, that Traeger. All right, I'll hold on...."

A moment later Jaworski relayed the address to Tori, who jotted it down on the back of an airline ticket. "Thanks, Denise," Jaworski said. "You're an angel. Now I think I'll talk to—what?" His expression changed from jovial to grim. "All right, Denise," he said, his voice muted. "Thanks again." He clicked off the phone.

"What did she say, just now?" Tori asked.

"She said I probably shouldn't talk to anybody else."

"I'm sorry, Kyle."

"Hey, at least I've got one friend over there. There must be a few other cops in the continental United States who aren't convinced I'm pond scum." He punched in another number. "Hello, Evan? It's Kyle. Yeah, I know. Of course it's bullshit. Listen, some day when all this is straightened out we'll have a few beers and I'll tell you the whole story. But for now, we've got another problem. A hot commodity may be arriving in the Denver area soon. It would be a kidnap victim, a child, and they'd be taking her down to Dunston. Yes, it's our buddy. It's Steen. Don't ask, Evan. Just be ready. Stand by. Probable cause? This call is what's known in our business as a Tip from a Reliable Informant. Probably within twenty-four hours. Thanks, Evan. We'll be in touch."

Jaworski's next call was to a deputy sheriff in the rural Virginia county that served as home to another Belke community. Then he called a contact in the Idaho state highway patrol. Finally he clicked the phone off and handed it to Tori.

"You just happened to know all these people?" she asked.

"I know Miller and I know the guy in Virginia. The Boise guy I called last week during the process of checking out Belke."

"So where do you think they'll take her?"

"Hard to say, but my money's on Idaho. Virginia is the largest community, but it's also a close and obvious destination. Dunston seems to be the most heavily armed, but we're more familiar with it. Idaho is the smallest, but it's also the most remote and defensible."

"I can't believe we're letting them do this," Tori muttered.

It was rush hour when they stopped at a mall near the Beltway and I-270 to purchase a pair of binoculars and some food. Twenty minutes later they approached the exclusive neighborhood overlooking the river.

Jaworski cruised up to a guard booth at the entrance to the gated community. An elderly uniformed man approached the car, his nametag identifying him as Ted. Jaworski produced his credentials. "Afternoon."

"Afternoon, Sergeant."

"All quiet?"

"So far."

"Listen, Ted. We've got a really sensitive situation here. It involves the family at 264—the wife mostly, but the children, too—you follow me?"

Ted nodded.

"I've talked to the uniforms and Secret Service who come through here, and they say you're a guy we can work with, that we can count on. My partner and I need to count on you during the next day or two. How late are you on?"

"Eleven."

"Great. Now, after we take a quick look, we're going to park over there, under those trees. If any member of the family enters or leaves, I'd like you to signal us. Can you do that?"

"Sure."

"We've had some reports—not serious, we think, but we can't take any chances."

"Of course. Anything else I can do?"

"Just keep your eyes peeled. You see anything unusual, just signal us. Don't go through the dispatcher—we'd like to keep it off the airwaves."

The man nodded and stepped back into the booth.

"That was slick," Tori said as they pulled away.

"A badge works wonders. So does a little respect—rent-a-cops don't get much of it. I hope we can count on this guy—there's no way we can just park out on the street in a neighborhood like this without somebody calling the cops."

"That's it, on the right."

Jaworski studied the large half-timbered structure with wooden shingles and a triple garage. "Nice place. Looks like somebody's home now."

"He's chief of staff to the President of the United States. Doesn't he get protection for his family?"

"Not around the clock. Traeger gets a government car and driver, and local police will drive by once in a while. They'll have all the latest security and communications." Jaworski continued past the house, circling the block.

They looped through the development and, with a wave to Ted, took up a position outside the gate. As the afternoon wore on, a steady stream of expensive cars made their way into the neighborhood. At the same time, a number of minivans and SUVs left, carrying families off to churches, picnics, and malls. Tori fought off mounting tension as well as fatigue. The car's interior felt hot and sticky, like the air outside; Jaworski had shut off the engine and rolled down the windows.

"What's going to happen?" she asked. "The girl disappears, just like Scotty?"

"Something like that, I suppose. But it will be elaborate, however it's done. We're talking big publicity and an even bigger investigation."

"High-risk," Tori observed. "Why are they doing it?"

"It's high-risk, but look at the stakes. We're talking about the next Leader of the Free World here. They need Traeger, badly. And what stronger hold could they have over him than his daughter?"

"Fair enough," she conceded. "But what about Larry? He wasn't exactly White House chief of staff. Just a software engineer. Why would they need a hold over him?"

"Beats the hell out of me."

At a little after six-thirty, a red Chrysler minivan emerged from the development, heading for the Parkway. Ted stepped out of his booth, nodded, and pointed. Jaworski started the car and cruised up to the booth. "Who was it, Ted?"

"One of the girls—the younger one, I think. She was with a neighbor and two of their kids."

"Thanks, Ted. And let's keep this between us, okay?"

"Of course."

They followed the minivan down a series of side streets, and ultimately onto the George Washington Parkway. "Do you think this will be it?" Tori asked.

"My first reaction is probably not. Out in public with three other people. But it's hard to say until we know where they're going."

The minivan's destination proved to be Montgomery Mall in Bethesda, at the intersection of I-270 and Democracy Boulevard. Jaworski stayed close behind as the van exited the freeway and drove into the Mall's parking lot. The van pulled into an aisle near the Nordstrom's store. Then its progress was momentarily blocked by a green SUV, which backed out of a space and left. The red van snapped up the prime front row space. Tori pulled out the new binoculars and watched four people emerge from the vehicle—a woman and three girls, all of whom appeared to be in their early teens.

"That must be her," Tori said.

"The blond?"

"Yes. She has braces, but you can tell she looks a little like Traeger. And the other two girls have to be sisters. They look like the woman driving the van."

"All right. You'd better follow them inside—make sure they don't leave by another exit."

"What if they do?"

"Get to a pay phone and call me. I'll drive around to wherever it is they're leaving, pick you up, and we'll follow them."

"Sounds a little convoluted."

"Get used to it. We may be doing this for a couple of days. Give them some room—don't be too obvious."

When the party had entered the store, Jaworski cruised up to the door and dropped Tori off, then double-parked at the end of the entrance row.

Tori spotted the four as she entered the Nordstrom's store. They paused briefly, examining some jeans before moving out into the mall. Tori felt her pulse quicken. They weren't going to stay in Nordstrom's. They could go anywhere. She followed, trying to look relaxed and unhurried.

Caitlin and her three companions next stopped at a Gap store, where one of her friends bought a pair of jeans. Tori felt butterflies in her stomach again when the three girls split off from the mother, who walked purposefully down the corridor toward Sears. The three girls stopped in a music store where, after due deliberation, Caitlin purchased a compact disc. Afterward, the trio sauntered out into the mall, where they purchased drinks at an Orange Julius stand and sat on a bench.

Tori, watching while browsing through a paperback at Waldenbooks, didn't know if she could stand much more. The three girls giggled and talked while they waited for the mother to return. Suddenly they stood up and started down a side corridor, past a Body Shop and an Old Navy store. Tori followed, and watched as they turned again, down a dimly lit, deserted hallway lined with lockers. They were going to the restroom.

Tori felt panicky. It would be a perfect place to snatch Caitlin, with no one around, only one easily blocked escape route, and a service door at the end of the corridor. She paused at the mall end of the hallway and watched the girls disappear through a doorway on the left. It wasn't a time to take chances; she walked down the hallway to the restroom door. She paused, took a breath, and pushed the door open.

The bathroom was dingy and cramped. Tori was relieved to see Caitlin and one of the girls standing at a mirror; the other girl was presumably in one of the stalls, whose door was closed. Tori smiled at the girls, who returned her smile, then resumed their conversation about a classmate and her cool boyfriend. Tori pulled a brush from her purse and began work at the mirror, fighting off the urge to warn Caitlin. This is madness, she thought. After a minute a toilet flushed, and the third girl—slightly older than the other two, Tori thought, emerged. "We'd better get back," the girl said, washing up quickly.

Caitlin and her friend nodded, and the three left abruptly. Tori, thinking about the service door just outside, left right behind them, then hung back as she watched the girls go back into the mall. She followed them back to the Orange Julius stand, where the mother was already waiting.

The mother, finishing up a cell phone call, appeared to be in a hurry, and the group set out immediately for the Nordstrom's store. Tori followed at a distance, more careful now about not appearing to be tailing them. She caught a glimpse of the foursome weaving through the store, leaving through the same door they had used to enter. Tori paused inside the door, around to one side of the entry area, feeling palpably relieved as the group neared the red minivan. They had gone to the mall without incident. From the corner of her eye she could see Jaworski, double-parked at the end of the row.

It took her several seconds to take in what happened next. Tori was knocked to the floor, glass erupting all around her. She picked herself up, feeling deaf and dazed. A ball of flame occupied the area where the minivan had been parked.

Her aching ears were able to pick out a distinctive noise. She staggered through the empty-framed door and realized the sound was coming from a car horn. Jaworski, leaning out of the Toyota, was screaming at her to get in. Without thinking, she ran forward and got in. She was thrown back against the seat as the Toyota shot forward.

"My God!" Tori shrieked.

"When did you see her last?" Jaworski said urgently. "I mean, really see her? One hundred percent, no doubt?"

"They went back to Nordstrom's."

"All four? You're sure?"

"Yes."

"Then they couldn't have gotten far." He floored the accelerator, and the Toyota shot down an aisle to the mall's ring road. "There it is!" Jaworski exclaimed. "That green van that blocked them and gave up its parking space." Up ahead, a green van without rear or side windows turned left onto Democracy Boulevard. Jaworski followed, barely making the turn on a yellow arrow. In the distance emergency vehicles, sirens screaming, headed toward the mall as the Toyota and the van headed away from it.

When both vehicles had taken the cloverleaf north onto I-270, Jaworski turned to Tori. "Are you all right?"

Tori looked at herself. There was blood on her right arm and leg. "I must have taken a little bit of glass," she said. "I was sort of standing behind the wall, peeking out." She cleaned herself up with a wet-nap and a tissue.

Jaworski said nothing. He dropped back, leaving a dozen cars between himself and the green van.

"Are you going to tell me what's going on?" Tori asked.

"It was a slick switch," he replied. "It had to have happened in Nordstrom's. That is, if you're totally sure all four of them went in there."

"I am. But what's this about a switch?"

"Not a switch, actually. But they pulled Caitlin out of there, somewhere in the store."

"Then...she's still alive."

"Oh, yes. Very much so."

"Thank God. But the other three...."

"Innocent bystanders," said Jaworski, his expression grim.

"How did they get Caitlin away from the other three? If there was a disturbance of some kind, I should have seen it, even at a distance."

"It was set up—Caitlin was expecting to go somewhere with somebody else, not to return with the other three."

"The mother got a call in the mall—that must have been a ruse of some kind. They left right away."

"Makes sense," Jaworski agreed.

"So then they blew up the minivan?"

"Oh, no. Way too obvious. They blew up the car next to it—a blue Buick LeSabre. The explosion will appear to have nothing to do with Caitlin or her friends. The investigation will focus on the Buick, which will probably be registered to a diplomat in some violence-prone country, or some Mob witness, or some other obvious target."

"But how did they—"

"The green van. It virtually forced them to take a space next to the Buick. And why not? It was a great spot."

Tori, her thoughts still swirling, said, "But when they find the bodies, and Caitlin's not there...."

"Oh, she'll be there, all right. At least there will be the charred remains of a twelve-year-old girl of Caitlin's height and weight, with dental work that matches records that will be found in the office of Caitlin's dentist."

"Then they...killed some other poor child. My God, what an incredible, evil scheme."

"Which is part of an even larger, more incredible, more evil scheme, which we don't understand."

"Wait a minute. Caitlin is in that van up there. Why can't we just call the police and tell them there's a kidnap victim?"

Jaworski's face assumed a pained expression. "We can't do that."

"Why not? Why do we have to let them take her to Idaho, or wherever?" Tori demanded.

"In all likelihood, she was taken out of that store by somebody she trusted, using a convincing story. She probably still believes she's on her way to meet her parents, or whatever. If they're pulled over, the police won't find a kidnap victim. They'll find a girl going willingly with a responsible adult. They will walk."

"But the body in the car—"

"Won't be positively i.d.'d as Caitlin for days, by which time they're gone. And by then, focus will have shifted to the identity of the person or persons calling in that tip."

"Us."

"And the heat on us is about to go up dramatically, anyway. It will only be a few hours before they've talked to that security guard in Traeger's subdivision. He'll report that we tailed the victims. And no doubt we were seen at the mall, driving away from the place after the explosion."

Tori stared straight out at the darkening landscape ahead. "It can't be like this," she said. "They kill at least four people and just drive off with an innocent girl. And we're powerless to stop them."

Jaworski paused before responding. "Tori, one of the first things you learn as a cop is that you can't save everybody. A fair number of cops can't handle that fact, and they quit, or start drinking, or get divorced, or whatever. We still have a chance to save Caitlin. But if we try too soon, we'll blow it. And then there'll be more Caitlins." Jaworski rubbed his eyes, and Tori suddenly felt exhausted herself.

Tori peered ahead through the traffic. "Do you think they've spotted us?"

"No."

"How do you know?"

"I'm good."

"Is your middle name Cocky?"

"No, it's Careful. You see that blue Mustang, five or six cars ahead?"

Tori craned her neck. "Yes."

"That's a trailer car. If they had spotted us, that car would have dropped back and taken us out."

"You're observant and thorough."

"Unfortunately, so are they. But now all we have to do is follow the Mustang. We can be out of sight of the green van."

Tori, to her disgust, found she was chewing a fingernail again. "But what if we lose them?"

"You're quite the worrier. There's really only one logical destination—a little airport off to the west. They'll take the last exit before Frederick."

It happened as Jaworski had predicted. The blue Mustang exited just before Frederick and turned west. The airport was about eight miles off the interstate. Jaworski dropped well back until the blue car was barely visible. Dusk was settling over the Maryland countryside, and cars were turning their lights on. Jaworski, however, kept his off.

The Mustang turned off to the right, toward a large flat area, with blinking lights visible in the distance. Jaworski stayed on the main road for another half-mile, rolling to a stop near a high chain link fence. Tori produced the binoculars and peered through them into the near-darkness. Two vehicles, barely identifiable as the van and the Mustang, were parked near a hangar, next to a small, twin-engine jet. She handed the binoculars to Jaworski.

"Looks like a Lear," he said. "The cars are leaving—they must already have her on board."

Tori tried to imagine what must be going through Caitlin's mind. Confusion, followed by suspicion, and ultimately by terror.

Jaworski put the binoculars down, and they watched the jet taxi to the far end of the runway, then reverse direction, accelerating and taking off right over them.

Tori took the binoculars, and looked back toward the hangar. "The van is gone."

"We'll see the headlights shortly. The Mustang will give them a few minutes' head start."

Again, Jaworski's prediction came to pass. As soon as the blue car's headlights returned to the main road and turned east, Jaworski started the Toyota and drove back to the airport turnoff. "If you don't mind, why don't you wait in the car," he said. "No sense in their being able to identify both of us. I'm the one with the badge, anyway."

Tori didn't argue. They passed through an unmanned gate and drove up to a small cinder block building, which was attached to a small tower. "This should only take a minute," he said.

He was back a minute later. "It's Idaho." As they started back toward the interstate he called his contact in Boise, giving him the arrival information.

"What do we do now?" Tori asked.

"We wait for our guy in Idaho to call." He glanced at his watch. "They'll be landing around midnight. You hungry?"

"Not really."

"Neither am I. We might as well eat anyway." They stopped at a coffee shop restaurant just off I-270 in Gaithersburg. Both left their food nearly untouched. It was close to eleven when they reached Susan's house. Tori collapsed into a chair in the living room and watched television, while Jaworski paced the house, stopping periodically to try to read the newspaper. Midnight came and went. Jay Leno didn't care.

"Damnit, he should have called by now," Jaworski said. He had barely completed his sentence when his cell phone, sitting on a coffee table, trilled.

Tori jumped. They looked at each other for a long moment. Then Jaworski picked up the phone. "Yes?" He listened intently, his expression changing from apprehension to fury. "What? Son of a bitch!" He clicked off the phone and looked at Tori. "The bastards crossed us up. They switched destinations in mid-flight."

Tori stood up. "What are you saying?"

"They landed in Colorado more than an hour ago. By now they're safely inside the Dunston compound."

CHAPTER 26

"You have to understand," said Evan Miller, turning sideways in the front seat to face them. "It's a political decision, not a law enforcement decision."

"That makes me feel ever so much fucking better," snapped Jaworski, slumped in the back seat of the unmarked car. "And I'm sure Caitlin Traeger will see that as a real comfort, too. Christ, Evan, this is about a twelve-year-old girl, kidnapped, helpless, and terrified. If this is any other case we've got plenty of probable cause."

"This isn't any other case. There's no way you can execute a search warrant out there without taking a lot of casualties."

"Since when has that been a factor in determining probable cause?" asked Tori, who was seated next to Jaworski.

"It's not supposed to be," Miller admitted. "But all you've got in this case is your uncorroborated testimony. In most cases that's good enough. But in this case, well...." Miller shrugged.

Jaworski stared out the car window at the heavy clouds that were rolling in over the Rockies. "So we just write off Caitlin."

"As far as everybody is concerned, Caitlin is dead."

"She isn't," Tori said, her voice rising.

"You didn't actually see her alive after the blast," Miller pointed out.

Tori looked at Jaworski for a cue. Ironically, she felt more rested than she had in a week. After receiving the call from Boise, they had driven nonstop to Denver. Each had slept for long stretches while the other had driven. Miller, meanwhile, had been in touch with Jaworski's superiors in Montgomery County, as well as the FBI, though not with Bertelson.

"Then what about the bombing?" Jaworski demanded. "I've given you the descriptions of two suspicious vehicles seen leaving the mall at the time of the explosion and driving to an airport."

"You were seen leaving the area, too. And the two vehicles—"

"Let me guess. Registered to a reputable Washington-based charity with a lot of heavyweight politicians on its board."

"Kyle, this isn't me talking. It's the Feebs. And the U.S. Attorney, for that matter. I'm just a cutout here—I have no jurisdiction whatsoever. You know that."

Jaworski nodded slowly, sitting up in the back seat. "I know that, Evan. And we appreciate it. But where the hell does all this leave us?"

"You don't have a choice. You have to deal with your superiors and deal with the charges. They don't seem to have much on either of you, to be honest."

"Sure," Tori said. "Just enough to have us arrested, tied up in court proceedings, bankrupted by defense costs, and our reputations ruined."

Miller hesitated. "Look, if you two are really convinced of your theory, I have an idea you might want to pursue."

Tori looked at Jaworski. "I'd say we're definitely open to suggestions, wouldn't you?"

"I work with a guy who is a cousin of Jim Traeger's," Miller said. "If you did a good song and dance for the cousin, you might get a chance to meet with Traeger. I mean, if there's any chance his daughter is alive, he'll want to pursue it, right? And if you can convince Traeger—well, he's got the clout to shift the investigation, and maybe to get you two off the hook...." He looked back and forth between them. "What? What did I say?"

"I'm sorry," Jaworski said, his voice weary. There was no use trying to explain the inexplicable. "We didn't mean to shoot you down, Evan. It's a great idea, and I really appreciate your being willing to do that for us. I can't go into it, but it just wouldn't work."

Miller gave them a dubious look, then shrugged.

Jaworski opened his car door. "I guess we'll be in touch. Thanks again."

"What are you going to do?" asked Miller, instantly suspicious.

"Head back to D.C., I guess."

"Whatever you're going to do, don't do it. Don't burn any bridges."

Jaworski let out a short laugh. "The fire was over a long time ago."

•

"Your diet is deteriorating," Tori observed as Jaworski wolfed down a large burrito.

"At least I'm eating. That's more than you can say."

Tori looked down at her half-eaten taco. Outside the Taco Bell restaurant, traffic whizzed by on South Broadway.

Jaworski wiped his mouth. "Decision time."

"There's no decision," Tori asserted. "We have to do it."

"We could keep trying reporters."

"A waste of time—time we don't have."

"The guy from the *News* seemed interested."

"Until he checked us out and learned we were fugitives from the law. Let's face it, the photographs of Scotty don't prove anything. They could be a hoax. And no reputable outlet is going to run a wild story like this without some facts. And even if they tried—"

"I know. They will call Traeger for comment, and he'll kill the story. I was just playing devil's advocate, Tori. I agree with you. My main concern is, are you up to this? Physically and emotionally."

Tori started to answer, then hesitated. Already, her breathing was shallow and her knees weak at the possibility of another encounter with Harlan Belke and Karl Steen. "I'll be all right," she said.

"You're bullshitting me. I'll go in myself. You can't risk your life and your mental health."

Tori paused, fighting to clear her head of half a dozen powerful, conflicting emotions. "I appreciate what you're saying. But you need me. I've been there."

"I'll get by."

She gripped the sides of the filthy orange plastic table. "Kyle, I need to do this. If I don't, they will always have power over me. I need to meet this, head-on."

"And screw yourself up for life?"

She gave him a sad smile. "Don't you understand?"

"Understand what?"

"The damage is already done."

•

The mountain air was cold as Tori and Jaworski stood by the rented jeep, checking their gear. Jaworski reached into the back for their jackets.

"So far, so good. If we'd met a patrol along the road, it was all over."

Tori walked over behind a fallen log, retrieving a backpack full of gear she had left on her last visit. "It's not a long stretch of road. Still, you'd think they would be extra vigilant now."

"I'm not sure about that," Jaworski replied, loading up their backpacks. "Thanks to your stashing the gear, they didn't know you had actually hiked over and seen the camp. All you were doing was driving along the road."

"They will have to assume the worst."

Jaworski slung the pack onto his back. Tori did likewise. They stood for a moment.

"You're looking at me like that again," she said.

"Sorry."

"It's...okay. You were right."

"About what?"

"You're for real. You're on my side, all the way. My God, when I think of what you've risked, what you've given up for me. And now, doing this...."

"It's for myself, too."

"It's for me."

"It's for us." He put his pack down. "Tori, if you could understand what it's been like these past couple of days, to be with you. This is worth doing; it's worth everything to me. It sounds crazy, but this is who I am; this is where I belong." He looked away.

She reached up and turned his face back toward her. Tori knew instinctively that he was right; somehow, in the past few days, in facing his demons, in being with her, he had achieved a kind of completion. He was no longer a core of obsession and guilt, topped by a veneer of smooth charm. He was...Kyle Jaworski.

They kissed for a long time.

Then they set off through the woods.

They hiked for an hour, Jaworski wearing the night vision goggles and Tori following close behind. It was past midnight when they sat down to rest.

Jaworski sipped from the canteen. "All we need is something tangible. Preferably Scotty himself, but even a hair off his head would do it. We were close to convincing the reporters as it was. I just wonder what we're going to find."

"I wonder if we really want to know. What will Scotty be like after all these years? Will Cindy be there? And what have they done to these people?"

"Then there's the sixty-four dollar question," Jaworski said. "When we get to the bottom of all this, peel back all the layers, what have we got? What the hell is the Bound?"

"It's a drug," Tori said.

Jaworski turned slowly toward her, trying unsuccessfully to hide his astonishment. "It's a what?"

"It's the only explanation that makes sense," she asserted. "Down in Mexico they kept talking about the Zest of Life, about discoveries by ancient alchemists. It's a drug, and the people who take it seem to like it a lot. They looked like they were high."

Jaworski stood up. "Christ, all this mystery, all these deaths, all these shenanigans, and you're telling me these people are nothing more than a bunch of junkies?"

"I'll tell you something else," Tori said. "All that stuff about the alchemists—it's all a crock. This drug was discovered by Rick Percival, when he was a pharmaceutical researcher for FuTek."

Once again, Jaworski's mouth dropped open. "Then why did they go to all that trouble, to cook up that bullshit story and convince people it was for real?"

"Who knows for sure? I'd guess it was just to awe people, make them feel they were part of something sacred and ancient. It also doesn't hurt that they're down in Mexico, away from the prying eyes of U.S. authorities."

"But where does Belke fit in? And what are they ultimately trying to accomplish? I mean, they must have a goal beyond just getting everybody stoned."

"I don't know," Tori said. "You can add that to a long list of things we don't know."

They resumed their hike, this time with Tori wearing the night vision goggles. She felt Jaworski's hand on her arm. "How much farther?" he whispered.

"We're almost there. See that little L-shaped clearing up ahead? That's where I watched them from last time."

Jaworski nodded. They had decided to observe the camp and its operations for a day before making their move the following night. They moved forward toward the small clearing, and instantly, they were blinded by powerful floodlights.

Then they were on the ground. Tori and Jaworski struggled, but it was over before they started. Within seconds the half-dozen figures that had sprung out into the clearing had separated, subdued, and handcuffed them.

Twenty minutes later, Tori was talking to Rick Percival.

CHAPTER 27

They took her not to the administration building, but to one of the long buildings forming the side of the quadrangle. She couldn't see where they were taking Jaworski. One of her two minders knocked on an exterior door, which was promptly answered by Percival. He wore jeans and a flannel shirt, and when he smiled Tori, incredibly, infuriatingly, felt once again the surge of desire she had always felt in his presence.

"Take the cuffs off," he ordered. One of the minions complied—reluctantly, Tori thought—and they remained outside the door when Percival motioned her inside. The place appeared to be a small apartment, well equipped and nicely furnished.

Percival gestured toward an easy chair. Tori simply stood, mute and terrified. "Please," he said, and helped her into the chair. He disappeared into the kitchen and returned a moment later with a glass. "Brandy," he said. "You need to soothe your nerves."

Tori felt herself begin to lose consciousness, and knew she was hyperventilating. Unresisting, she drank the brandy, which seemed to shock her back to alertness, while at the same time calming her breathing. Percival continued to stand over her, observing her carefully. "Tori," he said urgently, "whatever happens, you have my word that Belke and Steen will not touch you again."

Tori wasn't sure she believed him, but the reassurance helped. She took deep, slow breaths, gathering her wits, and Percival sat down in a leather wingback chair across from her.

"You're going to kill me," Tori said.

"That had been our plan," Percival admitted. "But I think I've persuaded Harlan to consider other options."

"Such as?"

"I have a lot to tell you," he said. "It will take a while for all of it to sink in, to the point where you can understand and accept it. But you're an extraordinary person, Tori. I think you're capable of comprehending and appreciating what we're doing here. Harlan knows you pose very little threat to us now. And in another year, none at all. You'd have to tell us everything you know, of course, and I'm afraid we'd have to confirm that with...medication. And then it would be necessary for you to remain under some kind of confinement or restriction until our plans are complete—again, in about a year, most likely. I'm still negotiating with Harlan."

"Why would he agree to that? Why would you do it, for that matter?"

"Harlan would be doing it as a favor to me. And I—well, I think you know why, Tori. As I said, I've developed strong feelings for you over the past few weeks. And I know you feel the same about me."

Tori felt fairly certain he was lying about everything. Still, why would he have kept her alive, talking to her, trying to convince her? What purpose could he have in manipulating her now?

"What about Jaworski?" she asked.

Percival, his expression grave, shook his head. "I'm afraid there's nothing I can do for him."

Tori felt herself beginning to hyperventilate again. She drank some more brandy, tried to relax, and forced her mind to ask for the answers she had sought for so long. "Is Cindy here?" she asked.

"As I've said, not really. You will see someone who resembles her—that's all. It's unfortunate she never understood the contribution she made, never knew what the Bound was really about."

"The Bound is a drug," Tori asserted.

Percival gave her a surprised look, but recovered quickly. "The Declaration of Independence is a sheet of paper. The Bible is a book. Those statements are true, but they don't scratch the surface."

"I saw those people you initiated down in Mexico," Tori said. "They looked drugged. Stoned."

"Again, an oversimplification. Most participants cannot find words to describe the experience. Yes, we gave them a substance—a very concentrated version of the Zest our people take on a daily basis."

"Why set up that cock-and-bull story about ancient Egyptians?"

Percival winced at the characterization. "For one thing," he said, "it

diverts attention

diverts attention from the fact that the Zest is a chemical, which would initially be a turn-off to many, if not most. It also solidifies group identity, which is critical to our purposes."

"People would never accept your 'purposes,' whatever they are, if they weren't drugged."

"Absolutely false, although it's true that the Zest is given only to people who are psychologically prepared to receive it."

"People with shallow moral roots."

Percival didn't disagree. "I would prefer to describe them as people who aren't closed-minded or irrevocably committed to dogma. Corman uses psychological tests and detailed interviews to select the participants."

"And the participants never have a second thought about it."

"Of course they do, especially because we ask them to do some painful things. After the ecstasy of the initial experience, many have second thoughts about the Zest. But a few days without it is usually enough to convince them of its merits. And their fellow group members reinforce them, help them through it."

"You keep them addicted."

He shook his head. "That's an inflammatory term, which implies neurosis or character defect. Our people make a rational choice that life is much better with it."

"Sounds an awful lot like crack or meth to me."

Percival's indulgent patience finally gave way, and he looked, for the first time, offended. "You just don't understand, Tori. The Zest is not about getting high. Do our people look like desperate, hollow-eyed junkies to you? I assure you, they acquire no physical dependence. The Zest has no resemblance whatsoever to a street drug, do you understand me? Getting high is not what the Zest is about."

Tori, exasperated, said, "Then what the hell is it about?"

"It's about happiness."

Tori, taken aback, said nothing.

"No one can fully explain it," he continued, "but there can be no doubt that evolution has left humankind programmed for misery. The level of human clinical depression alone is staggering, but overall, the fact is that most of us, most of the time, are not happy. We are not even close. Yet we've known for some years, at least since the development of the early MAO inhibitor drugs, that happiness is largely a physiological condition.

The development of the tricyclics and Prozac confirmed it. Some people on those antidepressants reported feeling 'better than well.' That should have tipped us off that we are no longer bound to misery. We can do better—much, much better."

"Come on," Tori said. "There's no happier person than a cokehead riding a high."

"In a superficial and short-term sense, that's true. But the coke high is not sustainable. You can flood the brain with serotonin, but there are feedback mechanisms, that require higher and higher dosages, that make it impossible to feel any pleasure without the drug, that generally screw you up. In the long run, no street drug works, because of the body's own mechanisms. Mother Nature seems bound and determined to have us plod through life in misery."

"But you decided to improve upon Mother Nature."

"Yes. I worked on the original team that developed Prozac, back in the eighties. But the people I worked with were dullards. All they could think about was marketability and liability. Profits and lawsuits. Results and side effects. None of them thought about what Prozac really meant. It meant mankind no longer had to be miserable. By the time I got to FuTek, I knew what I wanted to accomplish."

"And you did."

"Yes."

"By turning people into addicts. That must do wonders for their well being."

"Actually, it's pretty much the opposite. Overall, taking the Zest usually brings on an immediate attack of mental health. It eliminates the need for all the neurotic games, for all the mechanisms we use to try to make ourselves happy. Don't you understand, Tori? Happiness is the number one goal of mankind. Unhappiness is the number one problem. We have solved it."

Tori paused, trying to take it all in. "Is that all we are?" she asked. "Is that all personality is? A drug-crafted persona? Are we that malleable?"

"A very profound question," Percival said, "and one I've given a great deal of thought to. I'm convinced the self does exist, that it's not actually shaped or formed by drugs, although personality is much more biological and genetic than first thought. You would still be Tori McMillan, even with the Zest. Most importantly, free will still exists. That's what defines us as human beings."

"Free will? These people are addicted. Has anybody ever successfully quit?"

Percival hesitated. "A choice can be made to reject the Zest and the life that comes with it. But such a choice would be difficult and very illogical. Frankly, our research on that point is limited, since the reasons for choosing unhappiness over happiness are very limited indeed. Make no mistake, the Zest does affect will and personality. It elevates mood and smoothes out rough spots."

"If a drug alone can make people happy, how are they motivated to accomplish anything? Why should they even get out of bed?"

Percival smiled. "In fact, the Zest does increase contentment with the status quo to some extent. But it increases to the same extent the inherent pleasure that comes from creating, improving and striving. The difference is that people do these things for their inherent worth, not as a neurotic reaction to inadequacy and unhappiness. They do things because they are worthwhile and because they have an affinity for doing them. They don't do them to attract chicks, to prove themselves to their parents, to impress their peers, or compensate for being ugly or short. The Zest causes people to realize what really makes them happy, which is, potentially, everything."

Tori didn't know what to say. "I guess you've thought this all through. And Paradise is here. Whoopee."

Percival said, "I know I sound pompous and overblown, talking this way. But damnit, Tori, it's true. The Zest is the pinnacle of human evolution. It's a step up to a higher plane of existence. Even I didn't realize how powerful the impact would be. Bound people have problems like everyone else—they recognize them and don't like them, but they don't get depressed. They still feel happy. There are ups and downs—varying degrees of happiness. But they're still happy."

"I'm glad for them," Tori said. "But what about Cindy and Scotty. Are they happy?"

Percival had no answer.

"And," Tori said, "I hope Caitlin is happy, too."

•

No fewer than four soldiers accompanied Jaworski to the administration building. He was shoved through a side door into a large office. Behind a massive desk, Harlan Belke swiveled around to face him.

"Good work," Belke said to his men.

"The woman is with Mr. Percival," one of them reported.

"Naturally," Belke snorted in disgust. He nodded, and two of the men left the room. Jaworski remained standing near the door.

Belke leaned back in his chair with his hands locked behind his head. "Welcome to Amateur Hour," he said. "God, you two were predictable. All we had to do was locate your cache, get out the infrared scanners, and wait for you. What did you think, we were fucking idiots?"

"Did you spot us in D.C.?" Jaworski asked.

Belke shot him a wary look. "Spot you where?"

"Take your pick. At the mall. Following the green van or the blue Mustang. Out at the little airport by Frederick."

The racist leader's gaze hardened. "You're full of shit."

"Sorry, Harlan. We knew you'd make a move on the girl."

"And we knew you'd be stupid enough to show up here. Didn't even have to think about that one."

"Mister, you hate anybody with dark skin. You want to talk stupid?"

"Give me some credit," Belke said. "I hate a lot of white folks, too." He let out an explosive guffaw.

"Tell me something," Jaworski said. "Why did you pick people like Larry Stevens and Max Tuten to be in one of your cells? Jim Traeger—or even Nolan Bertelson—that's easy to understand. They can do a lot for you. But a software engineer, and a middle manager at the same company?"

"That's easy. Sattex is on the cutting edge of technology. They own the language that computers and ground stations use to communicate with each other. That's all under our control. Of course, the cell included people from Sattex's competitors, too. But the main thing is, we think long term. Max was a mistake, sure. But the concept is still valid. The guy wasn't the brightest, but he had great political skills, and he was cooperative. He could have risen to the top of Sattex some day. We were just looking ahead."

"Why did you let Cindy Stevens go, after she saw Scotty with Steen in Denver?"

He considered the question. "It was a judgment call. She saw them, sure, but they got away, and we figured she had nowhere else to look. We pretty much knew she wouldn't be taken seriously—hell, everybody knew she was obsessed with her son. But her death or disappearance might have raised questions. It might have given credibility to her claims to have seen the boy, which might have led to a serious investigation. She started out doing the expected—going to the police, then coming back to Colorado to look for the red SUV. But she ran into a dead end—the vehicle was registered to an untraceable dummy corporation. And, like we figured, she got nowhere with the police.

"When she gave up and went back to D.C., we lost interest. But then for some reason she started focusing on her husband. To this day, we're still not sure how she uncovered Larry's cell—probably from the same type of surveillance and research Tori did. Then she got desperate; hell, she became a mass murderer. Wiped out the whole cell, except for Max Tuten."

"Why didn't you just kill her? Would've been a lot easier. No loose ends."

Belke gave him a curious look. "You still don't get it, do you. What we do here, I mean."

"You use these people for research. That's what you do in the brick building."

"Yep. And as it turns out, Cindy was especially valuable. Same genes as Scotty, or some damn thing like that. I don't pretend to understand it all. But I do understand one thing, Jaworski. I understand power. And what we've got here will give us a lot of it."

"You own Hokanson, and he's going to become President."

"We own a lot more people than just Hokanson, but his election will complete the process. Especially with you and the woman in the bag. Hard to see what could stop us now."

"We've told the media," Jaworski said.

Belke studied him. "You tried, maybe. But if you did, you didn't get anywhere. You've got no proof—just a wild story. I don't think you knew enough to be much of a threat, anyway. But just in case, we'll let Steen and the boys have a couple of days with you. They'll find out what you know."

"Come on, Belke. Do you think we'd come here without telling anybody?"

Belke shrugged. "Maybe. Maybe not. But it doesn't make much difference. Because there ain't nobody gonna come in here and get you. Not unless they want to die."

Suddenly the room shook. Through the closed blinds, Jaworski could see bright lights. Outside, loud pops filled the air. One of Jaworski's guards ran to the window; the other trained his machine pistol directly on Jaworski.

A voice crackled over a radio on Belke's desk. "Mr. Belke? We've got incoming, sir, and aircraft on the screen."

Belke jumped to his feet and grabbed a handset. "What the hell?"

"Sir, we're under attack."

CHAPTER 28

Rick Percival drank scotch from a tumbler. Tori had refused further alcohol. She shivered in her chair, pulling her arms around her, even though it wasn't cold in the apartment.

"How did this start?" she asked him. "How did you get involved in this?"

Percival leaned back in his chair. "I was head of R & D at FuTek. Dennis Curry had recruited me from Merck. I agreed to take the job on one condition: I wanted to put together my own team to develop a happiness drug. It only took me three years. That's an incredibly short time. But I knew what I wanted. I'd been searching for my destiny."

"And you were willing to cut corners."

He looked her in the eye, with his saintly look. "Yes, I was. The first corner I cut was testing. Instead of doing these protracted, controlled human trials on the Zest, I just tried it myself. It takes effect within half an hour, Tori. I kept taking it for 30 days. It was the most glorious month of existence in my entire life. But I had to think about what to do next. I went camping down in Big Bend. I thought and prayed and meditated. And at the end of it all, I realized my destiny went far beyond merely living a happy life." Percival shifted in his chair. "In fact, my destiny didn't even include living a happy life."

"You went off it?" Tori asked.

He nodded. "First of all, to see if it could be done, which it can. Even so, it was the most difficult thing I've ever done. Ever. But I decided not to allow myself full happiness until I'd completed the fulfillment of my destiny. And, I decided, rightly or wrongly, megalomania or not, my destiny was to transform the world."

Tori shook her head, and Percival, becoming agitated, sat up and leaned toward her. "I know I sound full of myself, Tori, but you simply don't understand. You were happy with Ben, right? Imagine being three times happier. How about five times happier? How about ten times? What would you do if you discovered something that was literally earth shaking? That had a greater potential for good than anything in the history of the world? What was I supposed to do, turn it over to Uncle Sam? Start selling it and make as much money as I could?" He sat back and took another sip from his glass. "I decided not to release it through commercial or political channels. I decided to take it in a spiritual and moral direction."

"Spiritual?" Tori said, incredulous. "You entered into a scheme with a vicious racist."

"I called on Harlan because he's the most capable man I know, and I knew I could trust him completely. And I called on him because he understands power." He hesitated. "I honestly don't know whether Harlan really believes all that racial stuff or not, and I'm closer to him than anyone. In any event, it has no bearing on what we've done."

"You formed a cult."

"Not right away. The first thing I had to do was get control of the Zest and its production."

"Which meant getting control of FuTek," Tori said.

"That's where Harlan came in. He had the organizational know-how. As you know, I'm a little disorganized."

"You killed Dennis Curry."

Percival looked uncomfortable. "I had thought we could work with him, that he'd understand and be reasonable. You see, that's why I need Harlan. He knows people, and that includes knowing and facing up to their less desirable characteristics. Once we told Curry and he turned us down, there was no going back. We couldn't leave him in control of the Zest."

"So you and Belke got rid of him and took over the company."

"There was no alternative. Dennis couldn't see beyond the end of his nose. All he could imagine was making money off the Zest. Can you imagine that?"

Tori didn't answer, and he went on. "Once we had control of the Zest, we were able to implement my vision, to actually form the Bound. We knew existing institutions would be unable to cope with the implications *of the Zest.*

of the Zest. They would all have reasons to misuse it, like the Pentagon would, or to suppress it, as those puritanical control freaks who run organized religion certainly would, or exploit it, as big business would. This was something that had to be in responsible hands."

"Yours," Tori said.

Percival ignored her. "The Bound is not a cult per se—there's no specific object of worship. There's no charismatic leader—the members have no idea who Harlan Belke or Rick Percival are. They receive direction anonymously, from a voice they know only as Temple."

"You."

"Yes, I'm Temple."

"You're not answering my question," she said. "Why a cult?"

"Because it provides discipline, which is essential to getting anything done in life. Deferred gratification is the essence of the Zest; discipline and intensive education are needed to handle the power that comes with it. I wanted a spiritual focus; there's an obvious spiritual hunger in the world, and spirituality is the only way to ensure that the power is used for good, not for corrupt or self-interested purposes. And spirituality, along with the natural feelings and revised modes of thinking provided by the Zest, is what really forms the Bound between our members. I recognized early on that the Bound's purpose is nothing less than a sacred duty.

"I studied past movements, and I knew my group must not be based on personality. I knew it must respect, but not be a part of, existing religions. I knew the allegiance of our members must be permanent and absolute, even when they go back out into the world. So I knew my group had to be based both on absolute self-interest and on the good of all."

"High-sounding words," Tori said.

"More than words. I knew that a bond had to be formed among all the believers; that collective action would be essential in the new scheme of things. We'd need discipline, secrecy, and action. So we formed cells to take control of various sectors of society, such as the communications sector represented by Sattex and its competitors. And here in Colorado, we continued to study the effects of the Zest on individual and societal behaviors, and prepare for orderly transition. These are things a "free market" could never do. Without these efforts, the result would be chaos—barbarity, even."

"This research," Tori said. "That's what's done in the brick building, isn't it."

"Yes. By leading scientists I've recruited. This is a perfect location for secrecy and control—near a major metropolitan area, but at a place where we don't have to worry about external intrusions."

"Lovely, except that you ensure your researchers' loyalty by keeping them drugged, and you use unwilling human subjects for research."

A flash of anger crossed his face. "I'm disappointed in you, Tori. I thought you were bright enough, perceptive enough, to be able to see the big picture. Yes, I could have spent another ten years doing controlled tests on rats. Then another ten years of human testing under the watchful eye of the FDA, losing all control over the Zest. You've seen the state of our world—do you think we have twenty years? And do you think a world-transforming process like this is going to come at zero human cost?"

He stood up. "Yes, we use human subjects for research. And some of them are people who have tried to block us, even destroy us. And, yes, Tori, some of them are completely innocent, unwitting subjects."

"Children," she heard herself say.

He paced the room slowly. "Yes. It turns out that children—particularly adolescents—are especially critical for this type of research. But children are incapable of giving informed consent for pharmaceutical trials. The Zest is not a cure for a childhood disease. Therefore, by definition, we would never have been allowed to do the type of research we really needed to do. That's especially true of those we select using genetic tests."

"Like Scotty," she said.

"Like Scotty," he agreed. "And like Caitlin Traeger. It's regrettable, of course, but there can be no doubt that their participation will have saved countless lives, and enriched millions—even billions—of others, in the long run."

"And by happy coincidence, you have a hold over their parents."

Percival did not flinch from the question. "We prefer to see it as a test of loyalty. The supreme test. Most of our Bound members pass it with flying colors. You simply cannot understand the strength of the Bound, Tori. It allows our members to put these situations in perspective."

"And allows you to kidnap children and use them for testing."

He wheeled on her. "Don't get up on your high horse about these kids, Tori. We've used only a handful of genetically selected children from Bound members, who come from safe, loving, middle-class families. For the rest of these children, coming here is more a rescue than a kidnapping. Most of them were abused at home. Many of them would have died on the streets—"

"My God!" Tori shrieked. "Urban Hope. And these other social organizations your people are involved with—you're taking runaways. Kids who won't be missed by anyone. Your whole organization is a sham, a vehicle for kidnapping children, not helping them."

"What we're doing—"

He was cut off by the first explosions.

CHAPTER 29

Harlan Belke killed all the lights in his office except for a small corner lamp, then grabbed a small radio, clipped it to his belt, and attached a cord to one end. To the other end of the cord he fitted a headset with a speaker and microphone, then put the apparatus on his head. He flipped a switch on the radio.

"Assume defense positions!" he said, his amplified voice reverberating from loudspeakers outside in the compound.

The racist leader flipped another switch on the radio. "Report!" he barked. His expression turned grim as he listened over the headset. He pushed his desk chair aside and knelt behind his desk. Jaworski couldn't see him, but guessed Belke was accessing a floor safe. Belke emerged a minute later, holding what looked like a vinyl case for carrying compact disks or CD ROMs.

"I've gotta get to the bunker," he told the two guards, starting for the door. "You," he nodded to one of them, "take him to detention." To the other he said, "You're with me." He pushed past them out the door.

"Let's go," said Jaworski's guard, a slight, scared looking youth with dark hair and bad teeth.

Jaworski didn't move. "Don't be a fool, kid. We'll get killed if we go out there."

The guard, keeping the gun trained on Jaworski, backed toward the window, turned the blinds, and peeked around the corner. There were more explosions, along with the sounds of small-arms fire. He turned back toward Jaworski, who had backed into a corner, trying to stay away from the window and the line of fire. "I've got my orders," the guard said.

"Your orders are going to get you killed."

Just then Jaworski saw a flash of light streak up from the ground, and a huge explosion took out what was now revealed as a helicopter, which spun and crashed to the ground.

The guard looked back at Jaworski. "We're gonna kick their asses," he said, his mouth curling into a sneer. "We've got Stingers."

"Too late," Jaworski asserted. "Too many of them on the ground already. It's three in the morning and they've got you by surprise." He remained with his back to the wall. The automatic fire outside was nearly continuous, and all it would take is one stray bullet through the window.

"Let's go," the kid said, gesturing toward the door with the gun.

"Meanwhile, your fearless leader is sitting in a nice safe bunker, letting you take all the incoming."

"You're lying! And I said let's go!"

"No way, kid. I'd rather take a bullet from you than get cut to pieces out there. Go ahead, shoot. Of course, in the unlikely event you and Belke do survive this, you'll have to explain why you let a prisoner in your charge be killed. I'm supposed to be interrogated, remember?"

In the dim light, Jaworski could see the guard's expression change from surliness to panic. "Goddamnit, I said let's go!" he cried.

Another explosion ripped through the compound. The kid flinched, and Jaworski shot forward, kicking at his legs. The guard went down, and Jaworski kicked viciously at his face, then dropped to the floor as the firing outside grew more intense.

The guard was out cold, blood trickling from his mouth and ear. Jaworski retrieved the handcuff key from his belt, but couldn't unlock the cuffs himself. He threw his shoulders back, dropped his arms as low as he could, then sat on the floor, working his cuffed wrists underneath him. Then he got to his feet, his cuffed hands now in front of him. Now he was able to use the key to free himself. The scared kids who had captured him had been inexperienced; they hadn't known how to cuff a suspect. He ran to the window. The quadrangle was lit by intense flares, presumably dropped by the airborne attackers. Across the square, Jaworski spotted Percival and Tori going into a door on the side of one of the wooden buildings. Jaworski grabbed the guard's machine pistol and flashlight, then ducked out into the hall, looking for a doorway to the outside.

●

Tori, with Percival gripping her arm, ran along the back side of the building containing Percival's apartment, then into another, unmarked door. Then, inside what appeared to be a broom closet, Percival lifted a trap door. Cold, musty air drifted up into the closet. He flipped on a light, and they walked carefully down two flights of stairs, Percival first closing the trap door behind them.

Downstairs, in a small room lined with electronic equipment, Belke and Steen waited for them. Tori felt nauseous at the sight of Steen.

"What the hell's going on?" Percival demanded.

Belke removed his headset. "It doesn't look good," he reported. "They've landed in force. We managed to take out one chopper, but that's it. Casualties are heavy."

Percival exploded. "Goddamnit, Harlan. So much for you and your crack military force. Why didn't Bertelson warn us this was coming? And you said they'd never try this."

Belke, looking calm—even amused—shrugged. "Guess I was wrong."

"Well, what are we going to do?" Percival demanded. "Evacuate?"

"I guess so."

"You...guess?"

Belke, his expression suddenly turning grim, pulled out an automatic pistol. "Yeah, I guess. And I guess you won't be coming with us. I'm sorry, Percy." He fired three shots at close range.

Tori screamed and jumped back. Percival crumpled to the floor. Tori felt Steen's arm clamp around her biceps. Her knees weakened.

She felt two hard slaps across her face. Steen yanked her roughly across the room. "Stay with us, bitch," he hissed. "We might need you."

Belke was on his knees, going through Percival's pockets. "Yep, here it is," he said, producing a small disk. "This should be the latest stuff. Of course I've already got most of it right here." He dropped the disk into a vinyl waist pack he wore. "Well, let's go."

Steen, still holding on to Tori, opened a door at one end of the room and shoved her through it into complete darkness. Then a light went on, revealing a long tunnel, lit at intervals by light from bare electric bulbs. They hustled her through the tunnel.

"Hated to do that," Belke said. "Percy and I go way back. And I owe him—he invented the wonder drug and thought up the idea for the Bound. He was a genius, no doubt. But when the chips are down, when you need decisive action and clear thinking, he just wasn't the man."

"Where are we going?" Tori managed to ask.

"Away. That's all you need to know."

The tunnel seemed endless. After about ten minutes of walking, they came upon another stairwell. Shoving Tori in front of them, Steen and Belke ascended the staircase. They pushed open a door, then a second door, emerging in darkness from a small shed. They all glanced back at the floodlit compound; it appeared they had emerged on the far side of the complex from the main gate. The rat-tat-tat of small arms fire, along with an occasional explosion, could still be heard, but the fighting sounded less intense than it had previously. The large shapes of parked helicopters could be made out in the quadrangle and along the approach road. Armed figures occasionally darted across the open areas.

"Fools," muttered Harlan Belke. "They never seem to learn." He took the radio from his belt; the device looked like a television remote, with numbered buttons. He punched in a number, then hit a larger switch. Almost instantaneously, the brick building was consumed in a huge fireball. Seconds later, a wave of heat and pressure nearly knocked the three of them off their feet.

Belke clipped the device to his belt. "Let's go," he said.

"Jesus Christ!" Tori yelled as Steen shoved her along a path through the woods. "How many people did you just kill?"

"Enough," Belke said. "Enough to drag the FBI through all of it again, for having caused the deaths of innocent people."

"You caused it." Tori shot back.

"Sure. Just like Koresh did. Just like Weaver did. But who got blamed? There'll be more Congressional investigations, special prosecutors, cover-ups, resignations—the usual. Official mass murder, all to serve a couple of warrants on weapons charges."

"A couple of weapons charges? What about kidnapping? Drugs? Experimenting on children? Secret cells? Subverting the electoral process?"

"No evidence for any of that, I'm afraid. I just destroyed it all. All except for this." He patted the black vinyl waist pack. "I've got all the research data here, all the org charts, plus the formula for the Zest. The Feds will know nothing about the Zest, the Bound, the research, and least of all about President Hokanson."

They reached a rocky outcrop in the side of a hill. Belke held a flashlight while Steen began clearing away brush and boulders. Within a minute a small opening appeared. Steen went in first, pulling Tori behind him.

When Belke came in behind them, his flashlight revealed another tunnel, plus a waiting golf cart. Steen took the wheel of the cart; Belke got into the back seat with Tori. Steen started the motor, and they lurched forward, bumping slowly through the tunnel. Only the golf cart's headlights illuminated the path ahead of them.

"Where are we going?" Tori demanded.

"Through this old mine shaft to the other side of the mountain. Then to a helicopter, an air strip, a plane, and Mexico."

"What about all the drug research you just destroyed?"

"The research on the drug was finished a long time ago. For the past five years, our research has focused on genetics."

"Genetics?"

"Yep. Percy didn't want to use the Zest forever. He wanted to hard-wire this happiness stuff, make it so everybody is born with the capacity to eliminate the serotonin feedback mechanisms. That was his Utopian version: no drugs. Everybody bred for happiness. Born happy and built to stay that way."

Tori couldn't speak. Her brain struggled to process this latest shock.

"Unfortunately," Belke continued, "Percy, genius though he was, was a fool who didn't understand power or human nature. So I had to sort of tweak the research a little bit."

Tori felt ill. She could guess what came next.

"Our darker-skinned friends won't receive that kind of genetic engineering," Belke said. "In fact, they'll receive some race-specific gene therapy that will slow down their reproduction and increase docility. And after all that, their inferiority and social pathology will be obvious to everyone. Their status as an underclass will be reaffirmed and strengthened. The mud people will finally be where they belong."

Tori stared through the darkness at Belke, his face lit intermittently by the flashlight as they bumped through the tunnel. She wondered if he was insane. Probably. But what difference did it make? "All your research was destroyed," she asserted.

"Like I said, I've pretty much got everything I need right here. The fools attacked during the night, when all scientists are gone. Within a year we'll have quietly brought the researchers down to Mexico and set up shop there. This will set us back maybe a year—no big deal. And any problems can be smoothed out by President Hokanson."

They arrived at a set of double doors, which Steen unlocked and opened. Belke looked at Tori, smiling his weird grin. "Five minutes and we're off," he said. "And I have to say, I'm glad to have you along, Tori. You're a hell of a woman. I mean, you got away from old Karl here not once but twice, and he's the baddest dude I ever met. But you fucked us over. Somehow, you brought the Feds down on us, which is something I always thought they'd be too gutless to do."

Suddenly, he grabbed her hair and pushed her face up next to his. He hissed at her, his breath hot on her face. "One thing you gotta learn, lady, is that nobody fucks me over. Nobody. So we've got some unfinished business, you and I. All that fun we had down in Mexico—that was nothing compared to what we've got planned for you now."

CHAPTER 30

Jaworski reached the edge of the building. Most of the firefight was occurring between the quadrangle and the main entrance, but he could also hear firing behind the agricultural area, toward the creek. He peeked around the corner again, then dropped to his belly, crawling the thirty feet or so to the next building. Back on his feet again, he ran behind the building, then along the far end. Then he was back on his stomach again, crawling to the end of the next building, to the door he had seen Percival and Tori use.

The room was a utility closet. Yet he was sure he had seen Percival and Tori enter it. He dropped to his knees, feeling the floor, and within seconds had found the trap door. Lifting it up carefully, he could see nothing but darkness below. He wasn't surprised; Belke wasn't going to commit suicide, or stay and fight. He was getting his ass out of here, and using a tunnel to do it.

Jaworski carefully descended the stairs, feeling along the walls. Two steps down he found the light switch, which illuminated the staircase and the room below. He nearly tripped over Percival's body. He jumped back and looked around. The room was otherwise deserted; only a desk, a couple of television screens, and other electronic equipment remained. He took a closer look at Percival, who appeared to have been shot. Blood oozed in lazy trails away from the body. He glanced around the room and saw nothing interesting, then opened a door at the far end of the room, which revealed the tunnel. He found the light, then began sprinting through the tunnel. After a few minutes his sprint changed to a jog as the tunnel showed no sign of ending.

Finally he came to the staircase and climbed it. Outside, at the top, he rested and took his bearings. Then he was knocked to the ground by the force of a mighty explosion. He staggered to his feet and shielded his eyes; the brick building had become a fireball. He looked around but couldn't see the source of the blast; it had probably been caused by pre-placed explosives. He beat the side of the shed in frustration. All the evidence, all the victims, were destroyed.

Looking out at the rest of the camp, he saw chaos. Shouts, explosions, movement, and small arms fire filled the compound. After a couple of minutes, the activity began to sort itself out and make some sense. There was little activity at the main gate or the administration building, or at the building Tori had pointed out as the armory; that likely meant that the invaders had secured all three of those key objectives. The burning hulk of a helicopter, surrounded by shouting medics and victims, lay a hundred feet outside the gate, down the road. Small groups of soldiers were now spreading out around the perimeter, including several men heading in Jaworski's general direction. The place was being methodically taken over. Near the main gate, rows of prisoners lay face down on the ground.

Jaworski could see flashes coming from the rear of the camp, by the farm sheds and the creek. It appeared the defenders, at least those who had managed to assemble to meet the predawn lightning assault, had been driven out of the main part of the camp and were attempting to regroup.

Jaworski now turned around; Belke would be fleeing away from the camp, not toward it. He scanned the area with the flashlight, and spotted a dirt trail leading into the woods. After following the trail for a couple of minutes, he saw the opening in the outcrop. Peering through the opening with his flashlight, he saw a long tunnel, disappearing off into the distance. He was tempted to start running, but the passage, which looked like an old mining tunnel, could be miles long.

Jaworski trotted back toward the small shed where the original tunnel had emerged. The structure appeared to contain another room, opposite from where the staircase came up. He walked around to the other side and saw a large padlocked door. Stepping back, he shredded the door and lock with the machine pistol, then wrenched open the door. Inside were a riding lawn mower, a chain saw, tree trimming equipment, and a four-wheel all-terrain vehicle.

The keys were in the ATV, which roared to life when Jaworski started it. A minute later he was at the tunnel opening. He spent ten minutes enlarging the hole by removing rocks and brush, then, sweating and breathing heavily, he again mounted the ATV and entered the tunnel.

He didn't know how much of a head start Belke and Steen had. Obviously they had taken a vehicle of some kind through the tunnel, probably an ATV like the one he now rode. He drove as fast as he dared; the tunnel was bumpy and barely wide enough for the ATV. After about fifteen minutes he detected a slight variance in the darkness up ahead. He slowed the vehicle, and the outline of a door slowly came into view. Leaving the engine running, he dismounted and checked out the door, which was actually a set of twin doors.

The doors were unlocked; he opened one slightly and looked through. The entrance opened onto a gravel path, which descended steeply through a forest. About a hundred feet into the woods he could make out a clearing, illuminated by moonlight and a yard light posted on a pole. A shed or building stood on the far side of the clearing.

Jaworski pushed both doors open, then went back to the ATV. He took a deep breath, then gunned the engine.

●

Steen and Belke hustled Tori down the gravel path toward the dimly lit clearing, then over to a small building made of corrugated steel. Tori shivered in the damp, chilly predawn mountain air. Steen inserted a key into a padlock, unlocking a large sliding door. Belke pointed his gun at her. "Stand aside, right there where we can see you." Steen flipped a light switch, which illuminated the inside of the building. Tori could make out stacks of hay, rows of boxes, and a small helicopter inside. Keeping a watchful eye on her, Steen and Belke began to roll the helicopter out of the building.

The helicopter was halfway out when a foreign sound rumbled from the direction of the tunnel. Belke and Steen froze, looking at each other. Belke flipped off the lights and covered Tori while Steen scrambled up the slope. The sound grew louder. In the dim light Tori could see Steen taking up a position just outside the tunnel entrance. Jaworski, if it was Jaworski coming through the tunnel, would be a sitting duck, and she couldn't warn him.

The sound from the tunnel turned into a roar. Then a pair of headlights burst from the tunnel entrance. Steen sprayed the vehicle, whatever it was, with automatic fire, and the headlights veered wildly into the woods. Steen gave chase, and the vehicle, apparently an ATV, struck a tree and tumbled several times before coming to a stop. The headlights remained on, providing thin illumination for the woods between the tunnel entrance and the building.

Another crack sounded from the woods. Steen yelled and went down. Reflexively, Tori kicked Belke hard in the shin. He bellowed and hopped on his good leg while taking a futile swing at her. Then Tori saw an object on the ground. The gun. She lunged for the pistol, grabbing at it with her left hand, but then felt a sharp pain in her abdomen. Belke had kicked her.

Tori lay on the ground, gasping for breath, while Belke retrieved the pistol. His attention, however, immediately turned elsewhere. He cupped his free hand and shouted into the woods. "Karl?"

"I'm hit!" came the pain-filled reply. "Go!"

Belke didn't move. He wasn't going anywhere, Tori realized, with Steen alive to talk to authorities and someone, probably Jaworski, armed in the woods.

Then Tori felt the gun against the side of her head.

•

Jaworski peered out from the tunnel entrance, where he had jumped off the ATV, trying to get a fix on the automatic fire.

There. He saw a figure, probably Steen, dart toward the careening ATV. He aimed and fired.

Bullseye. Steen went down, rolling into the woods.

Jaworski, bent double, crept toward Steen. In his peripheral vision he saw movement from in front of the building, probably from Belke and, if he was lucky, Tori. There was also a large shape in the doorway. A helicopter.

There was no movement at all from Steen's direction. Then a voice, Belke's, shouted from the building, "Karl!"

"I'm hit!" came the anguished reply, and Jaworski had no reason to doubt it. "Go!" Steen added, but of course Belke wouldn't be going anywhere yet. Jaworski continued to advance toward the vicinity of Steen's voice.

"Jaworski!" Belke shouted. "Come out and drop the gun, or I shoot her!"

The detective froze. It was the moment he'd dreaded.

"Do it now!" Belke screamed.

Jaworski couldn't move.

"I'm going to count to three! If I don't see you in the clearing with your hands up, I pull the trigger! There won't be a four!"

Jaworski changed directions, wondering if he could get a clear shot at Belke. He could see the racist leader clearly now, his arm around Tori's neck, a pistol held against her temple. Jesus. He felt sick to his stomach.

"One!"

Jaworski resumed his stealthy advance toward the building. He clicked the machine pistol onto single-shot mode. He had to get closer, and even if he did, there would be the risk of hitting Tori. It was a risk he had to take.

"Two!"

Through an opening in the trees, Jaworski could see Belke shift his position, retreating into the shadows between the building and the helicopter. There was no chance now to get a shot off.

It was over.

"All right!" Jaworski yelled. "Don't shoot her—I'll come out!" He started to come up out of his crouch, then felt searing pain in his side. He went down, rolling in agony down the slope. Steen, fixing on his voice, had shot him.

Jaworski clutched his right side and felt wetness. The pain also seemed to be coming from his back, giving him hope that the bullet had gone all the way through. Breathing heavily, he looked behind him, where the shot had come from. He saw no one, but somehow the wounded Steen had moved around between him and the tunnel entrance. He glanced back toward the building and saw Belke and Tori emerge from the shadows. Belke still held the gun to Tori's head. Biting his lip to keep from crying out, Jaworski shifted, marshalling his ebbing strength for one shot. Belke stopped, looking around and listening. Jaworski sighted up the barrel, aiming for the head, and pulled the trigger.

Jaworski had no way of knowing if the bullet hit home.

He was already on the ground, unconscious.

•

Tori, the gun to her head, felt Belke's arm around her neck, pulling her back into the shadows. He was shouting to Jaworski that he would shoot her. What would the detective do? She still hadn't seen the figure that had driven the ATV through the tunnel and shot Steen, but there seemed little doubt who it was.

"Two!" Belke shouted. She felt the arm tighten around her neck.

Then, from the woods, "All right! Don't shoot her—I'll come out!"

Tori felt her heart sink. They would both die now.

She flinched at the sound of another shot. Then came a short yelp from the woods, and in the dim and waning illumination from the ATV's headlights, she saw movement that looked like someone falling and rolling.

Belke, maintaining his grip, shoved her cautiously along the side of the building, out of the shadows and toward the clearing. As they reached the corner of the building, there was another shot, and Tori sensed a bullet whiz by her head and imbed itself in the side of the building.

Belke reflexively flinched, loosening his grip on her neck, and Tori broke free, running for the woods. Gunfire exploded from behind her as she dived for the protective shadows of the woods, rolling behind a tree.

She immediately began crawling on her stomach, away from the building and into the woods. She stopped once to look back, and spotted Belke moving along the side of the building, entering the woods via a circuitous route that would not allow Jaworski to get off a shot.

Five minutes passed. Ten minutes. She slithered forward, soaked and scraped, hugging the ground, encountering stumps, branches, toadstools, pine needles, and dirt. She couldn't see Belke any more, but knew he was approaching her from the far side, away from the path where Steen and Jaworski had shot each other. And she was in the middle. She had to assume the worst, that Steen was alive and functioning, and that Jaworski was not. Increasingly, though, it seemed likely that both were either dead or unconscious; there would have been some activity from one of them by now.

Fifteen minutes. She still had not put much distance between her and the building; stealth had replaced speed as her primary concern. Belke had to be close now; he would fire at the source of any movement.

Twenty minutes. Tori's exhaustion finally overcame her survival instinct, and she was forced to stop for rest. She could hear Belke now; he, too, must have concluded that Jaworski posed no threat and was being less cautious.

"Tori!" She gave a little jump as Belke's voice pierced the silence. He was very close. She saw a flashlight beam, sweeping methodically back and forth across the woods.

"It's all over!" he said. "Come on out!"

Tori slowly positioned herself on the far side of a tree from the direction of Belke's voice. The flashlight beam swept slowly, inevitably closer to where she knelt.

"Tori! You cooperate with me and I won't kill you! Your life may not be a lot of fun, but you'll be alive! I'll give you one minute to think about it! After that, everything's off!"

Tori slowly pulled herself to a standing position, preparing to run. But it would be no contest. Running in the dark would be futile, and Belke would spot her immediately.

"Thirty seconds!"

Tori tried to control her breathing. She scanned the forest ahead of her, trying to pick out a path in the dim light. The flashlight beam would be on her within seconds. Her fingers closed around a jagged branch, the only weapon she had.

"Time's up!" Belke hesitated, then resumed speaking, in a much softer voice. He knew she was close. He said, "I've got news for you, Tori. You didn't know everything about your husband."

Tori felt as though the breath had been knocked out of her.

"Outstanding attorney with great potential. Real happy fellow, he was. That's because he was one of us. Had been for six years. We hated to lose him. He was Bound, Tori."

For Tori, time and space ceased to exist. The forest and the mountain were gone. Belke was gone. The only stimulus engaging her senses was a voice in the back of her mind, a small voice, which nonetheless overwhelmingly and permanently silenced any competing voices of denial, incredulity, or outrage.

Ben's voice.

It's true, Tori.

And she knew it was.

The forest and the mountain returned. Belke was back. And her entire being was filled instantly with a rage so profound and all consuming that reason and volition vanished, replaced only by a desire to kill Harlan Belke.

And then herself.

She sprang from behind the tree. Belke, startled, dropped the flashlight. He raised the gun in Tori's general direction, firing wildly. Tori, oblivious to the gunfire, lunged at him with the tree branch, ramming it into his face.

Belke screamed and fell backward, clutching his face. Tori fell upon him, driving the jagged stick into his face again and again, until he was motionless and bloody.

And then she was standing up, running, stumbling, falling down hard in the dark. She looked back at the object that had tripped her. A human form. Lying motionless, face-up, eyes open. Karl Steen, dead. She saw the pistol next to the body. Picked it up and aimed it. Pumped bullet after bullet into the body. Continued to pull the trigger, over and over, long after the clip was empty.

She stood for a moment, collecting her thoughts, then found her way back to where Belke still lay, motionless. She reached down, unclipped his vinyl pack, then fastened it around her own waist. Then she grabbed Belke's flashlight and began walking through the woods.

"Kyle? Kyle?"

"Tori? Over here," a voice answered. But not the detective's voice.

She thrashed through the brush, probing with the flashlight, trying to reach the voice.

Strong arms caught her. She struggled, then became aware of a man's voice, then words. "It's all right," the voice kept repeating. Then she saw the source of the voice. Special Agent Nolan Bertelson.

She sank to the ground, sobbing soundlessly, and the restraining hands let her go. After a long time she looked up; Bertelson was still there. There was activity all around: people, vehicles, lights, and a helicopter.

"Cindy," she managed to say at last. "And Scotty. And Polly. And Caitlin."

The FBI agent shook his head.

Still emitting gasping sobs, she looked down at the ground, unable to muster the energy or even the will to grab Bertelson's gun and shoot herself. It was an unnecessary act; her life had already ended.

After a minute she looked up suddenly. "Kyle," she said.

"Still alive," Bertelson answered. "It's touch and go."

Still alive. Would she ever be able to say the same about herself?

EPILOGUE

Tori, shivering slightly from a chill in the late afternoon breeze, pulled on the windbreaker she had brought along. The sunlight was beginning to acquire the filtered, diffused look of autumn as they walked the spacious grounds of the government hospital in suburban Washington, D.C. Kyle Jaworski, looking drawn and haggard, looked up at the man who pushed his wheelchair.

"We can go farther," Jaworski said.

"This is far enough," answered Nolan Bertelson. "I had to do quite a song and dance to get them to let you go outside at all."

Jaworski shrugged, using his good arm; his other was in a sling. They stopped near a gate leading to a busy street. Bertelson turned the chair around to face a bench, then took a seat on it next to Tori.

Tori, Jaworski, and other victims of the Dunston violence had been airlifted to a hospital in Denver. Harlan Belke had died en route; Karl Steen had been pronounced dead at the scene. Tori had been treated for cuts, bruises, dehydration, and exhaustion, while Jaworski had undergone emergency surgery for his gunshot wound. They had remained in Denver a week and a half; Tori had been discharged when they had returned to Washington, two days ago.

The media coverage of the Dunston raid had been sensational and unceasing. Video taken from circling news helicopters showed the smoking ruins of the Belke compound. Thirty-two of the community's residents and five law officers had been killed. The FBI claimed that due to the surprise and skill employed by the commandos, they had killed at most two or three community residents; the remaining deaths had resulted from explosives set off by Harlan Belke. Virtually the only resistance they encountered had been the Stinger missile that had brought down a helicopter, killing four of the five slain law officers. Critics from across the ideological spectrum, from right-wing extremists to left-wing civil libertarians, charged the government with a cover-up, and the inevitable congressional investigations were already under way.

In truth, the public knew very few details of the raid. Court papers filed just before the raid alleged numerous firearms violations and unspecified crimes related to "controlled substances." Large caches of illegal weapons were in fact found at the compound; nothing further had been said about controlled substances. During the past three days, Dunston had been pushed off the front page by another shocking development: the suicide of White House Chief of Staff Jim Traeger, less than two weeks after his daughter's tragic death in a terrorist bombing.

Jaworski squinted into the sun. "So, where've you been, Nolan?"

"The clean-up at the site has been a lot of work. So has the questioning of Belke's people."

"No, I mean where have you been? This raid had to be your baby, man. But with all the press conferences, all the investigations, you've managed to stay out of sight. How'd you manage that?"

Bertelson glanced at his watch. "For one thing, I'm no longer an FBI agent."

"What?" Tori asked, incredulous.

Jaworski answered. "You can only play both sides for so long. How long did you do it, Nolan?"

"Four years."

"So tell me about this Zest. Is it really better than sex or chocolate or heroin?"

"I've never taken it. I spit it out when they first gave it to me."

"But you played along," Tori said.

The FBI agent smiled. "No, no. There was no play involved. I was serious."

"But if you didn't take the—"

"The Zest had nothing to do with it. You saw that tape, Tori. Bound people love each other. They are closer than family. I may not have taken the stuff, but I love my group members. That's the sad part of it; they set up Corman with a great program for getting people to open up, to share, to really relate to one another. They wouldn't even need the Zest for that part of it. At any rate, I must have looked like an easy, logical target. And

I was. From all those tests and interviews, they knew I was having a crisis, with my faith—I'm a Christian—with my wife; with my work. I needed something. When push came to shove, I couldn't take the Zest. But I bought into the rest of it, totally."

"So how did it work?" Jaworski asked. "You came back from Cancún, went into your boss, and said you had a great idea for an undercover operation?"

Bertelson shifted uncomfortably on the bench, and once more glanced at his watch. "The first I told my superiors about it was a couple of weeks ago."

Even Jaworski was shocked this time. "Jesus."

"I might never have told them. I was already compromised, and the longer you go on without reporting it, the more compromised you become. But after the shooting at the picnic, I knew it had to end. Something seriously bad was going down. And I knew as soon as I told anybody, my career was over. I did manage to negotiate half of my pension. Otherwise I'm an unemployed, overweight, late-middle-aged, half-assed security consultant. But you know what? It's not as big a deal to me any more. After my experience with the Bound, I know what's important. My friends; my family; my faith. People."

"Christ," Jaworski muttered. "You can make guest appearances on Oprah."

The agent smiled. "Meanwhile, the clean-up proceeds. We managed to salvage some records from the administration building, but all of the research data, including the formula for the Zest, is gone. We do have what we think is a complete list of every member of the Bound. There are a lot of people in high places, like the Secretary of Defense, and Senator Hokanson, and Jim Traeger. And there are a lot of people who aren't well known, but who had the potential to be useful some day."

"Like Ben McMillan," Tori said, her voice emotionless.

"Like Ben," Bertelson agreed. "He was a brilliant young lawyer, maybe a future U.S. Attorney or more. From what we can gather, not that many members were actually asked to do anything to help the Bound. But everybody was on call, I guess."

"Especially you," Jaworski said.

"Oh, yes. I suppose I should defend myself a little bit, though. The Bound was very compartmentalized. You've got the Corman operation down in Mexico, and you've got a voice named Temple on the phone.

Other than that, all you've got is your fellow group members. And there was no way I'd do anything to harm them. And, at least in my group, there was no crime being committed, except by me."

"You tanked the investigation into Scotty's kidnapping," Tori said.

For the first time, Bertelson looked genuinely troubled. "I was asked to," he admitted. "I was told Scotty was safe, with loving Bound members, and it was imperative for all of us that he not be found. So, did I sabotage the investigation? I still ask myself that at least once a day. Was I going through the motions? Could I have done more? I actually had no decision to make unless we started to get close, with some solid leads." He looked up. "But with God as my witness, I'm telling you we never did."

He turned toward them, elbows resting on his knees. "God knows I've lied to myself enough over the years. But in this case, anybody will tell you we had nothing to go on, and I mean nothing. It was the perfect crime. Of course, we know now that's because the father was in on it. I could have acted more aggressively, maybe tweaked things here or there, and it would have made no difference. I still held out hope that Scotty was alive and that he'd surface again some day. I know what I did was wrong. I know I should have blown the whistle, said the whole thing was engineered by a voice on the phone named Temple, but if I had, I can guarantee three things would have happened: One, they would have killed Scotty. Two, Temple would have vanished. And three, I would have been dead. My God, if I thought I could have saved that boy...." His voice broke.

He stopped to compose himself, then continued, speaking directly to Tori. "Kyle knew, of course. He knew my heart wasn't in it, but it was mainly just my attitude—my ambivalence—that he sensed. There's really nothing I did that was inadequate or out of line. What Kyle didn't know, any more than I did, was that Larry was in on it. After the massacre at the picnic, Temple called and said all of the victims were Bound. That's when I realized what had happened. I knew I'd been used, and that this had to end."

Tori realized that Bertelson was no longer looking at them. He was looking through the gate to the street, where a dark sedan, followed by a long, black limousine, had pulled up. Three men wearing suits got out of the cars and entered the hospital grounds, scrutinizing the area.

"I never did tell my boss," Bertelson said. "That was what I feared most—that I'd confide in the wrong person. The Bound has people everywhere. Finally, after the picnic shootings, I knew I had to take the risk and trust somebody."

Vice President Norman Whitelaw strode briskly from the limousine, through the gate to the bench where they sat. He nodded to Bertelson, then extended a hand to Tori, who was too shocked to stand up. "You must be Ms. McMillan," he said. "Norm Whitelaw. Pleasure to meet you." Tori shook the proffered hand, and the Vice President turned to Jaworski. "Nice to meet you as well, Sergeant," he said. He was courtly, sincere, and Southern.

Whitelaw turned around and nodded to his security detail, which then backed off, just out of earshot. "I gave Agent Bertelson the go-ahead to fill y'all in," he said. "He came to me a couple of weeks ago with a mighty fantastic tale, which turned out to be true in every respect. He's done his country a great service. And so have y'all. I asked for a chance to meet you and thank you personally. We'll be assigning you a new FBI agent to handle things from here on. There's a chance you may need to do some testifying, but I'd just as soon keep your roles a secret." He smiled. "I imagine you wouldn't object to that too strongly."

Tori and Jaworski, though skeptical, returned the smile.

"Sorry to run," Whitelaw said, "but I have another stop to make. I have to go over and see Pam Traeger. You see, I considered Jim a friend, even though it's now obvious he was mixed up in this thing. After a double tragedy, I think Pam is entitled to a bit of good news, and I'm happy to be the one to bring it." He turned and nodded to a security man who stood next to the limousine. The man opened the back door, and said something to an unseen occupant inside. A moment later, a girl wearing a blue jumper got out of the car and walked over to stand next to them.

"Caitlin," Tori gasped.

"Hi," Caitlin said, looking back and forth at the three strangers. She looked pale and thin, but surprisingly confident. Whitelaw introduced them, one at a time.

"I guess I don't know you guys," Caitlin said. "But Mister Vice President said all three of you helped me after I was kidnapped. So...thanks, I guess." She looked up at Whitelaw, who put an arm around her.

"It's going to be difficult for everyone," the Vice President said. He shook hands again with the three of them, then left with the girl.

"So what happened?" Tori demanded when their visitors had left. "I thought Belke had destroyed the evidence—killed all the well-known kidnap victims."

"Except for Caitlin, he did," Bertelson answered. "She was still new—apparently hadn't been 'processed' yet, according to some of the community members we've questioned."

"She's your ace in the hole, isn't she," Jaworski said. "So far all you've gotten on them is weapons charges, and it looks like you won't be able to make any drug charges stick, either. With her you'll have kidnapping. That'll help you justify the raid and the deaths."

"She'll be helpful, yes—it's always nice to have a live witness. But this time the government did things right. We're not going to get pilloried—we have these folks dead to rights, and we'll be able to prove it."

"What do you mean?" Tori asked.

"We're still identifying remains from the brick building. We'll probably get positive i.d.'s on Cindy, Scotty, and Polly Kendrick."

At the mention of the names, Tori felt tears unexpectedly, embarrassingly, begin to form. Jaworski covered her hand with his. "It's better you never saw them," he said. "Percival was right—they were already dead, for all intents and purposes...." The detective sucked in a breath. "The Bound had to be stopped. We did what we had to do. But there have been a lot of times over the last couple of weeks when I've wished you never took those pictures of Scotty. I'll be haunted for the rest of my life, just by the images."

Jaworski turned to Bertelson. "How did you hook up with Whitelaw?"

The FBI man shrugged. "A friend of a friend got me a meeting. Like I said, I finally decided I had to trust somebody. I couldn't trust my superiors. Whitelaw is a politician, and I don't agree with everything he advocates. But he always impressed me as a decent man who stood for something, and he takes a strong stand against illegal substances. I got lucky, I guess."

"Very lucky," Tori said. "He also had a lot of incentive to block the President's endorsement of Hokanson. Which meant that discrediting Traeger would be just fine with him."

Bertelson nodded. "He and I put two and two together, and we concluded Traeger was probably involved, even before his daughter disappeared. But you know something? He pushed for the raid, and it wouldn't have happened without his support. The President is a cautious man, after all. Whitelaw pushed it through even though it was a huge risk, and will end up hurting him politically. We had a big meeting with him and the President and the Attorney General and the FBI Director. Whitelaw was wavering—he was scared like everybody else was. But then I told them we knew a twelve-year-old kidnap victim was being held there. That did it. 'We've got to get her out,' he said. He didn't know whose daughter it was. He just wanted to do the right thing."

The three of them were silent for a long moment. Rush hour traffic on the nearby road was picking up. Bertelson stood up. "Well, thanks for your help, both of you. I'm sorry for all you've lost, Tori. And to both of you, I'm sorry about my behavior. I know just saying that is inadequate. But I've got the rest of my life to live with it, to try to atone somehow." He reached for the handles of Jaworski's wheelchair.

"It's okay," Tori said. "I'll push him."

Bertelson nodded, started to walk away, then stopped. "The Vice President is a good man. I found I could trust him. The Zest won't go away, you know—we can't recover it from the ruins out in Dunston, but somebody will invent it again some day. And Percival was right—existing institutions probably can't cope. If we don't get control of these technologies fast, the Belkes will."

His eyes bored in on Tori. "Someone saw you mail the package, Tori. From the hospital out in Denver, the first day you were there. We don't know where you sent it."

Tori met his gaze. "You could probably find out."

"Probably," he agreed. He hesitated, then shook hands with both of them. "Good luck," he said, and walked away.

Tori and Jaworski didn't speak for a long time. Tori pulled the jacket around her shoulders.

"They'll be around," Jaworski said at last. "Bertelson may not want to pursue it, but his superiors will. You'd better think about what your response will be."

Tori nodded.

"Where is it? You'd better tell somebody."

Without looking at him, Tori said, "I buried it, in a little clearing in a little grove, on a farm belonging to Ben's grandparents in Pennsylvania."

"How did you get it there?"

"Drove up yesterday. And no, nobody followed me. I rented a car, just in case they bugged mine. And that package I mailed to myself contained nothing. I had the disks with me the entire time I was in the hospital, jammed underneath the sink in the bathroom. But they weren't even thinking about it until the last couple of days; they didn't know what they'd find in the wreckage out there."

Jaworski smiled. "You little devil. You have learned a few things along the way in this little adventure, haven't you? So what are you going to do?"

"Probably stonewall the authorities, and leave the disks where they are. It's an evil thing."

"Bertelson was right, you know. Somebody else will develop it again. You can't stop it."

"Maybe not. But I don't have to be the one to spread it."

Jaworski hesitated. "I don't know whether the Zest is evil or not. But it didn't make Ben evil."

"It was worse. It made him a phony." And she had been blind to it all, the little pillbox containing medicine for his mysterious allergies.

"You loved him," he insisted. "No one can take that away from you."

"It's already been taken away. It wasn't real. He wasn't real."

"Real?" said Jaworski, his voice rising. "What the hell is real? We're all a bunch of layers, levels, facets, hidden compartments. It's what we are. Ben happened to have a big layer, and a novel one. But it was part of the person you loved, part of who he was. And he loved you."

"He would have been happy with anyone."

"Maybe he would have—hell, I don't know. But if he wouldn't have been miserable with somebody else, so what? He wanted you."

Tori said nothing. They looked at each other for a long time. At last he said, "I guess it's obvious by now that I love you, Tori. I need you. But after what you've been through, I know I can't ask you to reciprocate. After the way you've been burned—betrayed—what do my needs amount to? Asking you to take a chance again so soon—I know I can't do that."

Tori's hands went to her eyes. Damn, here it came again. After a moment Jaworski wheeled around so their knees touched, then reached up with a handkerchief and dried her face.

Tori was finally able to speak. "I don't think I can do this by myself."

"Look," he said. "I deal with murder victims every day, and thanks to that I've become an expert on shattered lives. You think you are scarred for life, but you're not. Changed, yes, but crippled, no. You can survive this. You will survive this. You are the strongest person I've ever met. You will get help. You will start a new career and a new life, maybe here, maybe somewhere else. You will do what you need to do, and you don't need me."

"What if I want you?"

He took her hands in his. "If you do, you know I'm here."

"Don't go," she said quickly. "Please."

"I won't."

"You're for real. So was Ben."

He let out a long, ragged breath, tightening his grip on her hands. "I'll do everything in my power, every day, to prove I'm for real. If you'll give me a chance. And I owe you—you kicked my ass and got me to face up to my job and to myself. Besides...."

"Besides?" Tori asked between sobs.

"Besides, I got a call from Susan last night. She said, 'Kyle, I hope even you aren't enough of a thickheaded Polack to let her go. And if you do, I will personally rip out your beating heart and then hang you from the flagpole by your little toes.'" He managed a thin smile. "I guess I don't have much choice, do I."

Tori composed herself. "Yes, you do. So do I." She cradled his head in her arms. "But this is the right one."

Printed in the United States
3674